Thaxton Lee

This is a work of fiction. incidents either are the product of the author's imagination or are used fictitiously. Any resemblance to actual persons, living or dead, events, or locales is entirely coincidental.

Copyright © 2023 by Thaxton J. Lee

All rights reserved. No part of this book may be reproduced or used in any manner without written permission of the copyright owner except for the use of quotations in a book review. For more information, address: thaxtonjlee@gmail.com

First paperback edition February 2023

The Echo

The First Spark

By: Thaxton Lee

Contents

Prologue	6
One	18
Two	30
Three	37
Four	47
Five	56
Six	65
Seven	75
Eight	80
Nine	90
Ten	102
Eleven	111

Twelve	117
Thirteen	123
Fourteen	132
Fifteen	142
Sixteen	151
Seventeen	164
Eighteen	176
Nineteen	183
Twenty	193
Twenty One	201
Twenty Two	211
Twenty Three	227
Twenty Four	237
Twenty Five	250

Twenty Six	259
Twenty Seven	269
Twenty Eight	280
Twenty Nine	289
Thirty	301
Galactic Glossary	311

Prologue

The year is 100 E.E. (Empire Era) that is 2781 in common years.

Twenty four years ago on a planet called Nytar, a man named Xenos had a vision. In this vision, he saw a great being called Nylos. Nylos told Xenos that the Nytarians are his chosen people, and all those people who do not acknowledge Nylos as supreme are unworthy of his gift of life. The Nytarian race began a conquest throughout the entire galaxy. They went from planet to planet and slaughtered everyone who stood in the way of their *holy war*. This war has been called The Conquests. To this day, the Nytarians ravage the galaxy while the Empire scrambles to stop them.

In the far fringes of the galaxy, a Destroyer-class Nytarian battlecruiser, The Apocalypse, pulls out of warp-speed in orbit of Boloxia. The hulking mass of The Apocalypse goes from flying at 299,792,458 m/s to halting at zero in mere seconds. Four other much smaller, Nytarian light cruisers drop out of warp-speed behind it.

The Apocalypse is a tank of a vessel. Its hull is reinforced with the strongest metals in the galaxy. It is the single most powerful Destroyer class ship in the entire galaxy. Every single edge of this battleship is lined with Engergen cannons, ion torpedoes, and three shield generators that are placed in the bottom of the battleship. Its exact armaments are 750 x Energen pulverizers, 250 x Powernaught Railguns, and 500 x ionization cannons.

The vessel measures to be 19,520.97 m (19.52 km) in length, 3,580 m (3.5 km) in width, and 5,270 m (5.2 km) in height. Built to have a completely black metallic hull, so it appears almost invisible in the black void of space except for the small glowing strips and panels.

The ship's triangular silhouette clouds the sky above Boloxia. Its looming size casts a dark shadow over the face of the planet blocking the nearby star's light. Ten mid-sized troop transports slowly exit out of the underbelly docking bay of The Apocalypse. Each carries a platoon of Nytarian foot soldiers, but one has a special passenger. thrusters glow red with superheated gas on the back of the transports. Each transport flies through the vacuum of infinite space. Stars twinkle and shimmer in the distance.

The Nytarian transports enter the atmosphere of Boloxia. Residents of the planet below see the cruisers enter the space above their homes. The design of these particular ships are recognizable to almost anyone in the galaxy at this point. Families step out of their homes to gaze at the sky and see the transports land about a kilometer out from their village. As the ships make contact with the ground they crush all the fungal trees clearing a path to the nearby village.

The ten trooper transports land in a straight line one next to the other. The front hatch opens; it slowly falls to the floor like a drawbridge. Steam blasts from the hydraulic systems in the hatch. One Nytarian commander steps out of the transport. Clad in Zarium painted over black he carries an N-1 Energen powered ray-rifle. He wears a helmet that resembles a human skull. The eye holes illuminate red. Where the jaw would be is a respirator. A one-meter long plasma-laced blade is strapped to his back. Fifteen Nytarian soldiers step out of each transport ship. They all are dressed in the same armor as the commander except his shoulder pauldron is covered in red paint. He leads the soldiers toward the small Boloxia village. 150 troopers march in perfect formation behind him.

One person stayed behind the soldiers, high priest Xenos of the grand church in Nytar. The priest is covered head to toe in white-plated Zarium armor. Flowing pure white robes cover his body underneath the armor. A helmet metallic and tall sits on his head. The vision port on his helmet is in the shape of a cross and glows with purple light. As they approach the village the commander says,

"Go forth and round up everyone and bring them to the center of the village. In the name of Nylos!" All the soldiers sprint ahead with their guns on set to kill. They kick down the doors of the small huts and pull all those inside outside. Anyone who tries to fight back is immediately met with a bolt to the head killing them in an instant. Sparing no one they take everyone to the village center. At least a hundred innocent Boloxians are now standing in the center of their home village surrounded by the dead bodies of those who tried to resist.

The people of Boloxia have been aware that the Nytarians have been headed this way. Throughout the galaxy, there have been rumblings of Nytarian activity in this sector, but no one has seen anything.

A lone Boloxian shuttle takes off less than three kilometers out from the village. It is carrying twenty passengers aboard it, all are trying to flee. The shuttle is using its sublight engines to hopefully fly undetected past The Apocalypse. Within moments of the ship exiting the planet's atmosphere, the scanners aboard The Apocalypse sense the small ship's presence. The minuscule shuttle's reflective hull glimmers in the light of the crimson-red sun. Flying next to the gargantuan Destroyer the terrified shuttle looks like an ant next to a boot. A boot that could easily squash that inferior ant without even noticing. The chief gunner, Nator, sees this and charges up a single cannon just off the starboard side. The cannon illuminates with pulsating raspberry red light. Inside the shuttle the pilot sees a message appear on the screens in front of him. The ship's computer says in a robotic voice: SYSTEMS LOCKED! SYSTEMS LOCKED! The ship's systems alert them that The Apocalypse has locked onto their shuttle. The pilot hand dashes to a button on the control panel to activate the shield systems. The cannon fires. A bolt of pure whizzes through space and collides with the port side of the shuttle. An explosion of fire and sparks blasts from the ship as it is sent into hundreds of pieces. The fires immediately vanished due to the lack of oxygen. All those that didn't die in the explosion died within moments of being in the cold vacuum.

 The high priest steps out into the center area of the village. He stands three meters tall towering over everyone else. His snow-white silhouette is like a white ghost walking among the black armored shadowy soldiers. All the Nytarians around him know the glorious feats of Xenos. They all lower their heads in respect of his holiness. Xenos states in a glorious regal voice that booms across the surface of the planet,

"Hear me! Hear me! I preach to all those that are yet to be awakened! I am Xenos, the rightful prophet of god! As the great book says: 'all those who refuse to acknowledge the true might of Nylos shall be pardoned from this life they refuse to see the fullness of...' I am merely a messenger sent to carry out the will of Nylos! I pray that Nylos will look upon you all with merciful eyes!" Xenos raises his hand into the air and then clutches his fist. Only Xenos sees glowing strands of purple energy coalesce around his hand in the shape of a long pike. All around hear the sound of screams and shrieks of terror. None know where it comes from. This powerful energy vibrates violently. The strands come together and form a long sword. Suddenly everyone else around him sees a sword made of energy appear in his hand. The people before him cowardly lurch back in fear.

The Nytarian troopers don't understand what this power he uses is. Xenos only says it is Shrill Echo. They are this power as a godsend from Nylos himself.

Xenos says, "Mark them with the Stain of Death!" Three Nytarians priests dressed in flowing red robes walk out from behind Xenos. They each carry a wooden bowl full of crimson-red blood. Slowly, the priests move to each terrified Boloxians. As they pass each Boloxian, they dip their clawed thumb into the powder and put a dash across each of their foreheads. Once the priests finish, they walk beside Xenos, and the commander yells,

"Fire!" The dozens of Nytarian soldiers open fire upon the crowd of fearful people. All except one. A single man remains standing during the fire. The soldiers don't shoot him. After the ground is littered with the bodies of dead Boloxians, Xenos walks up to the one remaining man. He places his hand on the man's face and inquiries softy,

"What's your name?" The man looks up at him while tears pour down from his soft, tired eyes. His gaze is lost in the glow of Xeno's helmet. The man says,

"I-I-It's D-D-Darius..." Darrius' face washes over pale as he is filled with the truest of terror.

"Darius? I once knew a man by that name. You know I like you. I can feel it, the great Nylos has favored you. Go out and make it known to all those of this wretched planet that no one can hide from the just eyes of Nylos!" Xenos lets him go. Darius stands up, turns around, and runs away to the fungal forests. As he tries to escape, Xenos raises his hand to the fleeing Darius. From Xenos' point of view, purple strands of energy extend from his hand and wrap and constrict around Darius' body, but the purple strands are invisible to all except him. Xenos feels an intense rush of energy falls over his body. The strands vibrate erratically and violently. Everyone around can hear the faintest sound of screaming like it is coming from the strands. From everyone else's view, they just see Darius levitate into the air as he pulls at his neck. The energy curls around his neck and tightens like a boa constrictor to the point where he can no longer gasp for air.

In Darius' last moments his mind darts around, *What dark magic is this that holds me aloft? My friends and family have perished. What else is there to struggle for...* The spindle-like energy slowly goes into his ear. He has no idea what it is.

His mind rushes to think of all the time he lost with his family. All the suffering his people have endured. For a moment, he wishes for it all to be over. Tears roll down his green-skinned cheeks. He feels that he failed his family. As a father he was supposed to protect them, but he watched them be slaughtered right in front of his eyes.

As Darius has his last thoughts, a voice speaks to him inside his head, yet it is not his own, I pray that Nylos may have mercy upon your soul... Xenos has entered his mind; The one thing that is supposed to be secret and to yourself. The energy strands slowly fade as Darius falls to the ground dead of suffocation. Xenos whispers:

"This is the final price for rebellion against Nylos!"

This was one of the few demonstrations of the Echo shown by Xenos. After Darius falls deep to the muddy ground, Xenos stomps up to his lifeless corpse, pulls out a jagged knife from underneath his robes, bends down to the body, slices across Darius' chest, dips his fingers in the blood, and wipes it on his white robes.

He struts back to the transport. The commander struggles to keep up with his long, powerful strides. The troops march behind them. Everyone enters back into their transports; the hatches swiftly close shut. The clamps make a loud clunk as they grip onto the door to shut the airlock. The Apocalypse has control over the transports, so the chief captain issues an order for the transports to fly back to the battleship. Gravitational propulsion systems activate; it lifts them into the air about fifteen feet. The thrusters give off a low hum as they are flooded with Energen. Each transport vessel blasts off through the thick atmosphere. The transports cut through the atmosphere out into the planet's orbit. All ten of them fly underneath The Apocalypse and into the docking bay.

Xenos walks through the labyrinth that is the interior of a Destroyer. He knows the complete layout of all the Nytarian naval vessels from the numerous times he has visited each of them. Xenos' pure white robes make him look like a ghost walking through the dark halls. As he passes the soldiers stationed on the ship they all stand at attention and salute him. The dimly lit, black halls are illuminated by his glowing vision port. Blast doors open the moment he reaches proximity to them and shut with incredible force behind him and a loud crash. Small bots roll across the floor past him. Even the bots recognize the inherent power that Xenos carries with him. The lights around him seem to go darker as Xenos goes past them. Finally, he reaches the main bridge. The doors open slowly. All the people in the room turn and salute his highness.

The bridge is lined with computer screens everywhere with pilots, technicians, and gunners stationed on all the computers. A large glass-plated window that arcs around the room with an excellent view of Boloxia below. A single purple, spherical light is in the ceiling casting light into the room. Buttons flash and beep. A desk sits in the middle of the bridge with holo-screens and computers around it. In a swiveling chair sits the chief commander of The Apocalypse. The commander wears the standard uniform for Nytarian officers. He turns around to see Xenos walking towards him. He frantically stands up and salutes him. Xenos commands him,

"Take the planet!" The commander's brow furrows as he looks at Xenos in his blank glowing visor. Before he can even ask a question, Xenos turns around and struts out of the bridge. The commander says,

"Uh... your eminence, you want us to invade Boloxia?" Right before Xenos reaches the blast door, he turns around and yells to the commander,

"Set up a blockade around this system! Bring another Destroyer! I have plans for this one! Take an army to the planet and kill or capture everyone! Spare no one! I want you to see to it personally that this world is cleansed of all the pestilence that plague it! Siege Boloxia!"

Soon after getting this order from Xenos the Nytarian General sends three legions of Nyatrian troopers down to the planet's surface. Ten Behemoth-class tanks are carried down and dropped off outside the planet's capital city. The tanks push through the sparse mushroom forests; they trample anything in their way. As the Behemoths charge forward, a small village stands in their path. Instead of moving around it, they run right through. Anyone who isn't quick enough to get out of the way are crushed by the giant treads, and all those that got out of the way are either shot or stabbed by the soldiers.

The Empire has a small presence on the planet. There are a few outposts and fortresses on the planet. The Nytarians know that they must crush the Imperial outpost before word can be spread of their siege.

The Apocalypse zooms across the planet from where it was. It hovers in the space above one of the Imperial outposts. All the pulverizer cannons aim down towards the planet's surface. They all fire down at the outpost. Red lasers rain down like a storm from hell itself. Within moments of the bombardment beginning, the outpost is raised to the ground. Only rubble and debris remain.

The people of Boloxia try to run and flee but it is too late.

One

A light freighter cruises through the Mid Worlds sector of space.

The ship flies through Warp Route 66, one of the Empire's sanctioned warp speed routes. It soars past the most beautifully colored nebulae made of tiny stars and dust. Greens, blues, and reds swirl together in gaseous masses. In the helm sits the captain with his shiny boots up on the central console while he listens to some old Terran music. Next to the console lay piles of old newspapers and magazines that the captain loves entertaining himself with Terran relics.

Light blonde hair covers his head. He wears dark aviators that cover his eyes that are azure like the sea. His cheekbones are sharp, and his jaw is chiseled like a sculpture. A small dimple lies on his chin. He wears a fitted red jacket and glossy black gloves that cover his hands. Underneath his jacket, he wears a brown tee shirt. Black boots cover the bottoms of his dark khaki-colored pants that have two belts across them. Attached to the belts is a small holster, and lays a light blaster pistol. His pistol with the rest of the crew's weapons is all made by Apex Manufacturing.

As he bops his head to the music, someone taps him on the shoulder and says,

"Sir Captain, it seems we have entered Warp Route 66." The captain has a bit of an accent comparable to that of southern America from centuries past. The captain turns around and looks at the human-resembling bot and goes,

"SEE, you can just call me Xander." The bot's blue optical receptors illuminate in confusion. He tilts his head like an inquisitive dog.

"Sir Captain Xander?" says the bot in its synthetic, robotic voice. Xander puts his palm to his forehead, and he shakes his head in the slightest inclination of disappointment. Xander is a patient person with bots since he has had to work with them throughout his entire life. He says,

"Just Xander is fine, but you say whatever you want. Go tell the others I'm going to pull us down to the surface." As SE-3 processes this, he looks and thinks in his internal computers: Whatever I want? Want?... After thinking, he says,

"Affirmative, Just Xander." SE-3 is a repurposed assassin droid. Like all the other bots in the galaxy, it is built to resemble a human. His metallic outside has been painted to look like a Caucasian male. His face is chiseled, blue optical sensors for eyes, and he has slicked back hair which is pulled back wires. At each of his joints are mechanical gears so that he can move. On his upper torso is written: SE-3.

Oil drips from the exposed wiring. The crew members call him SEE for simplicity. SE-3 walks out of the helm through the blast doors. The doors open as he gets close and then close firmly behind SE-3. He walks down the corridors to the lounge area. The corridors aboard this ship are pretty messy. Exposed wiring hangs down from the ceiling and oil drips down onto SEE. The walls are plated with gray metallic panels. Yellowish ceiling lights shine down.

As he gets to the lounge he sees a large bipedal pig smoking a cigarette. He sits there on a couch polishing his minigun. He wears green camo-colored pants and Zarium-plated knee pads. His big nose is pierced with a big loop. An orange, dirty rag is what he uses to clean off his enormous gun that lies in his lap. He took out the belt and hung it on the wall. On the head of his minigun is a poorly spray-painted shark face. Across the room, another man is leaning up against the wall. His skin is dark mahogany, and he has a thick white mustache and bushy white eyebrows. A navy blue Imperial jacket with a pin that signifies his long-gone rank is what he wears. His left eye has been cybernetically replaced; the eye glows blue light as it darts around the room.

His face is covered with the scars of a hundred stories. Scars of war. Scars of pain. All stories he keeps to himself. Stories that will never be told; tales that are He is cleaning off his old Imperial laser rifle. Around his neck hangs old Imperial holo dog tags from old times of war.

The lounge floor is littered with old alcohol bottles and old snack bags. When SE-3 walks into the room the two of them look at SE-3. He says,

"Just Xander says to go man your stations. We are about to go." The two of them hop up and walk down to their stations around the ship.

Xander grabs the control wheel and sets a course for Las Nazara, the casino city on Coranthea. He sits up and takes his feet off the console. Xander presses a button on the console in front of him. It activates the ship's A.I. computer. An electronic beep sounds as it boots up. Speakers in the helm say,

"Hello Captain Xander, how shall I be of assistance?"

"Hey EQ, I need you to make the calculations for us to fly to Las Nazara." The A.I.'s designation is EQ-13. Xander refers to it as EQ.

"Of course, I can make the calculations; I am the number three greatest ranked A.I. in the galaxy…. Okay, calculations have been made, and we are ready for the warp.

Right as Xander preparing for the warp, SE-3 says,

"Captain, there is something on the radar."

Xander asks,

"What are we talking about here?" SE-3 looks at a screen on his holoscreen.

"It seems a ship has just warped in behind us." He is trying to get a read on the ship that is behind them. "Oh no..."

"What is it?" This ship is all too familiar to the crew of The Odyssey. The ship is a large, repurposed, Imperial, light, battlecruiser. It is covered in cannons and missiles. "Wally's back..." Xander rolls his eyes and sighs in deep frustration. He thinks, Not him again. "Sir, they are hailing us."

"Ugh, just answer him." Before they answer the hail, Xander quickly says,

"Everyone, Wally's back. This might get messy. John, Hogler head to gunner stations and prepare firing systems and Bre to your observation deck." They all head to their stations. The weapons systems boot up. John and Hogler head to the two gimbals (full 360 degrees) turrets on the sides of the ship, and they load the cells into the turrets. Bre heads to her observation deck where she has cameras to see all angles of the ship. SE-3 presses a button on his console, and a holoscreen appears at the head of the helm.

The old Imperial battle cruiser flies right in front of The Odyssey so that they directly face each other. The two bridges' faces are close enough that Xander can see Wally, and he can see him.

On the holoscreen, a tan-skinned man with short brown hair that has stripes of old white. A long scar runs down the left side of his face; it cuts through his dark eyebrow. And his left eye has been replaced with a cybernetic eye. He has a dark, scruffy five 'O clock shadow, and he is clad in rusty, scrappy armor. The man smiles grimly, and he says with a thick accent of Australia from ancient Terra,

"If it isn't Xander Holsmo! How have you been, mate?" Xander's brow furrows as he gets frustrated, but he puts on an apathetic smile.

"I'm good. I'd be a lot better if you were here right now."

"Oh c'mon mate, you know you're happy to see me!" Wally has a deep psychotic gaze behind his one organic eye. SE-3 scoots up next to Xander. He whispers in Xander's ear:

"Their weapon systems are coming online. We are waiting for your order." He walks back to his console. Xander says,

"Wally, what do you want?" Wally grabs a cigar from out of frame, lights it with a flamethrower in his cybernetic hand, and lights the end of the cigar. He blows a circle with the smokes and says,

"Let's cut to the chase. You know exactly why I'm here. You have something my clients want." Xander replies in an angry tone:

"We found that fair and square. It was out of Imperial space so it's a free game. You know better than me the rules of Free Space." (Free Space is the areas of space that no one has claimed.)

"My clients at Cryotech don't care about Free Space. You have something they are willing to do a lot for and I'm going to get it… the easy way or the hard way." Xander presses a button and it mutes his side of the call. He turns to SE-3 and says,

"Tell everyone… it's battle time!" Xander grasps his steering wheel. SE-3 hangs up on Wally, and he says transmitting over the crew's channel:

"Captain's orders: 'it's battle time!'" John and Hogler both angle their turrets straight at Wally's ship, Hell's Grace.

Inside his ship, Wally sits at the helm and flies the ship out of the way from the onslaught of bolts The Odyssey fires at them. Wally shouts,

"Someone do something!" People inside Hell's Grace scramble and rush around to the gunner stations. The turrets get a lock on The Odyssey. As Wally's gunners fire at Xander's ship, Xander blasts it down ducking past the bolts. Xander quickly zooms away, and

Wally follows. "Get over here, ya cheeky buggah," yells Wally to himself while he jerks around the steering wheel to hunt after them.

Xander flies fast when he tries to outrun Wally. John and Hogler swivel around and open fire on the fast-approaching ship. They miss a few bolts, but a few collide with the shield barrier.

The two ships spin around and chase each other as they exchange fire upon them. The Odyssey fires a torpedo at Hell's Grace. It passes right through their shield barrier and blasts a small hole in the hull of Wally's ship.

"Bloody hell! Xander you're going to pay for that," shouts Wally. Technicians in his ship rush to the hole and begin to patch the opening. They use a filler substance that can be sprayed and hardens into a temporary covering. Wally grabs a microphone, switches the channel he is in, and commands, "Send out the Buzzers!"

A cargo hatch on the bottom of the ship. When it fully opens, three Buzzers drop out of the hatch. Wally's Buzzers are repurposed Rock Wreckers, small starships built and outfitted to destroy asteroids. They have big clampers for grabbing rocks, and they have huge buzz saws on mechanical arms.

Once the Buzzers are out and in space, they activate their back thrusters and fly right at The Odyssey. They zoom onto the ship and clamp onto the hull. Their big metal hands dig deep into the thick hull. The Buzzers power up their saws. As they rotate at incredible speeds, they thrust them and start to cut holes into their hull. Bre shouts through the coms channel:

"Xander, we got Buzzers on us!"

"Yeah I see 'em," replies Xander. "John, Hogler, can you guys do something about them!" John says,

"Our turrets don't reach that far over." The two of them try to angle the guns at the Buzzers digging their saws into the hull. Hogler, who has an idea, hops out of his turret seat and rushes to grab his minigun. He shouts,

"I got an idea!"

"Oh no, this can't be good," remarks John.

"Lemme get in my spacesuit, get out there, and blow those skonkers up! Thoughts Xander?" Hogler shouts.

"Our guns aren't going to be able to get them, so if you think you can, you need to go ahead and blow some molopoo up." Hogler quickly suits up in his space armor suit in his bunk. He is now covered in Zarium steel-plated armor with a facial rebreather. He runs to a space hatch on the side with his hulking minigun in hand. On his feet, he wears bulky mag boots. As Xander nods. And he continues: "There is an asteroid field up ahead. My best estimates say we can lose them in that." Hell's Grace is proportionally bigger than

The Odyssey, so it could slip through the asteroids while Hell's Grace couldn't. Xander enthusiastically says,

"I like where your mind's at!" He pilots the ship, and it speeds to the rocky field.

Hogler is still on the hull, and now he is charging right at the last Buzzer. His rocket launcher and minigun are strapped to his back. His fists are clenched. After leaping onto the Buzzer, his mag boots lock on top. The pilot tries to rip him off the top with his big clampers. Hogler punches through the plated glass, rips the pilot out of the cockpit, holds him in the air, and punches him in the face with his big metal gauntlets. Hogler shouts,

"That's the last one down!" He runs back to the space hatch and goes back inside the ship.

"Nice job, head back inside. Things are about to get messy," says Xander. Now, Hogler is back aboard The Odyssey. Xander quickly engages his sublight thrusters. Wally also activates his sublight thrusters as he chases after him. The cannons open fire on The Odyssey's shield barriers. Many of the beams collide with the shield.

Xander twists and turns through the deep field of asteroids. Wally has to trail his ship behind a bit, so he doesn't crash into the rocks.

John and Hogler fire off an onslaught of laser beams. Both of them are good shots, so they land a few. The shield barrier begins to weaken on Wally's ship. Bre says from her observation deck:

"Xander rock on your left!" He moves the ship out of the way and dodges the incoming asteroid. "I think we're losing him!" Hogler fires a missile at one of the asteroids in the way of Hell's Grace. The missile hits the rock and explodes it, sending shrapnel straight at Wally. He dodges out of the way from most of the rocks.

Xander pulls the ship over to a huge meteor the size of a large capital ship. As he flies over it, a huge worm leaps out of a crater in the asteroid. It is a hulking space worm with bony armor plates over its body. Surprisingly, it moves incredibly fast as it zooms to The Odyssey with its huge, gaping, dual-hinged jaw. Its maw is full of sharp and jagged teeth.

With a quick reaction time, Xander can boost the engines and get out of the way of the worm's mouth. It crushes its mouth down just barely missing The Odyssey.

Wally, who was too focused on chasing Xander, didn't see the worm. The worm blasts up from underneath Hell's Grace. It snaps down on the escaping ship enclosing it in the damp prison that is the worm's mouth. Now, Wally and his crew are destined to rot for centuries while the worm slowly digests and melts them with its highly corrosive stomach acids.

Free from danger, The Odyssey slows down its thrusters. Xander takes his gloves off, wipes the nervous sweat from his bare palm. He deeply sighs and takes his hands off of the steering wheel.

The crew slowly converges back to the helm. Xander says with a proud tone;

"Good job guys! We had some great teamwork on this one!" They give a slow clap to themselves. "Now that we dealt with the crazy man, should we finally get heading to Coranthea?" Bre replies,

"That's probably best. We are going to need a lot of repairs from those stupid Buzzers. There should be an adequate spaceport we can dock at. I can check."

"Alright, I'll get ready for the warp... again. Before we jump, I will make sure to warn you all." Before Bre leaves, Xander stops her and asks, "Why do you think he was so persistent on getting that cargo?"

"With Wally... I never know. Maybe this was all just a ploy to chase us again... like he likes to," says Bre. Xander thinks, I wonder what is in there.

"Eh, you are probably right. He is one insane man."

"I know I'm right." The two of them exchange a slight chuckle.

"Yeah sure," remarks Xander. The crew disperses to their quarters. John goes and pours himself a steaming hot cup of coffee. In Hogler's quarters, he bench presses a slab of Zarium steel. Bre heads to her office to fill out some USG paperwork. Xander sits in the pilot's chair listening to some ancient Terran music.

Two

Xander presses a blue button with an icon of a microphone on it. A fuzzy microphone drops from the ceiling above. He says into it,

"This is your captain speaking, y'all might want to hold onto something we're about to warp." On the control console is a transparent hatch with a lever under it. He opens the hatch. Firmly grasps the lever and pulls it back really hard. "Now this is the fun part! Yeehaw!" As he pulls the lever back, the warp drive in the engineering room starts to shake and glow bright with quantum energy. He presses an arrow button on the console, and the loud music turns a lot louder. Now rock music from centuries ago is blasting through the ship.

Xander is looking through the glass-plated window in front of him. As he looks out the space out there starts to swirl like a whirlpool in the water. It looks to spin deeper and deeper. Space itself sinks back. Everything goes perfectly silent for a single moment; suddenly, the ship blasts through the portal at incomprehensible speeds. As they dash off, the stars streak like stripes in the sky. When the ship enters the portal, a flash of white light fills every corner and crevice of the ship. The light starts to fade away. Xander looks out the window to see Coranthea right there. "Now that's the miracle of space travel." Without the perfect calculations, their ship could have rocketed into a black hole or blasted straight into a planet. All or most ships with warp drives have some sort of supercomputer to make the calculations. EQ comes over the speakers and says,

"Warp successful. Now entering Coranthea." As Xander looks out into the abyss of space this all reminds him of his very first jump. Time feels like it is slowing down around him. As if he is watching every move slothful around him.

5 years ago (97 E.E.) in the Citadel, a student was preparing for his final test before graduating. Twenty-five-year-old Xander is attending the Citadel's School of Aviation, the most prestigious flight school in the galaxy. This is his final year before becoming a full-fledged pilot. Currently, he is top of his class; he has the fastest reaction time and is the best at tactical planning.

Unlike now, Xander is dressed perfectly in his Imperial pilot uniform. Black reflective aviator sunglasses rest on his nose. He has a thin 5 O'clock shadow. He walks to the docking bay where he will start his test. Walking through the garden-filled streets of the Imperial capital, the Citadel, Xander is making his way there; the

Citadel is the giant space station in the core worlds that serves as a city for millions.

Xander has lived here for the past four years where he has done the most rigorous training program in the galaxy. The tall street lamps that light the dark city at night shine onto him. The towering docking bay is where he enters. Waiting for him is Commander Jack Sonyan, the one who will be overseeing this exam, and one H-16 CloudJumper, a light starfighter that is to be used. The CloudJumper is a small blue colored ship with specks of chipping paint. When Xander approaches the commander he salutes him and the commander states to him,

"Private Xander Holsmo, you have passed all your classes with flying colors, but your place is not secured yet. You must pass this exam before becoming a true pilot!" Commander Jack is an old, grizzled Arlean man with a long scar that cuts across his nose. A standard Imperial naval hat sits upon his balding head. A fitted Federation uniform covers him from head to toe. "Go ahead and step in!" Xander nods to him. He walks up to the Cloud Jumper and takes off his sunglasses and puts them in his pocket. A metal ladder is propped up against it which leads up to the cockpit.

He climbs into the cockpit and shimmies into the cloth-covered seat. He places the helmet over his head and brushes his hair out of his eyes. After pressing a button on the ship's console, the cockpit closes above him. He flicks a few switches and the ship's engine starts to him as it is flooded with energy. The anti-gravitational systems activate, making the ship hover off the ground. Giant blast doors that are closed in front of the floating ship open slowly. As they slide open puffs of mist blast from the hydraulic mechanics. Xander firmly grasps the control wheel; he points it forward. It goes blasting off into the space outside of the Citadel. He reaches into his pocket with one hand on the wheel and pulls out a small data chip with the EQ written on it in marker. He plugs it into one of the ship's ports. A voice says,

"Hello Xander, what is the directive today?" After a moment of silence from the computer systems, Xander thinks, C'mon baby, don't let me down now.

"Yes, you still work!" Xander smiles widely. "EQ, you know you're my favorite A.I. in the galaxy. We've got a tough mission today: a double warp skip."

"My word, this is a difficult situation, but my systems will be more than capable of making those calculations." Within seconds EQ has made the calculations for a double warp skip. "Calculations completed." Xander puts the ship into full gear which activates the sun-light thrusters. After flipping off the hatch on a lever, he jerks back on the lever sending the ship into a warp. Xander's first ever warp, and it won't be his last. After completing the warp exam with outstanding results he graduated from the school and became a pilot. He had no idea how difficult it would be to make a living as a pilot, even a good one at that. He began taking up odd jobs from strangers he met at diners across the galaxy. After purchasing his first ship, the Odyssey, he found a crew that now travels the galaxy working jobs for the United SpaceFarer's Guild or USG.

Now in Corathean space, Xander aims his ship's bow at Las Nazara. He flicks a small metal switch that activates the thrusters on the stern side of the vessel. The thrusters glow bright with power and the light freighter blast off toward the planet's surface. The three suns barely peek out from behind the planet. They cast an intense light into the ship. It is about a two-minute drive down with the thrusters activated. It is a pretty smooth ride but the ship shakes a bit; it needs some repairs. Xander confidently says,

"Another successful warp! Welcome to Coranthea, the planet of sin as they call it." He dusts his gloved hands off. With the ship being piloted by EQ, Xander hops up out of his seat and heads to the lounge room. Behind his station is another console where SE-3 sits. Xander walks through the blast door and down the hall. An open hatch in the corridor fires a blast of hot mist into his face. He tries to swat it and exclaims, "Ugh we need to get this hunk of junk fixed!" A drop of dark brown oil drips onto his forehead from the ceiling above. He wipes it away with his gloves. He walks with inherent confidence. Xander reaches the lounge area and John, Hogler, SE-3, and Bre are sitting there. John is sipping on a cold Bizzle Juice, SE-3 is trying to repair some of the ship's insides, Bre is typing on her holocell, and Hogler is lighting a cigarette... again. Bre Evenguard is a human, same as John and Xander. Her flowing blonde hair shimmers in the light as it rests on her shoulders. She sports a shining spacefarer uniform with a black leathery belt across her upper waist. One light pistol is the same model as Xander's. A small USG logo is placed on the breast of her uniform. Golden earrings dangle from her ears. She looks over to Xander as he walks in and remarks,

"What's got you so happy?" He glances over at her while smiling and he adds,

"You know I love the feeling of a successful warp! I can't be happy!" As they are talking the ship shakes and rumbles as they approach the landing bay on Las Nazara. As he feels the ship shake, John sets his drink down on a nearby table. He looks over to Xander and questions,

"If I may ask sir: what is the purpose of our trip to Coranthea?"

"Well, I thought we could use a bit of a vacation. Honestly, I've been craving a zapple pie from Dina's Diner down there, and I thought maybe we could pick up a contract down at the SpaceFarers station there." Bre proposes,

"I think we can do that. We just need to update the Odyssey's transcripts, so that we can travel the galaxy legally." Xander nods,

"That's the problem, it's a flat 1,500 credit deposit to renew the transcripts. We only have 1,000 out of pocket." Bre replies,

"Well, if we can get a lucrative enough contract we'll be able to pay off the transcripts and have some extra." The ship lands at docking bay 35 near the outskirts of Las Nazara. Las Nazara is a bustling city. It has some of the biggest casinos and gambling spots in the whole galaxy.

Huge super yachts land at some of the pads nearby. Loud music blasts from giant speakers, and cannons shoot fireworks from the yacht's top deck. Drunken patrons stumble off the ship into the space port.

Three

Before they leave the ship and go to Coranthea, Xander says to Bre while they are at the helm,

"Hey Bre, should we open up that cargo container before we leave?" She thinks for a moment and then says,

"Yeah sure, let's head down to the scooper. The scooper is a section on the bottom of the ship that can pop out to grab cargo. Right now, a meter-and-a-half tall, two-and-a-half meter long, and one-meter-wide box sits in there.

Bre and Xander both walk down to the scooper bay. The crew picked up this metal container as they were just cruising on their way through warp route 66. It was in the wreckage of a derelict ship. On the way down, Xander asks,

"So what do you think's inside?" Her eyes wander around while thinking. A

"Uh... I have no idea. I'm hoping it's like Nexite, and we can just go seek that." As they approach the blast door to the airlock where the scooper bay is, Xander takes out a node and presses a button. The airlock door opens, and they see the container.

They both walk up to it. They walk around it as they examine it. On one side, they see a logo. It is a cartoonish picture of an ice cube and beside it is the text: Cryotech, Save your place in the future. On another side, is a blue glowing panel that still seems to be active even though the container seems old. Xander sees a glowing button that says: Open. He motions Bre over and says,

"I think I found the open button." Instinctively she presses the button. The top of the container is lifted by inside mechanics. The two of them step back as light blue, sub-zero mist pours out. Blue light shines from inside. They peer into it from afar. They look at each with the look of: do we look? After thinking for a moment, they walk up to the container.

As they get closer, someone inside sits up frantically and takes a big gasp of air. Both of them jump back like scared cats, draw their ray guns, and aim at the person. A man in a white sweatshirt with a red baseball cap sits there inside the container. He has bright blue eyes and fluffy brown hair.

He looks around the room confused like he's never seen a ray-gun or spacefarer. Once he sees two spacefarers with ray-guns pointed at him, he screams, and Bre and Xander scream in response. Xander says,

"Woah, Woah, calm down! Who are you?" He lowers his gun and motions for Bre to lower hers which she does. After he stops breathing heavily and calms down, he says with an accent that resembles New York of ancient Terra,

"Who the hell are you too, some space larper?"

"Larpers," asks Bre in an inquisitive voice. Her nose and forehead scrunch up in confusion.

The out of place man responds,

"Ya know, those losers who dress up and play games at the park?" Bre and Xander glance at each other puzzled. Xander says,

"Nope never heard of it. Who are you?"

"No, no, no I asked first! Ya gotta tell me!" The man starts to get out of the cryopod. He is wearing sweatpants and socks with sandals. Xander puts his palm to his chest and says,

"I'm Xander Holsmo, captain of The Odyssey. And this is Bre Evenguard, my first mate and USG representative." Bre shines a comforting smile on the man. He smiles back uncomfortably; he shivers and is pale from being inside the cryopod. "Now, you go."

"Me... I'm Brooks Jackson. Now, where on Earth am I?" Xander and Bre both make a realization. She says,

"Wait, where are you from?" He studies her with a befuddled expression and notices the unknown holocell on her waist, and the unusual jacket that she wears. He says,

"Uh... New- freakin' -York. Ya know it, baby!"

"As in Earth?" He begins to look more and more bewildered as he is bombarded with questions he thinks as normal. He thinks, What is she talking about? Of course Earth. Where else would it be...?

"Yes, Earth. Where else would it be?" Xander butts in:

"Okay, what year were you born?" Xander's eyes widen in interest deeper than the seas of Galatia.

"In 1998. What is with all these weird questions?" Bre and Xander exchange a mortified glance. They both think, Oh no, I know what's happening. Bre scoots over next to Xander while Brooks looks around and examines the room. She says to him,

"You got what's happening?"

"Yep, he's been out for 700 years. This is going to be an interesting day with him." Brooks wanders over to a wall full of technology and trinkets. "What are we supposed to do with him?"

"I don't know, we can't just throw him out into the galaxy... Maybe he could be useful to the crew?" He thinks, Maybe he can....

"Bre, you're too kind. If we all voted on this, we'd probably just drop him off at the nearest spaceport." She grins.

"I know. it's my lot in life; I'm too kind." Xander smiles back. "So I'll let you deal with this while I get everything set up for going out, and I'll tell everyone else about him." Xander rolls his eyes in annoyance.

"Don't leave me with him," he says as she walks out of the scooper bay. Xander turns to Brooks as he is admiring the ship's interesting inside. "Brooks was it?" He nods at Xander. "Brooks, Do you want this the easy way or the hard way?"

"Want what?"

"An explanation..."

"Give it to me straight," Brooks says while trying to look strong despite having no idea what's happening.

"Okay well, this is The Odyssey, a light frigate ship—"

"As in a spaceship in space?" Brooks' eyes widen in interest.

"Yes, this is a spaceship. We are in the orbit of Coranthea which is about 8,000 lightyears away from Terra or as you call it Earth." Brooks tries to wrap his mind around this.

"I want to go home." Brooks notices Xander's shift to a more solemn expression. He begins to feel anxious. "What is it?"

"That's the problem, Terra is gone. Some 200 years ago it was destroyed. Not to mention it is about 700 years past when you were born." In disarray, Brooks takes a seat on the lip of the container. His mind spirals thinking about this.

"They said it would only be twenty years." What have I missed? My son... My wife... My friends and family... all long gone, thinks Brooks. Xander sees the distress on his face. Brooks thinks of the hundreds of years he lost. The generations of the family he missed. He says,

"I'm sorry... but on the bright side; there is a whole galaxy out there for you to explore." The frown on Brooks' face begins to fade. Maybe I can reconcile my past with this present. Brooks says,

"Let's say I want to stay here. What do I need to know?" He begins to smile as he tries to forgive himself for his past mistakes.

"Well if you are going around the galaxy, you're not going to want to piss off the Empire."

"Wait like the Galactic Empire from Star Wars is real?" Xander looks puzzled by his reference.

"Star what now?"

"You know that movie from like forty years ago? The one with the lightsabers and Death Star?"

"Well for you forty years ago is more like 740 years 'cause of the whole cryosleep thing, so most of the stuff you know is probably long forgotten."

"If it's not the thing from Star Wars, what is it?"

"Well, I don't know what empire you are thinking of, but this is the governing authority over the entire galaxy." Brooks thinks, *So exactly what I'm thinking of.* "It is ruled by the twelve house heads." *That's a little different,* thinks Brooks. "I'm just warning you to watch out for Imp-pols, pretty much the police."

"What else do I need to know?"

"I'm assuming you don't want us to drop you off somewhere... alone?"

"I'd rather not."

"That's what she thought also. If you are going to be on my ship, there are some things you're gonna want to know." Brooks listens attentively as Xander takes him on a small tour of The Odyssey. "First, one of the other guys in here, Hogler, be careful around him. If you don't want him to rip your arm off, don't call him a pig."

"Why?"

"Just don't. You'll figure it out soon enough. Second, don't go into the reactor room."

"I feel like a room called the reactor room is a given not to go in."

"You'd be surprised. The last guy who went in there when we were in a warp was incinerated instantly, so I wouldn't recommend it."

"Noted." Xander shows him where the bathrooms and kitchen are.

"Since you are a rare find, you aren't going to want people to know who you are exactly."

"You mean me being the literal oldest guy in the galaxy?"

"Yeah that. I'm sure some people would love to get their hands on you as an attraction... it wouldn't be the first time something like that has happened in this galaxy."

"Again noted." Xander takes him to his captain's quarters.

"Right now we are docked in Las Nazara. It would be a very dangerous place for someone as inexperienced as you. No offense." Xander reaches into one of his drawers and grabs out a ray gun pistol. "Here, take this." He hands him the gun.

"Thanks." He looks at the ray gun with the amused look of a child.

"Now, do not just go shoot someone. As I'm sure you can assume, that is still illegal, and you will be arrested."

"This place does seem weird, but I think that was still a constant."

"I don't know how your society worked so I'm just making sure." Xander chuckles a bit. "Last few things before we head out if someone offers you Coco, say no. Always." Brooks nods nervously. "Another thing: this is space. There will be many aliens and creatures you have never seen before. Don't overreact, or make a big deal because that's rude and will give away that you aren't from 'round here." They walk back to the helm, and Xander tells him almost everything he will need to know how to survive in this galaxy.

At the helm, the rest of the crew waits for them including John, Hogler, SE-3, and Bre. Xander coaxes Brooks into the helm reluctantly. Xander pretty much pushes him through the blast doors. The rest of them watch as a man out of his time walks through the doors.

"Guys, this is Brooks. He's from Earth some 700 years ago," says Xander. Brooks awkwardly waves and says nervously,

"Hey." They all respond by saying:

"Hey, Brooks!" Before he came in, Bre told John and Hogler to be on their best behavior for the new guy. They both put on an apathetic smile as their eyes look dead inside. Hogler remarks,

"John, there's finally someone older than you!" He slaps John on the back and laughs obnoxiously loud. John glares up at Hogler who towers over everyone else.

"I'm not laughing," he says with no emotion. Bre steps up and says,

"Let's try to make Brooks feel at home as he acclimates to our galaxy." Brooks smiles as he feels comforted by the crew.

They all head down to the ramp that leads outside. Xander and Brooks stay back for a minute. Xander says,

"I know you probably want to see the city and everything, but I think it would be best if you stay on the ship for now." Brooks sighs and rolls his eyes.

"Ugh, I was looking forward to seeing it."

"I'm just saying for now. In due time, you'll be good to go out. Okay?"

"Yeah sure, I'll stay on."

"Thank you." Xander walks down to the ramp where the others are waiting.

Four

With the ship docked at bay 35, the landing strip extends from the hatch on the belly of the ship. Hydraulics pull the metallic walking down. Steam shoots from the mechanics. Xander comes walking down whilst brushing the dirt on his tan pants. Behind him, John, Hogler, Bre, and SE-3 follow. John carries a small metallic ray gun by his side. He is seldom seen without a gun and Hogler is still chewing on that old cigarette.

As the footramp lowers, a wave of humid air blasts in their faces. The smell of sea foam and saltwater fill their senses.

The triple suns pierce through the thin clouds above. It is relatively seventy-five degrees Fahrenheit. It is a truly beautiful day in Coranthea, but every day feels amazing. After stepping off the walkway, a young mechanic girl approaches Xander. Her eyes shine like diamonds in the hot sun. Pointy ears poke out from behind her frizzy brown hair. She is carrying a metal clipboard with a holo screen on it. She stumbles up towards him somehow tripping over her own feet. She looks at him with a nervous smile and says incredibly fast,

"Hello, I am Cinise. I work with the docking corporation here in Las Nazara. I've come to inquire if you need any repairs or fixes on this beauty of a ship you have here?" She looks up to the Odyssey, a hot rod red, round-shaped light freighter. Some of the bright red paint is chipping off the hull, and bits of carbon scoring are scattered around the hull. It measures sixty-five feet long, twenty feet wide, and twenty-five feet tall with metallic stripes across its body. Two powerful thrusters are attached to the back of the vessel. At the helm a glossy black window curves around the port. There are two cannons, one on each side of the ship. A tall tail sticks up from the back of the freighter. Small windows sit dotted around the hull. Xander looks up at her and inquires,

"Yes, we do need repairs and many fixes, but you seem very familiar. Where have I seen you before —That's it! You applied for the engineering position through Excellent aboard our ship didn't you?" Excellent is a job search application used by many across the galaxy.

"Oh, that makes a lot of sense! Your ship looks very familiar and that's why," she exclaims. Xander smiles at her and says,

"If you are still looking for a job we still never found an engineer, and we're still hiring?" She looks up from her clipboard and her eyes widen. A huge smile grows across her face. She frantically says,

"Oh my sir, that would be amazing! You have no idea how hard it is to find work in this galaxy! I would love to see the galaxy aboard a ship like the one you have here?" Xander replies,

"Woah Woah, calm down. If I recall your recommendations were highly thought of, and what I saw of your work was great. We do need an engineer, but it seems you already have a job doesn't it?"

"Yes, indeed that is true. I've been working here for a while now, but if you're offering I'll drop this job in a minute" As Cinise says this, she turns around and darts off to the main office at docking bay 35. As she runs off into the distance they hear her holler, "I'll be back with my stuff in two hours". As she runs off to who knows where Xander looks to the other standing behind him and he goes,

"Ok, we can deal with that whole thing later. Right now let's focus on why we came here. Bre, you go to the USG station and pick up a contract. John, can you go buy up some new ray guns down at the shop? Hogler, you go do whatever just don't blow anything up. SEE and I will head to Dina's Diner and the pool house. Let's meet back here in about— I don't know— three halons. Everyone make sure you have your coms on channel one. Okay, break!"

Each of them put little black earpieces in so that they can stay in contact. They all split off and go their separate ways. The landing bay they are standing in has piles of rusted scrap metal, old ship parts, and deactivated cells. Mechanics of all species work and tinker with ships.

At the exit of docking bay 35, there is a big sign atop tall posts. In big neon letters, it is written on the sign: Anything Goes. SE-3 looks up at the sign with his big optical lens. In his computer mind his thoughts go to: Anything goes? Humans say the darndest things... maybe they're onto something.

Though Coranthea is a planet in Imperial space, they don't have much of a presence in this world. There is a small Imperial checkpoint two clicks away for Las Nazara. Small patrols of Imp-pols (Imperial police) patrol through the city. Imp-pols wear sapphire blue, steel armor with white stripes along it. They are simply there as an intimidation tactic. Most people aren't going to start a fight or deal drugs if an Imp-pol is nearby.

With Las Nazara being such a popular planet, giant advertising hover blimps soar through the sky's above. These huge remotely piloted ships have giant screens on each side. The screens play ads and commercials. The city is littered with body mod shops and black markets.

Bre pulls up a map of the city on her holocell. She walks out of the open air bay with her head down in her holocell. Xander is following closely behind since they have to go in the same direction with SE-3 behind him. When she looks up from her holocell, she looks at the streets around her. Hoverbikes and speeders line the street as they lean up against the metal buildings. Flashing neon lights point to all the many casinos and bars. Little patches of sand and grass litter the streets. Tall Coranthean palm trees sprout from the patches. They walk past Destolacians, Plastarians, Roxians, and all other sorts of species. A Roxian, a race of reptilian humanoids that are incredibly strong, drags a cart past them. The Roxian stands approximately six feet tall. Its skin is dark green with lime-green spots. The hovering cart is full of scraps such as warp drive motivators and rusted deactivated canisters. Bre halts and says,

"This is my stop! I'll see you in a bit." She waves at Xander as he strides down the streets. He turns around and waves back at her. Bre enters the USG station. She walks through the saloon doors that open as she reaches them and shut them firmly behind her. Inside the station is a jukebox playing some Bizz Bop music. Neon lights hang from the ceiling illuminating the room. A female Cenianite, a race of semi-aquatic humanoids with long tentacles that stretch from the back of their heads, stands behind a counter with a computer sitting atop it. The woman has thick blue eyeshadow and bright red lipstick. As Bre enters the station the lady looks at her with an annoyed expression and states in a monotone voice,

"Hello and welcome to the USG station on Coranthea. Please submit your crew's ID number before interacting with our terminals" she says this as if she is reading from a script that she hasn't practiced. Her voice sounds like she has been a long-time smoker and is very deep. Bre replies,

"Our ID number is 18960." The lady types it into her computer. The keyboard clicks loudly. "We would like to take a contract." The lady looks up from her computer and glares at Bre. She says to Bre,

"Well, it seems here that your USG transcripts require renewal. Your crew is going to need to get that renewed as soon as possible, or else the fees go up." Bre slyly says,

"Ok—" Bre squints and looks at her name tag. It reads: Clirise. "— Clirise. Is it? That's the problem: if you get the payout from a contract we can pay off the fee." Clirise rolls her eyes and sighs. "If you give us an extension and let us have a contract we can pay it— please." Clirise types something on her computer; she looks back to Bre and says,

"Ugh, I think we can manage that."

"Oh thank you! What kinda contracts do you have?" Clirise looks down at her computer screen and reads,

"The first one: pick up crates of Nexite from Boloxia and deliver them to the Citadel for 20,000 credits. Second: stop a rebellion on Destolace for a payout of 50,000 credits—" Bre cuts her off:

"Is there any way we can take both of them?" She looks at her with a nervous smile. And taps her fingers on the counter anxiously. Clirise responds to her,

"Ugh" she rolls her eyes at her again. "Fine take 'em both, but you need to renew the transcripts as soon as possible." Bre nods and sticks her holocell into a data port on a terminal in the corner. All the information from the contracts downloads onto her holocell. She exits the station out into the city streets. As she is leaving, she hollers to Clirise,

"Thank you!" Clirise goes back to her duties on the computer.

As Bre completes this deal at the USG station, it reminds her of the first time she worked with them. Flashback to three years ago (100 E.E.). Bre is twenty-six years old. She was struggling to make ends meet in this harsh galaxy. Eventually, an old friend of hers told her there was an opportunity for a mining job on Moxous IV.

After taking a shuttle to the Trench of Moxous IV, she began terrible work as a miner. The conditions in the Trench are horrendous. The hours are unimaginable. The pay was only 8 credits an hour. There was never any safety equipment to protect the miners from the caustic gasses released in the mines. It was unbearably hot. Bre was lucky she wasn't killed due to the conditions. Throughout her year of mining in the Trench she remained optimistic as she always did. Even as a young human female she still was one of the most effective miners in the Trench. Everyone else in her troop noticed this about her. Word started to spread around the company. Even the mean old executives of her company noticed this; they began to promote her up the ranks. She eventually became a manager of her own mining company. She got many opportunities and job offers from many sorts of people. A few weeks after her promotion a USG recruiter asked her if she would want to join the guild as an overseer. Of course, she took this job immediately. The pay is much higher (18 credits an hour); she would get to travel the galaxy. Now working for the USG she had to find a ship that was already in the guild to work from. That just so happened to be the Odyssey. She joined their crew and became their USG representative. Now for the past year and a half, he has been working with the USG and flying through the galaxy with the Odyssey.

Before Bre leaves through the doors of the USG building, Clirise says:

"Oh also, the Empire sent out an email to all private companies that everyone needs to renew their weapon licenses on all ship's underneath us. We're going to need that as soon as possible. None of us are looking to have the entire Empire on us." All ship's under the Empire must have licenses to authorize the use of their highly deadly weapons. Bre says,

"Okay, we'll have that done right away." She walks out of the door and heads to docking bay 35.

Five

John walks through the city streets heading north. He uses a map on his holocell. He is looking for Dexstar's Pawn, a popular pawn shop in Las Nazara that is most notable for selling ray guns. The shop is not in the best part of the city. He walks through a dark street. Tall buildings and overhanging canopies block the triple sun from above. The dimly lit street is only illuminated by the small holes in the canopies and the bright neon lights. John passes by drug merchants sitting on the street curbs. Hoods they wear shroud their face in shadow. As he is walking, a hooded figure approaches him. The man pulls a light ray gun out from his holster and aims it at John. As he holds the gun out, his hand shakes nervously. He says,

"Give me your money!" He drops the hood down. He is a human; his face is scarred with a patch covering his left eye. John looks at him with a small smile. The guy doesn't look angry or happy to do this. It's just what he has to do. It looks as if he had been on Coco or something (Coco being a very powerful hallucinogenic drug crafted from the toxic flowers grown on Boloxia). John has seen what someone on Coco looks like too many times; he is all too familiar with it. John slowly says,

"I don't have any money." The man squints at John and says,

"Ugh, that ray gun— that's probably worth some credits. Give it to me!" John slowly reaches for his holster. He unclips the strap holding it secure. Once he pulls it out, he tosses it in the air at the guy. As he looks up to catch it, John dashes at him. He moves at incredible speeds as he closes the distance. John quickly disarms him of his weapon, throwing it to the ground. He also grabs his gun from out of the air. After John sweeps his legs, the guy drops to the floor. John stands above him. The man reels back. Johns calmingly says,

"I'm not going to hurt you. What is your name!?" He looks at John with terror behind his eyes and hesitates for a few moments and mummers,

"Bareen— My name is Bareen." John reaches into his jacket pocket. As he does, Bareen lurches back again. "Don't shoot!" Bareen notices his Imperial jacket and thinks, Oh no, he's an Imp-pol. He'll take me away for sure.

"I'm not going to hurt you." He pulls out a small data card and tosses it to the guy. Bareen catches it and looks up at him confused. "Take this and don't go on and waste it. Get yourself a meal or something." John turns around and continues walking. He can almost feel Bareen looking at him, but he does not turn to look back.

As he is walking, he passes a Rock Shack. It's pretty much just a fancy name for a brothel. The flashing neon lights outside the building flash in his eyes. John purposely avoids it. He gives the building a sort of glare while he walks past. He takes his holocell out of his pocket and pulls up the city map. Dexstar's Pawn is straight ahead. John walks up to a metal building with glass-plated windows to show off the merchandise. Neon signs above the canopy that hangs over the door say: Dexstar's Pawn, the galaxy's 3rd greatest pawn shop.

When he opens the glass door a little bell dings. He looks around the open room. Across the room is a tall counter with a computer and register on it. The counter's body has a sliding glass door with a compartment that had all of his wares on display. A tall, bulky, four-armed, bipedal, male, humanoid, alien stands behind the counter. He is a Driodite. He has burnt orange skin and bright yellow eyes. Clad in a light blue polo shirt with holes for two extra arms. A navy blue tie lays around his neck. Two black ink pens hang in his left breast pocket. When the bell dings the alien spins around to look at John entering. The moment he recognizes that it is John he grows a big smile with his small shiny white teeth. And he says excitedly,

"John Tyler! Look who wandered back into Dexstar's arms again! I assume you're here to buy your usual items, but I would love to interest you in these new ray guns that just came in!" He says while gesturing to the glass case below him. Dexstar's voice sounds like that of a used car salesman who is always hunting for a sale. "We have state-of-the-art cryo-blasters, new and improved plasma-laced blades, and our newest item— the personal deflector shield!" John's eyes widen as Dexstar says this.

"You know I never like to buy any of your knockoff items, but that shield piques my interest."

"I knew it would!" Dexstar slyly smiles.

"How much for it?" asks John.

"Since it is new, it would be 200 credits, but for an old friend, I'll make it 175 credits! Is that a deal?"

"Ok, I'll take it!" John pulls out a data chip from his pants pocket. He plugs the chip into the register on the counter. Dexstar clicks some buttons on the register and 175 credits are transferred out of his data chip. He opens up the glass compartment from behind; he pulls out the personal shield generator. It is a circular lustrous metallic disk with a glowing blue center and a strap so that it can be worn. After taking it out, he sets it on the counter, and John grabs it. "I'm also looking for a heavy repeater ray gun. If you have one?" Dexstar presses a button underneath the counter with his lower right arm. The overhead lights dim down. The wall behind him spins around, and it reveals a wide emporium of blasters. A strip of flashing yellow lights lines the sides of the enormous weapon rack. John's eyes open wide as he takes in the huge assortment of wondrous weapons. "So which one ya want?" He says while gesturing to the rack of guns. The assortment ranges from light handguns to heavy assault rifles to long-range snipers.

"That one!" John says while pointing to a big heavy repeater of the XO-1 model. Dexstar grabs it off the wall, presses the button to put the wall back, and sets the gun on the table.
CLICK-CLICK-CLICK! He presses some keys on the computer with two of his hands whilst the other two are cleaning the repeater off. Dexstar says in a convincing tone,

"So that's gonna run ya about— uh— let's say 200 credits." John puts his data card in the register again and the allotted credits are transferred. Which puts John's total balance on his data chip at 225 credits. John puts the repeater on his back with the strap that came attached. Before he leaves the shop, he walks up to some of the shelves on the sides.

As he walks out of the store, Dexstar yells:

"Thank you! I might be back again!" Dexstar waves his four arms at him as John leaves through the doors. He says,

"I'll see you when I see you!" He turns around and walks and exits through the glass door out front. John was happy he got a good deal on this equipment, but Dexstar changed him about 25 more credits than it would've cost at a retail store. With the items in hand, John heads to the ship.

As he is strutting back to The Odyssey, he recalls some he should probably do while he is here on Coranthea. *While I'm here, I may as well check in at the station.* He changes his path of travel towards an Imperial station on the planet. His face reads of annoyance and disdain. While he is walking, he groans and puts a hand to his back. John murmurs,

"I'm getting too old for this." He continues walking through the metal-grated streets until he reaches the tall Imperial station. It is an elegantly designed, white, metal base. Blue Imperial banners hang from the edges of the roof. Two Imp-pols stand on the sides of the glass doors. As John walks through the doors, he nods to the Imp-pols. When they notice his Imperial jacket, they give an affirmative nod.

Inside, it is pristine and white, and much nicer than the city of Las Nazara. Fine couches sit in the corners of the room. Holo screens of the Imperial Heads stand in powerful positions. White lights fill the room with a cool glow.

A young Arlea man stands behind a tall white desk, but he is facing the other direction because he is working on a computer in the back. He wears a black suit with the Imperial crest on it. John walks up to the desk. Before he can speak, the man swivels around and says:

"If it isn't John Tyler, what are you doing here?" When he turns around, John

"Eh, just the usual, Tom. I'm just picking up my monthly package."

"Oh well that's ironic, that one just shipped in a few days ago." Tom swivels back around and walks in the back room. He scavenges through the large pile of gray plastic boxes with different stamps and labels. John leans against the desk and taps his fingers on the desktop. He loudly says:

"Tom, how's Avara been?" In the back, Tom scoffs and says:

"John you have no idea. Avara and I are good I'd say, but the kids are a lot to say the least." Tom loudly shuffles through the pile. "Imagine trying to keep track of three kids while working a 9-to-5 with the Empire."

"I think I can imagine that." John puts a hand to his breast pocket and feels a small paper photo. He thinks of what used to be.

"I get home after working with all these annoying people all day, and then immediately have to take care of them. I hate to complain, but it can be a lot sometimes."

"Yeah, I get that." Tom steps out of the back holding a small gray box. He sets it on the top of the desk and opens up the computer. And he begins typing on it.

"Lemme just pull up your profile, and we can get this all sorted." Tom pushes the box over to him. John opens it and looks inside. There are multiple metallic credit chips, packs of food rations, and Energen ammunition cells. He confusedly looks at the credit chips and says,

"Why are there so few credits here? There were like 7,500 last month and there's only 5,000 now."

"Well, high-ups in the Empire have been making a lot of cuts recently, so they've had to cut the retirement packages by twenty-five percent." John begins to feel a deep frustration grow in him. John raises his voice:

"What! How can they do that! I worked my ass off fighting for this." Tom presses a button to authenticate that John has received his package.

"I'm sorry. Things are really getting out of hand with the Nytarians. The Empire has been going to their farthest lengths to defeat them."

John understands. He will always advocate for the Empire. After his decades of service, he almost feels obligated to have firm allegiance to the Empire for all his days to come.

It is true that the Empire has been going all out to destroy the Nytarians. They have doubled or even tripled their blockades and enlisted billions more into the galactic army. They all know of the power the Nytarians possess and aren't looking to underestimate them again...

He picks the box up underneath his left arm and walks out of the glass doors.

"See ya, John. I'm sorry about that," says Tom before John leaves. He turns around, gives him a smile and nod, and leaves. Now outside the Imperial Station, he heads towards The Odyssey with guns and boxes in hand.

Six

Hogler is here for one reason and one reason alone: to soak in the natural hot springs. He headed straight for the springs as he had known where they were from previous visits. Even though Hogler is big and broad his strong, powerful legs propel him through the streets. Sand that is spread across the streets keeps getting uncomfortably stuck in between his hoofs. He slides by Talasians and surprisingly Boloxians in the city streets. He put on some dark sunglasses to protect his eyes from the harsh tri-suns. As he runs, his hoofs make a loud banging sound as they hit the metal roads. Warm steam caresses his face as he enters the outside of the springs. The natural pools are crystal clear and azure blue. They are like little divots in the ground. All of them are full of tiny sand particles. Vents in the pools connect deep underground to the nearby dormant volcano that heats the pools with steaming magma.

Tall metal fences surround the boiling-hot water pools. Vacant hover bikes lean against the fence. Metal lamps stand out of the ground and cast a dim light below. Little sea bill nests lie atop some of the lamps. A concrete room where all the fences converge at.

Sitting in a chair sits a human wearing an Aroa and a pair of sunglasses. She is loudly chewing gum and listening to music with an earbud in. Completely oblivious, she bops her head to the bizz bop music. Hogler walks up to the human and says,

"How much to go in the pools?" He waves at her to get her attention. "Uh, hello. I want to go to the pools!" He bangs on the glass, "HELLO!" She takes out her earbud and looks at him very annoyed. She stares daggers at him, and she snarls,

"What the skonk do you want?" She looks at him disgustedly.

"Uh, what do you think? How much to get into the pools?" She rolls her eyes at him and says,

"Ugh, it's 15 credits." Hogler takes out his data chip and hands it to her. She plugs it into a register; 15 credits transfer off it. She hands it back to him; then he puts it in his pocket. She clicks a button inside the room, and the gate opens swiftly. Hogler walks through the gate, and it shuts behind him. Once he leaves, she puts her earbud back in.

Now inside the gates, Hogler walks over to the pools of bubbling, hot water. A quick breeze blows over the ground; it blows warm steam onto Hogler's face. In the pools sits one man: a human with tan skin and bright blue eyes. Hogler walks past the pools into a small hut; where he changes into a complimentary bathing suit. Now changed he walks back to the springs. As he slowly gets into the pools; his eyes widen as the heat crawls up his legs. He lets out a relaxing sigh as he lets his worries melt away in the boiling water. The man across from him looks over to Hogler and gives him an acknowledging nod; Hogler nods back to him. After moving to the side, Hogler put his arms up on the sides and leans his head back on the rim of the spring. His eyes slowly close when he falls into a relaxing slumber.

Golden beams of light rain down from the triple suns that are held in the sky. He senses the light fall over his face and he slowly wakes up. A quiet sound of the sea bills cawings above. The small feathered creatures glide on the cool breeze that travels throughout the sky. He lets out an enormous yawn. The guy across from him glances over at Hogler. An inquisitive expression lies on his face. He takes a long deep breath before he says,

"You were on that big ship that pulled in not too long ago?" Hogler lifts his heavy head and opens his tired eyes to look at him. He growls,

"Yeah who's asking?" The man across from him smirks,

"I'm just a traveler looking for travel. . . I see you have a ship. . .? I'm not looking to impose on you, but just curious If you have room for one more old soul aboard your vessel?" Hogler grins and his large tusks poke out of his mouth. He thinks, *I think we would all love some more money on the ship.*

"Before, do you have credits?" The man glances at a bag next to him.

"I'll have enough."

"I hope so. You could get anyone to do anything with enough credits."

"Sadly, that is too true," whispers the man. "No one cares for anything anymore unless money is involved. It is the root of all evil." He quotes ancient texts from Terra's past. Hogler somewhat recognizes the quotation.

"You said you were an Akara?" The man nods. "It sounds so familiar. What is it?"

"We are the guardians of the Echo. Seekers of wisdom. Keepers of knowledge." All of that flies right over Hogler's head.

"So what, you're a monk?"

"Some of us are. Some of us aren't."

"Well that's weird. I'm not one to care much for the mystical. When I head back to the ship, come with me, and the captain will see if we have room. Also, what's your name?"

"Just call me Davenk the Akara." Hogler looks at him somewhat confused; his brow furrows and a small crease appears on his forehead. He thinks, Akara... Where have I heard that before...? The word sounds somewhat familiar, but he doesn't know where it comes from. Davenk senses the confusion amidst Hogler and says, "Maybe if I go on the ship with you, I'll be able to tell you about Araka..." Hogler nods to him in affirmation before sinking back down into the bubbling pool. As Hogler rests in the pool he hears Davenk whisper, "The truest test is the one that is in your mind..." Hogler feels a sort of mystery about this man but he isn't sure why.

In Boloxian space, two more shuttles have tried to escape. These were now armored with light cannons but cannons at that. A low-power deflector shield made from blue energy hexagons surrounds the full area of the ship. As the two shuttles exit the atmosphere, they emerge from the thick green clouds. Once in range of the looming battleship, they open fire on the giant ship. The bolts whizz through the vacuum and strike the thick energy field that surrounds the Apocalypse. These shuttles are slightly bigger than the ones before but not anything in comparison to the Apocalypse. The blasts barely register as damage on powerful shields.

Aboard the bridge, Chief gunner Nator gives the command to fire the ion cannons. Ten of the bow ion cannons lock onto the shuttles. Five cannons for each of them. After Nator gives the order, the ion cannons open fire until the small ship's shields are down. Now that it is rendered defenseless, the Apocalypse charges up one of its belly-side Powernaught rail guns. These 25-meter-long barrels hold a 5-meter-long steel bolt. Magnets inside the barrel flick on. Electromagnetic currents flow down the rail or barrel. Parallel conductors fire the electricity through the long barrel. The steel bolt blasts through the barrel at incredible speeds. A 68-kilogram projectile zooms at 13,000 m/s. The bolt flies out of the barrel; it collides with the first shuttle. The amount of kinetic energy obliterates the shuttles. After this swift demonstration, the shuttle activates its sublight thrusters. It zooms past the Apocalypse. What no! Dead... My brother, friends, and family are all dead to those vile monsters— how could they do such a thing? They will pay for this act, the pilot thinks. Nator halts the guns not to fire, so that it may escape and tell what has happened here. Now a shieldless shuttle speeds away from the Apocalypse to safety.

Xenos is meditating in the presence of Nylos. In the Chamber, Xenos lies in a pool of water. His mind is perfectly still like a still pond. The Chamber is pitch black beside the lanterns that are suspended with gravitational disruptors. This is the time when Xenos prays with Nylos. We still haven't found the Stellaris. As it is your will we will find and destroy them. Suddenly Xenos senses two life forms outside the chamber. He feels two janitorial Nytarians; one of them says,

"...I'm telling you, don't go in there! Xenos said 'Do not disturb me'."

"Yes...," says the other. "...But I'm pretty sure he would want to know about this."

"If it's that important, just tell him when he's done!"

"I could, but this is urgent! I'm going in!"

"Don't come whining to me when he gets mad." The one janitor opens the door. As he steps his foot out into the open door, Xenos senses him. He raises his hand in the air. Invisible, chaotic, purple strands of Echo energy zoom to the janitor. The strands wrap around the sides of his neck. They pull back, snapping his neck which kills him immediately. In his last moments before he reaches the Veil, he hears a voice that isn't his own. *Though you fail, you are still forgiven.* The other janitor sees his friend drop to the ground dead. He immediately averts his sight away from the door and shuts it. Xenos calms down and goes back to his meditation.

In the far reaches of the galaxy, the Nyatrians are mobilizing their troops on the planet Nytar. A heavy rainstorm looms over the planet.

The Tarkos Mountains are the tallest and biggest mountain ranges on the planet. The tallest ones can be up to 10,000 meters tall. Many Nyatrians have tried to surmount the perilous peaks but none have ever made it to the top.

Deep within the Tarkos Mountains, lies an expansive hollowed-out cave. For centuries, miners worked to hollow this vast cavern. Originally it was made for harvesting the resources of the mountains, but now it has a new, holier purpose. Inside, it is damp and cold. Wind echoes throughout the barren tunnels like roaring lions. Moss and vines crawl up the sides of this cavern. Spiders spin their spindly webs.

The sound of howling shouts billows throughout the tunnels.

In the dark recesses of the caverns, thousands of Nytariansoldiers lie face up in shallow, frigid water that only reaches just below their mouths. Inside this deep cave, is a perfectly carved-out section. A thin layer of water has been spread across the chilly stone mantle. The Nyatrian soldiers are all naked except for thin, tight loincloths. Their eyes rest closed, and they breathe calmly and slowly.

At the front of the water pool, is a tall stone podium. A Nytarianpriestess stands upon the stone. This is Nalara, second to Xenos in the Nytarian Hierarchy.

Nalara wears the standard priestess gown with the black veil that shrouds her face in the darkness.

While she stands tall on the podium, she holds an old book with a leathery cover, and the pages are brown and weathered. She reads from it with a voice that echoes throughout the entire mountain.

"You shall not be fearful, for I grant you all the power you need to vanquish all of you enemies in my name, Nylos!" In the far corner of the cave room, is an enormous pile of dead bodies. None of them are Nytarian, there are Humans, Diodrites, Hessoths, Roxians, Boloxians, Arleans, and hundreds more aliens from across the galaxy; their blood of many colors pools underneath the pile. "You will be anointed in the blood of the unworthy! Their sufferings will fuel you to become the warriors you have been destined to become!" She reads from the holy texts that Xenos wrote from his communions with Nylos. "You will be reborn through your enemies' blood!"

Other priestesses in red draping robes who hold wooden bowls walk up to the pile of bodies. They fill their bowls with warm pools of blood. The priestesses wall around to all of the men laying in the shallow water. As they walk past each soldier, they pour the blood across the soldier's bare bodies.

Water slowly drips off the ceiling into the pools below.

"You will fulfill your true birthright as Children of Nylos! As my devoted followers, you must purge the galaxy of those who refuse my doctrine!" she shouts.

After a few minutes of the priestesses anointing them, all the soldiers rise out of the water. Blood drips off their lavender skin and falls into the cold water. The soldiers are filled with the dark presence of Nylos and holy rage. They breathe heavily and growl.

Nalara sets the book down and yells:

"Now go prepare for the Conquests! Suit up in your armor! Sharpen your blades, and be ready to have the galaxy bend down before Nylos!"

The soldiers rush to put on their heavy armor and ready their blades. Thousands of enraged troopers flood onto Nytarian attack ships as they prepare for battle

Seven

Back on Coranthea, Brooks wanders around The Odyssey as he tries to find something to do. He sits in Xander's pilot chair; he pretends to fly the ship, and Brooks makes laser sounds with his mouth. He stares out the huge glass-plated window in the helm at the interesting landscape of Coranthea. He says to himself after he gets out of the chair:

"I can't believe he's making me stay on the ship." Begins to sulk around the ship. "I mean, how would he even know if I left?" Brooks begins to hatch a devious plan. He starts to plot. "That's true. He would never know. There's a whole city out there waiting for me." Brooks decides what he has to do. He walks to the landing ramp. After searching for literally five minutes, he finds the button to lower the ramp. He lowers the ramp completely. Once it touches the metal landing bay floor, he presses it again to start closing it back up. Brooks dashes through the closing door. As it is about to shut, he slips through the steel ramp.

Now on the ground, Brooks looks around at the surroundings. He sees bots that baffle his young mind. Back on Earth, he would have never imagined that robots and androids could have ever existed.

He notices the huge sign that says: Anything goes! And he assumes that's the exit, and walks through it. He passes all sorts of aliens: Driodites, Hessoths, and many more. He tries not to stare while also examining them. Some do notice him and see his odd choice of outfit as no one dresses like that anymore.

Bored, he tries to think of something to do. Hmmm... what to do. What to do.

Brooks eventually reaches one of the roads where hovercars blast by. He walks up to the crosswalk where a traffic light is. Other humans and aliens wait at the crosswalk where Brooks stands. The light stays green for an obnoxious amount of time. A Florbod, humanoid aliens that are all hairless and come in many colors, next to Brooks says,

"What is with this Skonking light? Some people have places to be!" He constantly looks at his watch and taps his foot. A few moments later, the light turns red and the walk sign pops up. Brooks sprints forward the moment it changes. Though all the hover cars should have stopped, one hover truck didn't and keeps going.

As Brooks is sprinting through the crosswalk, the hover truck comes speeding by. It almost hits him, but the driver stomped on the brakes just before. With the sudden stop, it falls and tips on its side. The doors in the back of it fly open, and everything in it dumps out onto the road. Everything pours out on the road except mattresses. Hundreds of tiny credits chips and dozens of green cubes fall out of the open doors. All the hover cars around honk in frustration as he blocks the entire road.

The truck is a transport truck. On both sides of it, there is the logo for Mr. Marshy's Mattresses, a galaxy-wide mattress firm.

A very angry human in an Italian cut suit with a small fedora comes stomping out of the driver's side seat. He strides over to Brooks with a ray gun in hand, and he yells,

"What are you doing? Ya knocked over my skonking truck!" The man gives Brooks the middle finger. Brooks is at first surprised that it is still used nowadays. "Hey wise guy, you gotta pay for all this!" Another man in the same suit who looks freaked out hops down from the other seat and starts to frantically pick up the stuff that fell out.

A small patrol of four Imp-pols who all carry ray rifles notices the ruckus and the stopping of traffic. The four of them clad in blue and white armor march over to the accident. One of them with a purple shoulder pauldron which indicates he is of higher rank, walks over to the man yelling at Brooks. He butts in and state,

"What is happening here?" The man puts on a suspicious smile and turns up to the Imp-pol; he says,

"Sir, there is no problem here. This fine gentleman and I were simply talking some things through. You know how it can be." The man talks with the slightest indication of an Italian accent. He sounds very persuasive.

One of the other Imp-pols is looking through the fallen over stuff. He picks up one of the green cubes and scrutinizes it. He stands up and walks over to the leader with the green cube in hand; he says,

"Sir, you might want to look at this." The leader swiftly grabs it and looks at it. He says to the anxious-looking man and says,

"What is this?" The man scratches his collar nervously.

"Oh, it's mattress stuffing." The longer he looks at it he begins to realize.

"This is Coco isn't it!" ask the Imp-pol.

"No, no it's not!"

"Are you aware that lying to an Imperial officer is a federal crime?" Brooks, who realizes he is in the middle of a drug bust, begins to try and scoot away. As he starts to walk away, the driver man notices and says to the one cleaning it up:

"Don't let him get away. He needs to pay for this!" The man hops up and begins to chase after Brooks. The other one chases after them. As he dashes ways, the Imp-pol shouts,

"You are under arrest! Come back or we will take lethal action!" The man momentarily turns around but then continues to run after the panicking Brooks. "Run after him!" The four Imp-pols run after the men who are running after Brooks.

The two men open fire on Brooks with their ray pistols. Laser bolts fly past Brooks. He yells,

"You have lasers! What isn't there?" The bolts barely miss him. One of them pulls out a metal gun-type thing. He fires a small steel bolt; it attaches to the back of Brook's shirt which he doesn't notice in all the action.

Right after they see the man shoot, the Imp-pols open fire with their ray rifles. Since they are a much better shot than the man, they hit both of them in the legs with a stun bolt which knocks them both to the ground in the back alley they are all in. The Imp-pols rush to the stunned man and put Imperial cuffs on them.

Brooks sprints far away from the alley. He runs as fast as he can; he pushes through anyone in his way which pisses off a lot of people. He tries to remember the way back to where The Odyssey is parked.

After about five minutes of wandering throughout Las Nazara, he finally finds his way back to docking bay 35.

After he presses a bunch of buttons on the landing legs of The Odyssey, eventually he found one that opened the landing ramp. He rushes aboard the ship and goes to the bunk that Xander gave him. He falls asleep immediately after he lies down.

He is asleep for about twenty minutes, and then he wakes up due to an odd sensation on his leg. When he wakes up, he remembers that his cell phone is still in his pocket from 700 years ago. He takes it out, turns it on, and sees that somehow there is still 62% left in it. He thinks, How is there still battery left? He scrolls through his screen pages, and he sees that he has 25,5675 missed notifications from Bereal. He begins to freak out and quickly swipes over to another app, Snapchat. Once he opens it, he falls to his knees and yells,

"Noooooo! I lost all my streaks!" He looks through all his other apps seeing what he missed.

Eight

Xander and SE-3 first walk up to the main building in the docking bay. A sign above the building reads: Brandy's Landing. Xander walks up to the metal front door. He knocks. Inside, they hear rustling and someone stomping towards the door. It swings open, and a tan, heavyset human steps out. She has emerald green eyes and brown hair. In one hand she holds a whiskey bottle and in the other is a smoking blunt. Xander smiles and says,

"Hello, I'm guessing you are Brandy?"

"Yep, the one and only."

"Wow, you are one fine girl," charmingly says Xander. She holds back a smile.

"Oh, I know I am." SE-3 notices her interesting attire. He notices her thin white, shirt, her tight leathery pants, and the dual holster that is strapped around her thick thighs.

"We were wondering if you guys do repairs here?"

"It depends."

"On what?" She eyes them both up and down.

"Do ya got credits?" Xander feels his pockets.

"Yep!" Her ears perk up after hearing money is involved. She leans into the building, flips a lever, and sets her whiskey down. After the lever is flipped, a sign underneath the other sign lights up. This one says, And Repairs. She smiles and says,

"Welcome to Brandy's Landings And Repairs! What can I do for you?"

"Well, we need a full Energen to refuel, hull repairs, and ammunition reload." She walks around the base of The Odyssey. She inspects it.

"Goodness, what did you do to this beauty of a ship? Oh my, you've got chunks of your hull missing." she rolls her eyes. "For all that stuff ya asked for... it'll be 2,000 credits."

"Okay, that sounds good."

"I'm assuming you'll want Zarium plates for the full covering?" He nods. "Actually, make it 2,500."

"Woah, don't you think that's a little much just for Zarium."

"I would, but you've seen the economy. Zarium prices have skyrocketed ever since the rebellion on Moxus."

"Yeah, that's fair. It's a tough galaxy." Brandy persuasively asks, "So 2,500?"

"That'll do." She whistles very loudly. Suddenly, a bunch of bots comes pouring out of a hatch on the floor. All of them hold tools. They immediately begin repairs and refuels on the ship.

Xander and SE-3 turn around and begin strolling through the city down to Dina's Diner which is just a little past the USG station where Bre is. SE-3 pre-downloaded the city's layout map onto his internal hard drive. SE-3 leads ahead of Xander since he knows how to get there. A hoverbike zooms past them. Driving it is a human man clad in black leathery clothes. The smell of salty water is blown throughout the air. Grains of sand blown in the wind brush up against Xander's face and SE-3's retinal receptor. Though the suns are beginning to set over the horizon, it is still very bright out due to there being thrice as much sunlight and very few clouds.

Though the Empire doesn't have a strong presence on Coranthea, six-foot-tall holo signs stand on the sidewalks. The holo signs flash propaganda posters to join the Imperial navy. One of them has an Imperial officer standing at attention and written on it in big font reads: "Join The Empire Now! Come And Protect Your Galaxy From The Threats That Want To Take Your Home!" Xander glances over at one of the holo signs. Seriously Imperial propaganda out here. They've got the Outer Worlds too. He shakes his head at the holo signs. Xander doesn't have any real problems with the Empire if anything he likes how they have bettered the galaxy. How they have established good warp speed routes, provided a galaxy-wide currency, and they provide protection to all.

    The diner sits on the corner of 39th and 3rd street. After waiting for the speeder and hoverbike traffic to clear, Xander and SE-3 approach the front of the diner. Above the canopy that shades the front of the place are the words: Dina's Diner written in big curved neon letters. Revolving doors are placed at the entrance. The two of them spin through the doors into the restaurant. The moment they enter, the sound of Cyber Heads band playing in the background. Their music is an interesting take on the galactic classic of Bizz Bop. The music is overshadowed by the chattering patrons and guests. The warm scent of pie fills the room. Checkered black and white tiles line the floors. Along the length of the diner is a raised counter with bar stools placed every meter or so. A red vinyl cushion is on top of each stool. Thin metal lines the counter's top. Scattered across the countertop are mustard and ketchup bottles, napkin boxes, and salt and pepper shakers.

    Places like this are hives for people from all over the galaxy. All sorts of people sit at the counter eating their delicious food and sipping some delectable drinks. Xander walks up to the counter and hops up on a stool. As he presses the metal bell in front of him, It dings, and a small red light illuminates on top of it. The moment it lights a bot springs up from the floor behind the counter. The bot is tall and thin with a small black bow tie around its "neck". Made of shiny metal rods, it stands in front of Xander. On its torso is the manufacturer sticker that says: "Model # CP-5". Its retinal receptor looks down at him; it says in a stale tone,

"Welcome to Dina's Diner. What would you like today?" Though it has no mouth, Xander feels as if it is "smiling" at him. Xander looks at the hologram that is projected on the wall behind the silvery robot. Xander says,

"Uh... I'll have one slice of Zapple pie, and can I get a hard Bizze Juice."

"Oh of course. Just one moment!" CP-5 says while falling back into the floor.

While Xander awaits his order, a person on his right scans his wrist on a credit register. People paid for that crap to go in your body. I was certain no one paid for that Hellstorm chip, Xander thinks. A dark brown hood shrouds his face. The tip of his nose pokes out of the shadow. He sees Xander looking at him scans his wrist chip and remarks,

"What the skonk are you looking at!" Xander replies,

"Nothing, I'm just waiting for my food." He turns his head to look at Xander. The entire left side of his face is cybernetic. Light from the lamps above cast down onto the shiny, reflective metal. A cybernetic eye stuck in his artificial socket rotates to look at Xander. Similar to John's eye, the center glows.

The man spins around on the stool to turn around. He hops off of it and walks through the spinning doors. *Oh thank goodness that could have been bad*, Xander's thoughts wander.

As Xander looks around the diner, he notices an old man with thin white hair and is dressed in a black, pristine suit. He glances at a golden pin on the man's breast pocket. Immediately, Xander recognizes the pin as the Hunters Club pin.

I'm not going to want to mess with this man. He could take me out in a heartbeat. Xander knows when not to mess with people, especially not someone in the Hunters Club, but he has a reputation of messing with certain people.

Moments later, a hatch opens up in the counter and a platform arises out of the opening. A porcelain plate rests on the platform. On the plate sits a steaming hot slice of Zapple pie. Chunks of yellow fruit are embedded in the delicious filling. Flakey, golden-brown crust surrounds the filling. The glorious scent wafts into his nose. He thinks, Wow, that smells good. I haven't had a good slice in ages. Small arcs of electricity shoot from the pie slice.

The Zapple fruit is native to the fruit fields of Arlea. The yellow fruit grows on huge trees that can grow up to 20 meters tall. The juices in the fruit are unique conductors. While the Zapples grow, they collect static electricity from the air, and when they are harvested the shock is carried with the fruit.

Next to the plate is a tall glass. An orange carbonated liquid rests still. Fog clouds the glass's exterior. Tiny bubbles shoot to the top and pop with a tiny sound. As he grabs the cup and lifts it to his mouth, his hand is chilled. A long sip of the fizzy drink trickles down his throat. He gives off a long sigh. Oh, that's good... He picks up a shiny metal fork that is sitting on the platform. Xander cuts a piece of that pie and lifts it to his mouth. He takes a slow bite of it. The warm, delicious pie shocks and tingles his tongue. While he is eating it, he hears a holo screen behind him turn to the INN or Imperial News Network. Xander turns around to look at the holo screen. A human male in a black suit sits at a desk in a tower somewhere on the Citadel. The suit he wears is perfectly tailored and fits him like a glove. His skin was fair and pale. Hair black like the void of space covers his head; it is glossy and combed over. He is clean-shaven with a sharp jawline. Perfectly plucked eyebrows right above his dark brown eyes. This is Chet Chapson, head news anchor for INN. Chet looks deep into the camera and says in a joyful yet serious tone,

"Welcome back to the show citizens of the oh-so-great Empire!" As he starts talking, the band stops playing and everyone in the diner looks at the holo screen. "Here on INN, we will give you…" he points to the camera. "The latest scoop on all the galactic news! First, those evil Nytarians have been spotted in the Mid Worlds… How will the Empire react to those vile beasts entering their territory?"

When Chet mentions the Nytarians approaching the Mid Worlds, everyone in the diner gasps. Many in the galaxy are blind to what happens outside of their bubble of life. Chet continues:

"Not only have Nyatrians been in the Outer Worlds, but they are going for the beloved planet Zulara. The Empire is sending its finest vessels to crush those savage beasts! In other news, the new Imperial occupation of Destolace has been met with hostile force. The Empire has purchased Destolace and the natives are not too happy about it. We wouldn't be surprised if the Empire just destroys them all. Now to transition to the weather: on Rone, there is a seventy-eight percent chance of meteor showers; the comet Centaris is set to collide with the northern hemisphere of the planet in two days." While watching the news, Xander continues to eat his delicious pie. "Coranthea is just as beautiful as it always is. Seventy-two degrees and the three suns are shining down. And of course, the Citadel's skydome keeps it at the perfect temperature all the time!" Chet continues to list the weather for every planet in the Empire. His voice shifts from joyful to incredibly bored as he lists the weather for 1,089,124 planets. All planets underneath the Imperial rule. One after another, "...And finally Talasia with its usual negative 50 degrees and not sunny ever." His plastered smile slowly comes back as he announces, "Well that's all for this episode. We'll see you for the next segment after his quick commercial break!" The holo screen fades to black. Then it turns back on to a commercial. A male voice exclaims very enthusiastically,

"Come one come all, get the latest product from Apex Foods! FOOD GOO! The one goo that is pretty much food! One out of ten doctors doesn't recommend consumption! This slimy substance is almost considered food! It has less than one of the necessary components to be considered real food! Food Goo comes in five delicious flavors: meat, vegetables, bread, home-cooked dinner, and best of all regurgitated sea bill vomit! Call now and get one capsule for free with ten easy payments of 7.99!" Most people divert their attention away during the advertisement, but one person burst out in cheering applause. In complete silence, one guy in the corner of the diner is just cheering and everyone looks at him. Some other guy shouted,

"Shut up you Molo-milker!" The guy proceeds to shut up. Xander finishes the slice of pie and takes the last sip of his Bizzle Juice. He sets everything back onto the platform, and it descends back into the counter. Xander grabs a data chip from his left pants pocket. He inserts it into a small metallic register with 10 credits transferred off of it.

During Xander's meal, SE-3 has been standing in the back of the diner waiting for Xander to finish. He is plugged into a charging port. It is transferring power into his central core since he had been running on low power for a while now.

Xander hops off his stool and calls SE-3. He shouts,

"SEE, let's move!" When SE-3 recognizes his voice calling him, SE-3's systems boot up. As he turns on, he mutters,

"Power on..." He walks over to Xander, and they both exit through the revolving door.

Nine

Outside Dina's Diner, Xander puts his hand up to his ear, presses the comlink, and calls Bre. As she is walking back to the ship, she hears a beep on her communication channel and then hears,

"Hey... Bre?" She waits a moment, takes a long breath, closes her eyes, and then says,

"Yes, Xander?" She replies,

"Now that I'm walking back to the ship, I passed a casino. I was wondering..." She thinks, Not this again. "...if you wanted to come to play some blackjack with me?" A few moments of silence later, she sighs and says:

"Ya know what? Sure, I haven't gambled in a while. I'll come to play with you." Xander mutes his communications and yells,

"YES!" He turns his communications back on and says, "Alright sounds good, I'll meet you at the casino, and I'll send you the directions." Xander pulls out his holocell; he looks through his contacts, finds Bre's name, and sends her the locations of the casino he is at.

Bre opens up her holocell and sees the casino's location. She thinks, Oh no. The text from Xander says: Hey, so I'm at the Golden Shores Casino. Once she sees it, her heart drops. Damnit Xander, she thinks. She stands there in the middle of the street just thinking for a moment: It's going to be fine... It's going to be fine... Normally Bre is calm and collected, but whatever is happening with her and this casino can't be good.

This part of the city is lined with dozens of huge casinos. Outside the Golden Shores Casino, Xander is leaning up against the exterior wall scanning around looking for Bre. Next to him on Xander's right, SE-3 stiffly stands as he is powered off. Suddenly his lowered head pops up, and his systems boot on. His optical lens illuminates yellow inquisitively; he turns to Xander and says in his robotic voice:

"Captain, what is it we are doing here?" Xander's vision darts over to SE-3; he looks confused by SE-3's inquiry. He thinks: I thought I had powered off. He slowly says to SE-3 in a cautious tone,

"Uh—We are here to gamble..." SE-3 turns his head like a curious dog. His lens changes color to an amber hue. He says,

"Hm... I have never understood the human compulsion to risk your capital resources over a simple game of cards." Xander looks worried of sorts. He says,

"Well, it's not your job to understand… us." He gestures to himself and everyone around. SE-3 just stands there. He slowly starts to mimic his stance of Xander; SE-3 says one thing:

"Interesting…" Thankfully a few moments later, Bre strolls up to them. After glancing at the two of them, she enthusiastically says,

"What's with the long faces? Aren't you glad to see me!" Xander looks at her; his eyes widen and dilate.

"Of course I am," he says. Bre thinks, Maybe he won't even notice. She rolls her eyes and then says,

"Don't give me that look." Xander quickly shakes his head and wipes that look off his face. He thinks, Stupid! She taps her foot on the floor quickly and in anticipation. She says,

"So are we gonna play or not?"

"Alright, let's go!" Outside the massive building which stands hundreds of feet tall. It is a towering building with hundreds of windows that line the building up and down. Huge elaborate fountains blast the water all around the outside of the courtyard. Tourists clump together around the exterior with holocells taking all sorts of photos and pictures. At the top of the building, a huge sign sits there. Written on it in glowing, pulsating lights says, Golden Shores Casino.

The three of them make their way through the revolving doors at the entrance. First, Shannon and Xander walk in, but SE-3 waits back a moment. Inside his internal systems he thinks, Hm... anything goes! Xander looks back and exclaims to him,

"Are ya comin'!" After his sonic receptors pick up what he said, SE-3 bumbles after them. Now as he walks, his movement resembles how Xander strolls everywhere. "I don't know what is up with him, but SEE has been acting kinda weird." She says,

"How so?" Xander is about to answer when he walks into the casino and is hit with the intense smell of smoke. The two of them both cough. They are somewhat used to the smell of Hogler and John always smoking something, but this is much worse. They are overwhelmed by the obnoxious sounds of ding slot machines and shouting patrons.

They all notice directly in the lobby of the Golden Shores there are these metallic pods. Glowing blue lights line the edges of the pods. Above the pods, a sign says, The Machine. When Bre notices this, she remembers what it is, but then a holoscreen appears above the machine. On it is a beautiful woman in a lab coat with black-rimmed glasses and her hair tied back. She has a clipboard in one hand and the other is on her hip. The lady on the screen says in a persuasive tone,

"Introducing Hellstorm Industries' latest invention: The Machine! Do you ever come out to one of these wonderful casinos, but then you realize you are short on credits?" A small crowd of patrons gathers around the holoscreen. "Well, we just fixed that problem. Now with The Machine, you can trade a few of those unnecessary years off your life, for a whole bunch of credits!" The obnoxious sound of cash registers dinging plays, and the credit symbol appearson the screen. "You know what you want... Hellstorm Industries the new way." The screen fades to black as the Hellstorm logo appears.

Bre thinks, Disgusting. I can't believe people will throw their life away for a few credits to gamble. She disappointedly shakes her head as she watches an eager, young human turn the dial to twenty. He walks in. The pod gives off a vibrating hum. Steam and mist blast out of the exhaust pipes. After he comes out, she sees that he looks exhausted, sweaty, and twenty years older than before, and a credit chip pops out. She watches him dash over to one of the slot machines.

Once they enter, their vision darts around at all the different patrons and tourists. All of the employees wear golden-yellow suit coats with a small black bowtie and sleek black pants. One of the workers walks up to the three of them and says in a regal sort of voice:

"Would you care to have some refreshments?" Xander reaches up his hand to the silver platter the worker is carrying. On the platter, small little hors d'oeuvres sit on it. Bre quickly swats his hand and says,

"We're good." The worker nods his head and walks away to the next person behind them. Frustrated, Xander turns to her and exclaims,

"What was that for? They looked good!"

"That's the point! Let's just make this quick!" Xander rolls his eyes and says,

"Ugh, fine. Let's go over there." He points over to a blackjack table to the left of the casino. They all walk over to it.

Near the entrance, an older male human dressed in a clean-cut, black suit, a white undershirt, and a black tie. stands against a wall. He has pale skin that is hued almost green and a clean-shaven face. On his feet, he has freshly polished dress shoes. In his mouth, rests a thick brown cigar; smoke wisps from it. Behind him stand two other similarly dressed men except they don't have a cigar, and they have big dark sunglasses. The older man immediately noticed the three of them as they entered the casino, but his vision was partially focused on Bre.

Xander, Bre, and SE-3 walk up to the round half-circle table. Bre looks tense and uncomfortable. At the table is a Driodite who wears the same outfit as the rest of the workers. With his four lanky arms, he shuffles up the unique Golden Shores-themed cards; he quickly flips them from one hand to another.

Now up next to the table, Xander says to the Driodite:

"Hey, can we join?" The Driodite glances up at them, nods, and motions with two of his hands at three open white, leather chairs. They all sit down in the chairs. In two of the other three chairs sit two human patrons. The dealer says,

"Alright, place your bets." Everyone around the table pulls up a small data chip out; they place it into a metal container. Once they do this, a few black and red chips pop out of a hatch; they catch them and place them into the small betting box on the table. The dealer speedily hands out two cards face up to each of them from his left to right.

A few moments later, the black-suited old man walks up and sits in the empty chair on Bre's right. His two bodyguards standing behind him. Once the dealer notices, he looks flustered and says,

"Oh Mr. Bercham, you're playing?" Once Bre sees him sitting beside her, she looks distraught. Xander glances over at her. Mr. Bercham says,

"Indeed I am. Just cause I own the place doesn't mean I don't play." The dealer hands out two up-facing cards to him with three of his arms. Mr. Bercham turns over to Bre and says, "It's been a long time." He stares daggers at her with his marble-green eyes. As he blinks like normal humans, a thin transparent membrane blinks sideways like a hawk. She winces as he talks. Bre mummers,

"That's the damn point!" Xander looks confused and looks down at them. He thinks, What is going on? After pausing for a moment he says,

"Bre, who's this?" Mr. Bercham looks down at Xander with a wide smile; he says,

"Ah, you didn't tell him." He extends his hand to Xander. They shake hands. Mr. Bercham's grip is cold and firm. "I am Mr. Bercham. I own this very casino. And I was Bre's first employer." Her expression shifts to that of anger and disgust. Xander's brow furrows in confusion. He says,

"What exactly did you guys do together?"

"Oh, that's not the important part!" Mr. Bercham places his chips in the betting box. "Let's play," he says. Bre is uncomfortable; she reluctantly stays to play. The dealer begins the game.

A little bit after the game starts, Bre is playing; her cards: are six hearts and a jack of diamonds. As her turn just finished, she feels something poking her right side. Mr. Bercham presses a small handheld ray gun up her side underneath the table. Xander is caught up in the heat of the game and is not paying attention. His two bodyguards stand in the way so that no one around could see. Mr. Bercham whispers to her:

"If you move, I shoot. If you scream, I shoot. You're going to listen to what I say. Understood?" She barely indicates a head nod. His voice is breathy and raspy like an old smoker. "Two. I'm going to give you two days to get as far away from here as you can." His voice is stern and forceful. "At the end of the two days, I'm going to send my guys to come after you. When they get to you, you will give them the Shroud. If you do, you will go unharmed. If not, which I would hate to happen, we will make you disappear. Understood?" He presses the gun more forcefully into her side. She closes her eyes and slowly nods her head. He maliciously smiles and says, "Good." He pulls the ray gun away and tucks it into his suit coat pocket. He pulls back the sleeve on his right forearm; it reveals his elegant gold watch.

After he glances at it, he pops up from his seat and says, "Sorry for the abrupt leave. I've got an appointment."

He walks away; his two bodyguards follow closely behind. As he walks away, a small thumb-sized green insect crawls out of Mr. Bercham's pant leg. It is small enough so no one sees it. It scurries on the floor and jumps on the back of Bre. It just hangs on the bottom of her jacket.

Bre turns to see him leave. The moment he's out of sight, she gets up, grabs Xander's hand, and they both walk towards the door. Xander turns around as they are leaving and says,

"SEE, I guess we're going!" SE-3 quickly stands up from his leathery seat almost in the same fashion as Xander. He thinks, Ugh, humans and their random pursuits.   He speedily runs after them.

As Bre is holding Xander's arm and taking him through the entrance door, he stops and says,

"What is going on?" She clenches her teeth and says,

"Okay, you know before I was with the USG, I was working in the Trench, right?" He looks confused and then says,

"Yeah, you've said that."

"Well, in between when I left the Trench and joined the USG, Mr. Bercham offered me a job... to be a Spore Runner." Xander's eyes widen in surprise. His jaw drops; he says very loudly in the center of the street outside of Las Nazara:

"You were a Spore Runner!" She rolls her eyes.

"Ugh, yes I was. Before you go assuming anything, it wasn't for long and I didn't like it."

A Spore Runner is normally someone who works for a larger corporation, in this case Mr. Bercham's cartel. They will deliver and ship Spores to whoever will pay. She continues, "...I only did it because I needed a start in this world."

"Oh Woah, I never would have guessed. You don't come across as that kinda person." Bre sighs in relief.

"And in two days he will send his best guys after me..." Shocked, he says,

"He's what and why?"

"Back when I worked for him, he had me steal his device he calls the Shroud. Instead of bringing it to him, I took it and joined the USG. It is experimental; it is supposed to be able to cloak a ship and turn it completely invisible on any scale."

"What! Does it work?"

"It hasn't been tested."

"If that does work, this is insane. Something that powerful could cloak an entire battleship or something." He thinks: Imagine if the Nytarians got it... "Where is it now?"

"That's the thing, it's attached to your ship..."

"You did what," Xander shouts angrily. "You put some molopoo on my baby." She thinks, I hate it when he calls it that. "We're giving it back to him! Right?"

"I mean we can't. A powerful device is dangerous. We'll figure it out; let's just leave this forsaken planet before he changes his mind. Can you not say anything to anyone else?" Xander pauses for a moment and then says,

"I promise I won't." Bre smiles and responds,

"Thank you." Bre, SE-3, and Xander slowly make their way to docking bay 35.

Ten

The flagship of the Americorps, the Liberty, is landing at Neo York. Neo York is the capital city of Rhea. The people of the Americorps name most of their cities after the cities and states of Terra from centuries ago. The Liberty is a huge Dreadnought-class battleship. It is 8,732 m (8.7 km) long, 2,892 m (2.8 km) wide, and 1,587 m (1.5 km) tall. Its armaments are 100 x pulverizers, 200 x ion cannons, and tons more torpedoes. The front hull of the ship is shaped to be like an eagle's head. The eagle's eyes are glass ports to see out of because the eagle's head is the ship's bridge. Red, white, and blue stripes are painted across the vessel's hull. An Americorps flag hangs off the back of the ship.

The Liberty is currently in orbit of Rhea, and it is heading in for the grand landing bay. Aboard the bridge of the Liberty stands President James Jackson of the Americorps. Similar to their ancestors that adopted the title of president to their leaders.

James is a tall, tan-skinned man. A thick-brimmed cowboy hat rests on his long dark brown hair. Long teeth of Grygons, native predators of Rhea, are attached to his hat. His eyes are bright sea blue like the oceans of Galitia. He has a bushy, brown handlebar mustache with a thin toothpick that hangs out of his mouth. A deep scar stretches across his face seemingly from a plasma-laced blade. He is clad in a black suit with sleeves, and his hairy arms are covered in tattoos of eagles and Americorps flags.

President James is looking out the glass-plated window at the field planet Rhea ahead of him. Technicians and officers rush around the bridge as they are maintaining all the complicated systems. James looks to one of the chief pilots and questions,

"Hey partner, how much longer till touchdown?" The pilot says to him,

"Three minutes till landing, sir!"

"This is the best part!" James announces. The Liberty angles towards the surface of the Rhea. They activate the thrusters. The huge vessel rockets toward the planet.

As they reach the atmosphere, the fire burns on the hull of the huge ship. They activate the heat deflector shields which protect the ship. The Liberty shakes and rumbles while it's entering. James stands perfectly balanced while everyone else is bumbling around like dominoes falling into each other. He has flown on this ship so many times; he knows its exact movements of it.

After a minute of them blasting through the atmosphere, they reach the central docking bay in Neo York. The deflector shields deactivate. The hulking ship activates its gravitational suspenders to slow its descent as it barrels toward the docking station. Once it is about 1,500 km out the suspenders kick in. It goes from flying hundreds of thousands of kilometers per hour to halting in an instant.

In the docking station, huge Zarium clamps blast out of the metal floor, clamp down on the bottom of the ship, and lock the Liberty in place. The clamps pull the hulking ship into the belly of the station. Steam and mist blast from the hydraulic mechanisms. Once it is fully locked in, the side exit ports open up; thin metal bridges extend from the ports. The crew members aboard walk off the bridges into the city. Men and women dressed in pristine Americorps uniforms pour out of the bridges.

Hundreds of mechanics emerge from the station around the ship. They all carry blow torches, wrenches, hammers, and all other sorts of repair equipment. The repairmen fling zip-ropes on top of the Liberty. The ropes lock onto the ship's top. They surmount the massive ship with the zip-ropes and begin repairs. Sparks fly. Steam blasts. A swarm of drones fly around to the back of the ship where the gargantuan thrusters are. The drones have mounted extinguishers on them. Once at the back of The Liberty, the drones blast a bombardment of white foam to the red hot thrusters to quickly cool them down.

After a few minutes of being docked most of the nonessential crew left the ship. Soon after James comes walking out on one of the top bridges. He is followed by eight other Americorps troopers. They all carry scattershot guns. Scattershots are most similar to the shotguns of the late planet Terra. The Americorps are one of the only factions to still regularly use slugs, physical lead rounds, in their guns. Most other groups only use blasters.

James walks on the bridges to the streets of Neo York. He is heading for the huge capital building where he has to delegate with the rest of the Americorps council. He swiftly strides down the streets of Neo York. His leather hat protects his face from the blistering heat of the nearby star, Callous II. Normally someone like the president of a planet wouldn't just walk through the city like a commoner. James believes that as he is the leader of this society that the most important thing is respect. And how will they respect someone who refuses to even walk the same roads as the people. His guards aren't the biggest fan of this choice, so they insist on escorting him anywhere he goes.

As the walk past some of the fields of golden wheat, James puts his hand out to brush past them amber grain stalks. He recalls his childhood when he would play outside for hours in these fields. The rough spikes of the stalks poke his hand as he glides it past. A feeling to most would be uncomfortable, but James feels the opposite. It is pure nostalgia. The simpler times when he didn't have to worry about who was trying to kill him or what everyone thought of him.

James thinks of the times when he and his father would hunt wild Grygrons in the fields behind their house. He wonders, Would he be proud of me now? Suddenly one of the guards behind James taps him on the shoulder and says,

"Mr. President, we need to move. The senate is waiting."

"Alright," says James. "I don't need Senator Lakely screaming at me again." It is about a five minute walk to the senate business. The senate building is a marvel of Americorps architecture. It is modeled after their ancestors from Terra but with their own twist. Outside of it stands a fifteen foot tall statue of the first president of the new Americorps and the one who found Rhea, Kane Halloway. The building is big and made of white bricks. Bricks that were sourced from the ground of Rhea itself. Atop the building is a perfectly crafted dome.

They walk into the building and James makes his way to his desk which is in the center of all the other senators from around Rhea. As he sits down, music starts to play, and everyone in the room rises to stand. Speakers placed around the room play the national anthem of Rhea, which is really just that of the United States of America just changed a bit. They all place their right hands over their heart and look at the Americorps flag which is on one of the walls. The speakers play,

"O say can you see, by Callous' light,
What so proudly we hailed at the twilight's last gleaming,
Whose broad stripes and bright stars through the perilous fight,
O'er the ramparts we watched, were so gallantly streaming?
And the rocket's red glare, the missiles bursting in air,
Gave proof through the night that our flag was still there;
O say does that star-spangled banner yet wave
O'er Rhea, the land of the free and the home of the brave?" The music concludes and everyone is seated. Around James' desk are twelve more desks. At each of them sits one of the ten senators for the ten Americorps sectors of Rhea. Mere moments after they are

seated, a man dressed in a fine, black suit stands up; he is Terry Conray, the head of the senate. Now stood up, he says,

"Mr. President, we must now discuss why this meeting was called." He looks to one of the other senators; she is dressed in a black suit. She is Mary Brookson, senator of Sector 3. Terry sits down as Mary stands up out of her leather chair. She says,

"President Jackson, on the southern border of Sector 3, seven of our cargo transports have been hijacked and stolen by bandits." James sits up in his chair a bit straighter. He inquisitively tilts his head and looks at her; he inquires,

"What were we shipping in those transports?" She responds,

"Energen. We were sending canisters to sector five to fuel their ships." James glances over to Robert Artins, the senator of Sector 5. When John looks at him, he nods back acknowledging what Mary said. James clasps his hands into a steeple position and says,

"Well, this is not good. If these bandits are stealing our reservations, they could be looking to cripple out planetary defenses by trying to keep us from leaving Rhea." Mary says in response:

"Mr. President, what do you suggest we do in response to this?" The room's attention is immediately directed to James. He says in a confident tone:

"We will send a decoy cargo transport with a tracking device on it, so then it will hopefully lead us to these bandits. Once we have found them we will detain them properly." All the senators nod in agreement with the statement. Terry Conray stands and says,

"To the next matter of business, we need to address the growing Nytarian threat. Mr. President, as I'm sure you are aware of the rumors that there have been Nytarian scouts spotted in the Outer Worlds." As he finished saying that, another senator pops up out of his chair. This is Senator David Hartly of Sector 7. Everyone turns their attention to David. He says,

"Preposterous! The Nytarians wouldn't dare enter our space!" Frustrated, Terry exclaims,

"That is what I am saying! But if these rumblings are true we need to be prepared!" He looks around at everyone. "We have all seen the might of the Nytarian fleet. I know the Americorps is good. We are very good, but we need to be ready for an attack. Mr. President, what do you think?" Terry slowly sits down. The room turns to James. He says,

"Senator Terry, you are right. We can't ignore the fact that if they wanted to, the Nytarians could destroy us if we are not prepared. I say, if we get real proof that they have sent scouts to the Outer Worlds, we will activate the shield." The Americorps has a planetary defense shield that can be activated to protect the entire planet. "There is no way even their weapons could pierce the barrier. The twelve senators all nod their head in affirmation of this plan. This meeting of the senate is shortly concluded after a few more topics have been discussed.

Eleven

After their travels throughout Las Nazara, the crew of the Odyssey all meets back up at docking bay 35. Xander and Bre enter the bay with SE-3 following close behind, and he sees the small pointy-eared Cinise standing right outside the Odyssey. When Xander enters the bay, he pulls out a small metal node. He clicks a red button on it. On the back of the Odyssey, lights flash twice and the foot ramp extends from the ship's underbelly. Before he reaches Cinise, he turns to SE-3 and whispers to him:

"SEE, while I'm talking can you do a quick scan of the ship?" SE-3 responds,

"Of course I can, but what is it I am looking for?"

"Just check the hull. I've never been too trusting of these big corporate run docking bays. Look if there's anything out of place like a tracker or something." SE-3 nods his stiff metal neck; he walks up to the back of the ship and begins to scan for anything out of place. Xander walks up to her, and he says while smiling:

"Cinise, How's it going?" She scratches the back of her neck in a nervous manner, looks to him and says,

"Actually really well." Her voice resonates with enthusiasm. "The repairs you requested were a success. We got you a full refuel, resupplied your reserves, and gave the whole thing a fresh new coat of paint!" Xander looks up to his ship. The suns shine down onto its new hull. The rose red paint glimmers. Xander says,

"Wow, she hasn't looked this good in a long time!" She can see in his eyes how happy he is. He thinks: I don't know how we are going to pay this off. We barely have anything on us right now. I hope Bre got a good paying job. We're going to need it. "So I know this was no cheap task. What's the damage to my wallet looking like?" Cinise says in an uncomfortable tone:

"Well, first the docking fees which will be fifty credits per hour." Xander thinks, Oh no. "...and you've been docked for five hours so that's another 250 credits." This isn't looking too good. "Then it is 100 credits per kilo of Energen, and your full refuel was fifteen kilos. That is another 1,500 credits on top of that. And then the paint clocked in at pretty cheap; it was only 200 credits. In total I think that'll be 2,050 credits." Xander exclaims,

"Oh my!"

"If you head inside the main station there is a terminal for the credit transfer whenever you are ready," she replies. Then Xander says,

"That's the problem... we technically don't have 2,050 credits on us." Cinise sighs and rolls her eyes. "Before you get mad, we just got a contract for some new jobs that will be high paying." He thinks: I really hope Bre found something good because we will be in some bad trouble if she doesn't. "I think since we so graciously offered you a spot on the crew of the Odyssey. I think you could give us a small extension on the payment." Cinise reluctantly says,

"That is a very good point, captain. I am very thankful for you allowing me to join you all in your adventures across the galaxy. I think I can put in a request to my manager to let you have an extension." Xander smiles in relief. He says,

"Oh thank you. We will be very glad to have you on board the Odyssey." As he says that, Hogler, John, and Hogler's new friend Davenk. They all walk up to Xander, SE-3, Bre, and Cinise. Xander looks at her and says, "Bre, please tell me you got a good contract." She smiles wide and responds with:

"Xander you already know I do! I grabbed two actually. They shouldn't be too much of a hassle and if we complete both of them, the payout will be 70,000 credits!" Xander feels a weight lifted off him. He lets off a long sigh and thinks, Thank the Light! Xander responds,

"Alright, this can be a stroke of luck!" John looks around at the group. He looks at Devenk and is confused. He says,

"Who are you?" Davenk pulls his hood down. He says,

"I am Davenk the Akara. I am just a simple traveler, looking for passage across the galaxy." All of them look at him with a confused expression. When John hears him say that he thinks, Akara? Where have I heard that before? It sounds so familiar... John responds with:

"Okay 'Davenk." He says snakily with finger quotes as he says his name. "We don't speak cryptic. Who are you really?"

"I only look for travel. I seek to spread the word of the Echo. Your friend Hogler said there would be room for me aboard your vessel." Xander looks at Hogler and stares daggers at him. He thinks: What were you thinking! Hogler shrugs at Xander. Xander says,

"Davenk, I am the captain of this vessel the Odyssey." He motions to the ship behind him. "My name is Xander. As it seems Hogler has already made you aware that we have an extra bunk aboard our ship." Cinise looks up to Xander with a worried expression. He sees her and understands what she's trying to say. "Well technically we have two open bunks, but someone has just taken one," he says while looking at Cinise. She looks relieved. "But my question for you, Davenk, is: do you have the money for the rent?" Davenk reaches into the pocket of his poncho and pulls out a small credit chip. He says,

"Will 700 credits do for the first month?" Xander's eyes widen. He says,

"That'll be just fine." Davenk tosses him the chip. Xander pockets it.

Bre looks at the walkway that extends into the Odyssey. Right next to it are three gray boxes. All of them are packed to the brim with little stuff. Bre motions to Cinise to come to her. Cinise walks up to her and Bre says,

"Hey, I'm guessing that is your stuff?" She points to the boxes. Cinise nod. "How 'bout I take you to your bunk and we get you all set?" Cinise smiles and says,

"I would love that! I've worked on so many different ships, but I've never been on one!"

"I think we can change that." Bre picks up two of the boxes, and Cinise grabs the other one. As they are walking up the walkway way up, Bre says to her, "it's going to be nice having another girl aboard the Odyssey." Cinise giggles. She says,

"It can't be that bad... right?"

"Living with them is not terrible, but they can be annoying sometimes, says Bre.

"How so," Cinise inquires.

"Hogler can be pretty loud. When Xander is in one of his arrogant moods, and John's a bit bleak at times."

"Well I'm sure this will be a good adventure." The two make their way to the empty quarters and start unpacking her stuff. Once inside the ship, the small, green insect that is attached to the back of Bre's jacket jumps off. It scuttles around the metal grates, and then it climbs up a wall into one of the air ducts.

Twelve

Hogler shows Davenk to the other vacant bunk once they get to the room. It is just next to Hogler's room. Hogler says,

"So this is it!" Davenk scans around the room deeply looking at everything. There is a metal desk in the corner, a bed in the wall, yellow tinted lights in the ceiling, and gray metal walls. Davenk says,

"It's homely. I think I'll manage here." He thinks, I think this will do for my needs. Hogler looks around and realizes Davenk has no personal stuff with him, unlike Cinise who had multiple boxes of little trinkets. Hogler says,

"Did you not have anything with you?" Davenk looks at him with his yellow-hued eyes that almost glow; he says,

"I prefer not to. I live the life of a nomad, journeying from planet to planet. I seek to meet new people such as you and your crew. Then I learn about their culture and way of life." He turns away and whispers, "...And hopefully to find them..." Hogler inquires,

"What was that?" Davenk thinks, I can't say. He responds to the question with: "Oh it was nothing." Hogler couldn't care to investigate so he continues to think about what he always does: guns and explosions. Davenk sits down in the chair that is in the room. He spins around to look at Hogler; he says,

"So Hogler, tell me. Who are you really...?" That simple question makes Hogler's mind spiral. He thinks, Who am I? Who... am I? Who is Hogler? Why am I? Davenk watches as his face goes blank. "Again I ask: who are you?" Hogler's vision starts to fade to black as he thinks about the past. He hears Davenk say, "Feel the Echo of your memories..."

Hogler has a fuzzy memory of a dark room. Above him hangs a blinding white light that shines in his eyes. The room is uncomfortable and damp.

Cold.

He is laying on something cold and metal. The ambient sound of chattering fills his senses. The sound of footsteps walked all around him. He sees the blurry image of someone with a bluish face mask covering their nose and mouth. The person has glasses that are fogging up as he heavily breathes.

Davenk watches Hogler shiver and wince as he remembers this. He looks at him with a deeply confused look. His eyes illuminate with a yellow glow. Though Davenk can't see what Hogler is remembering, he can sense the emotions that Hogler is flooded with. He thinks, Highly interesting... he doesn't know...

Hogler remembers hearing the sound of power tools and machinery. He sees the person pull a syringe out. It is full of some sort of glowing green substance. He watches the person shake the syringe around before he feels him inject it into his neck. Hogler tries to thrash and move, but he is restrained. He remembers losing the feeling in his arms and legs. He feels his whole body tingling. The sound of loud saws and machines by his head. Slowly Hogler falls unconscious.

He wakes up in an empty room. The lights are barely on. He looks and sees a damp tiled floor. Once he looks down at his hands. He was thinking, Hands! I have hands! He sees his four-fingered hands. He wiggles and moves his clawed fingers. As he moves them, he hears the quiet sound of mechanics and motors in his hand. Who is I? Am I me? What does me even mean? Hogler... Hogler? Am I Hogler? I am Hogler! How is this even possible? What is this... thoughts? What is thinking? Since when does Hogler think? He looks down at his legs. What are these? Are these mine... Hogler? All the thoughts that have ever been thought by anyone are all flooding into Hogler's mind all at the same time. Hogler thinks, He said I was Hogler. Said? What is said? Say... said... say? Can I said? Can I say? Hogler sits up straight on the metal table. He opens his mouth. Confused beyond anything anyone has felt, he touches his throat and feels his vocal cords vibrate as he struggles to make a humming sound. With his mouth open, he moves his tongue around. A sound exits his mouth:

"Ah..." He thinks, Was that me? Did I 'Ah'? Again he says, "H-h-h-hog. Hogler." I said! I can say! "I is Hogler!" He shouts with all his might: "I is Hogler!" He stumbles around until he shifts himself off the metal table. When he touches the table with his hands, they make a loud clunk. Walk? What is walk? Can Hogler walk? He shifts his body off the table. He hits the tiled floor with his hoofed feet. Instead of the sound he thought to expect when he hit the floor, it made a metallic sound. Though hoofs are natural keratin, they sound made.

Now he is barely standing. He wobbles around.

"Hogler Walk!" He puts his leg out to take a step. He takes another and another. Step after step he walks forward in the dark room. He thinks, Who was that? Man...? Was he man? Who was he? Mask. He had mask. Doctor? Is he Doctor? Doctor did this to me. How is Doctor... good or... bad? Doctor bad. I'll find Doctor. Hogler runs. His body is covered head to hoof in muscles. He looks to his arms, and tubes of a green liquid are being pumped into them. What is this? Green? He says, "I feel strong!" In an impulse, he puts his shoulder up and runs right at the south side wall. Miraculously he is not injured one bit. Instead of just bumping against the wall, he crashes right through it. He remembers just feeling like he needs to go, so he bolted. Where? That isn't important to him, he just kept running. The last thing he recalls is looking back and seeing Doctor standing there yelling,

"Come back! You are my creation!"

Suddenly he hears a voice:

"Hogler, that's enough." In an instant, Hogler feels himself travel through the years back to this moment. He looks at Davenk with the most distraught expression. His eyes welling up with the smallest of tears. With a furrowed brow and mouth hanging open, he slowly turns to look at Davenk sitting calmly in the desk chair. Hogler slowly says,

"How? How did you do that?" Davenk raises his jaw and opens his eyes. Eyes that once looked to be a soft yellow hue now shine with the light of a star. Davenk elegantly rises from his chair. He softly places his right hand on Hogler's burly shoulder. He says,

"Hogler, you thought the Akara sounded familiar." Hogler thinks, I never said that, how did he know? Hogler nods. "I'm sure in your time in the galaxy you've heard crazy people talking about something called Echo." Davenk watches glowing, golden strands of light appear around his hand. The strands slowly and elegantly swirl around, and then they flow into Hogler's ears. Hogler is completely unaware; he says,

"Yeah, I've heard of it. What is it?"

"The Echo of Creation is what it is formally called. To truly explain would be to explain the history of the galaxy. Think of it as a woven blanket; each fiber represents one of us. There are trillions all sewn together to make something wonderful. The Echo connects the past, present, and future that is how I saw into your past." Hogler pushes Davenk's hand off his shoulder and he says frustratedly:

"Cool, you do magic or whatever, but keep your little Echo out of my head!" Hogler storms out of the room. He has his hand on his forehead; he feels a migraine forming. Click-Clock is the sound his hoofs make as they collide with the metal floor grates. He strides through the ship's hall down to his gunner station preparing for takeoff. His mind wanders: He's lying. Magic is not real. Especially not something that can see into the past... Now that Davenk is alone in his quarters, he pulls out a holocell from a pocket on his pants. He holds it up to his mouth and says into it:

"This is Davenk, I found her. I repeat I found her...."

Thirteen

Xander, SE-3, and John walk into the Odyssey. Once they enter the ship, Xander presses the node again and the foot ramp is pulled back up into the ship by hydraulic mechanisms. Their boots make a stomping sound as they walk through the ship's metal halls. Xander turns to John and asks,

"Go tell the others to be ready to leave in ten minutes, and tell Bre to meet me at the helm as soon as possible." John responds with:

"You got it. What would you like me to do after?" Xander's eyes float around as he thinks.

"Uh… just prepare the weapon systems in case these contracts get a little dicey." John nods in acknowledgment. He turns around and walks towards the bunk area where everyone lives. In Cinise's newfound quarters, it is slightly bigger than some of the others. Yellow-hued lights embedded in the ceiling illuminate the room. It seems no one had occupied this bunk in ages. The room was spotless yet dusty.

About thirty seconds later he reaches Bre's quarters. He sees her help Cinise unpack her stuff.

"...So where are you from," he hears Bre say to Cinise. She grabs a small framed holo-photo from the box of Cinise's stuff. Bre glances at it for a moment. The picture is of a young Cinise, her mother, and her father. They are all smiling and hugging each other. It seems to be taken on the beaches of Coranthea outside a small villa house. As Bre looks at this, a thin smirk appears on her face. Cinise responds to what Bre said:

"I was born and raised here on Coranthea."

Bre says,

"Are these your parents?" She points to the holo-photo. Cinise looks at it, and her joyful smile starts to fade. She pauses for a moment then she says,

"Yeah— they are." Bre notices her change in expression. "But when I was really young, we used to live on Destolace. But in the first wave of the Nytarian conquests they attacked our home town. Both of them were killed in the mass bombing. I've lived with my grandparents ever since then." Tears start to swell up in her eyes. One slowly falls down her face. Bre isn't sure what even to say. She thinks, *Someone this young shouldn't have to deal with this. How does she maintain such a happy attitude?* John stands outside the door and hears them say this.

"Cinise," Bre says. "That is horrible. Someone so young should never have to deal with this sort of loss." Without a moment of hesitation, Cinise moves up to Bre and embraces her. She whispers,

"Thank you." Bre thinks for only a moment and then she wraps her arms around her. A small tear rolls down Bre's face. In a soft voice, Cinise murmurs, "...but they taught me to always be positive and have a happy outlook. Though this galaxy may be tough, it all depends on how you look at it." Bre grins widely and says,

"I've seen a lot of things in my time, but I've never seen someone say that. I needed to hear that." After a long moment, Cinise releases. She saw John waiting outside the metal framed door. Bre with her back to the door turns around and looks at him. He awkwardly says,

"I don't mean to interrupt, but Xander says he needs to talk to you in the helm whenever you are available, and we need to be ready for take-off in about five minutes." Bre nods and says,

"Okay, I'll head there now." John steps out of the way, and Bre steps out of the doorway. She turns around and waves to Cinise as she leaves; Cinise waves back. As she makes her way down to the helm, she takes out her holocell and checks the INN news application. She scrolls past a few articles until one catches her attention. The title reads: Americorps Report Nytarian Scouts Spotted In The Outer Worlds. She reads through a little bit of it:

President James Jackson of the military nation, the Americorps, has made a public statement saying, '... out the top of the line scanners have picked up the unique signature of Nytarian scout ships'. This was all that he told us, but only from this we would tell all those currently in the Outer Worlds to be on their best watch. Only as a united galaxy can we tackle this growing threat of the ruthless Nytarians. For a second she doesn't even believe what she reads. For most people, it is so wild to believe that a group hell-bent on the destruction of all those who don't follow their ways would destroy innocent lives. These monsters, persecuting innocent families for what... not believing in the same deity, she thinks.

Bre reaches the helm. Xander is sitting in his pilot's chair. As he hears her enter the helm, he swivels his chair around to look at her. Xander thinks of himself as a pretty charming person, yet he never has had the best of luck. That is mainly because he messed up a six-year relationship with the love of his life. When he sees Bre walk in he thinks, Damn, she's pretty. Ever since he's had to work with Bre, he has had the biggest crush on her. When she walks up, she looks at him and says,

"You're staring again." Dang it, He thinks. He quickly looks away and turns redder than a bolt. She awkwardly scratches her neck and blushes.

"So why'd you call me up here?" He looks at her but can't manage to look her in the eyes. He responds,

"I was just wondering about the specifics on those contracts?" Bre pulls out her holocell and opens up the USG application. She scrolls through until she gets to her current contacts. She says,

"Well, the one I was thinking of is we do the first one on Destolace. It is a mission to just go to Destolace and deal with a rebellion against the Imperial outpost that has just been established there. We will be working closely with Sentinels, the Imperial troopers." Xander rolls his eyes while smiling and says,

"I know what Sentinels are." She chuckles a little.

"Just making sure. This shouldn't take more than a couple of hours depending on the resistance or the... well resistance. This is the 50,000 credits one."

"To be paying that much to these rebels must be a real problem," says Xander.

"Yeah, no kidding. It says bring them in alive preferably and let the Empire take care of them, but I don't know if Hogler will abide."

"Yeah," says Xander. "I'm curious if John will be glad to get back in the fight or be all cryptic again."

"I'm not sure, but just keep in mind his time in the Imperial army did take a toll. It'll be weird for him to revisit old battlefields."

"I know, you're right, so what about the other one?" Bre scrolls a bit further down the contracts page. She says,

"This one is to collect a package from Boloxia and deliver it to the Citadel." Xander's expression turns to that of an inquisitive look.

"Boloxia is in the Outer Worlds." Bre nods as he says this. "And you've seen the rumors that Nytarians have made their way to the Outer Worlds where we will be going?"

"Yes, I have, but those are just rumors. It's nothing to worry about. We will still go do that one."

"Alright," he says. "I'll have EQ plot a course to Destolace. If you see Cinise, tell her to come up to watch us warp." Bre smiles.

"I'm sure she'll like that." She turns around and walks through the blast doors.

Xander flicks a switch on the console in front of him. As he does this, a voice comes over the speaks in a robotic voice:

"Captain, how will my services be of use?" Xander replies with:

"I'm going to need you to calculate a warp jump to Destolace. Find the quickest route because we'd like to be there as soon as possible." The speakers beep with electronic tones and EQ says,

"Give me about 2.653 minutes, and I will have it done." While EQ is calculating, Xander grabs the control wheel. He hears the sound of tiny footsteps running down the hall. As he turns around, he sees

Cinise running up to the helm's windows. She presses her face up to the plated glass windows.

Xander pulls back on the wheel. As he pulls up, the back thrusters lightly activate along with the gravitational disrupters. The ship starts to lift into the air. A low hum is heard coming from the back thrusters. Now hovering about forty meters above the landing bay, Xander reaches for a lever; he grasps it, pulls back, and it clicks as it locks into place. He expresses,

"You might want to hold on to something!" Cinise glances over at him then she scurries and hops into one of the seats behind Xander's chair. Xander takes a quick look behind him. Once he sees she is buckled in, he flicks a switch and it activates the A.L.T. ALT stands for Atmospheric Light Engines; there is one on each side of the back of the ship. Their main purpose is to propel the ship through the thick atmosphere of planets before they can reach space and use the S.L.E. or the Sub-Light Engines.

With the ALTs on, the Odyssey zooms through the upper atmosphere. As the ship rockets forward, Cinise sinks into the crackling leather seats. A huge smile is on her face as she is experiencing something she has waited for, for a long time: space travel. She looks out the windows to her left and sees the clouds and sky zoom past. Everything I've ever known left in seconds, she thinks.

The Odyssey cuts through the clouds like Galitian Trout bursting through the water. It slightly vibrates as the thrusters blast so much power. Once they burst through the clouds, they exit through the atmosphere. Xander pushes the ALT lever into its original position, and the ALTs turn off. He quickly flicks a switch on the left side of the console. Then the ship smoothly accelerates forward through space.

As Xander always does, he pulls down his microphone and speaks into it:

"Everyone hold on to something. We're about to be in Destolace space." He glances over to Cinise. She is gripping her seatbelt tightly in excitement and anticipation. He chuckles. He thinks, *Was I that excited for my first time?*

Right before Xander activates the warp, SE-3 stumbles his way into the helm. His metallic feet clank and clunk as he walks over the steel-grated floor. He says,

"Captain, wait for me." Xander turns his head around to see SE-3 about to sit down. He rolls his eyes and sighs. After reaching the communication station where he is stationed, SE-3 grabs the seatbelt, clips it over his metal legs, and says, "All ready to go, Captain."

Xander flips open a transparent hatch, grabs the lever underneath, and yanks back. Cinise stares out the window at the front of the helm. She sees the abyss of space slowly start to shift and swirl before her eyes. She thinks, It's amazing. Moments later, the space in front of the Odyssey starts to spin faster and faster. Suddenly, they dash forward through a wormhole. The stars that surrounded them streak past like stripes on a Terran zebra. Her jaw drops. A blinding white light blasts around them. As they open their eyes from the blinding light, they see Destolace hanging ahead like it is being held up by a string.

Fourteen

As the Odyssey exits the warp, they enter the surrounding space of Destolace. Now that this planet is officially under Imperial control, all access in and out is monitored by the Empire. SE-3 clicks and presses some buttons at his station. Bre, Hogler, John, and Davenk all walk through the blast doors into the helm. They all sit down in the chairs at the back except for Davenk who stands and leans up against the wall. Now the whole crew of the Odyssey is present at the helm.

Xander turns his chair to Cinise and is about to say something, but he is interrupted,

"Captain, it seems we are being hailed for a video call." Xander takes a deep breath and then swivels his chair in SE-3's direction. After pausing for a moment, he says,

"Who's hailing us?" SE-3 types something in on the keyboard in front of him.

"It is coming from the Imperial outpost down there," says SE-3.

"Put 'em up on the big screen." Once SE-3 clicks a small blue button on his console, a large holo screen pops up at the front of the helm. The screen is white with three small ellipses that are pulsating while they are connecting. The video call connects; they see a Caucasian man in the standard uniform for Imperial Sentinels. As The image pops up, Xander recognizes him. He says in a thick accent that resembles that of Terran New Jersey,

"Hello, this is—" Xander interrupts him:

"Mark? Mark Johnson? Is that you?" Everyone else on the bridge is confused about who this is. The Imperial Sentinel looks surprised then he says,

"Well, I'll be, its Xander Holsmo." A moment later they both say,

"What are you doing here?" They both are surprised and laughing. Mark says,

"Derek, come look at this!" He turns around and motions to someone behind him. A moment later another man appears in the frame. He is young, has chestnut skin, and is dressed the same as Mark in an Imperial uniform. When Derek sees Xander, he says,

"You've got to be kidding me, Xander! I didn't think I'd see you again!" Xander thinks, Man, such a vast galaxy and I somehow meet these two dudes again. After he says this, Bre stands up from the chair and walks up to where Xander is; Bre says,

"I think I speak for everyone else: what is going on?" Xander turns around and says,

"We all went to the Citadel School of Aviation." Derek chuckles and says,

"Yep, the best there was! Class of 97 baby!" Xander swivels back around to them, and he goes:

"So what are y'all doing here?" Mark says,

"Well once we all graduated, we tried to enlist in the Imperial Navy."

"Yep, but we both flew with them for a few years. Annoyingly, they said 'we don't have the guts'," Derek says with finger quotes. Mark continues,

"Then they sent us here, The Purple Desert. We're supposed to be overseeing the construction of this new outpost. As they said, there was a lot of resistance from the natives here." Derek finishes,

"They kept intercepting our shipments, so Higher Authority allowed us to call for some assistance. Yeah, so what the snonk are you doing here, man." Xander says,

"It's kinda ironic isn't it? My crew and I work with the USG." The rest of the crew gives a small wave to Derek and Mark. "It seems we're here to help y'all." Mark and Derek both smile; then they say,

"Nah, you're kidding!"

"Nope," says Xander. Then Mark says,

"Alright man, let's get your USG codes for confirmation." Xander turns to look at Bre. He mouths to her: You got the codes? She walks up to his console. Plugs in her holocell to a small port. She says to Mark:

"I'm sending them over now." A few moments later, Mark says,

"Here they are." He clicks a few buttons. "Oh great, everything checks out; I'm sending the coordinates for our landing pad. We will have a bot waiting for you when you arrive." Xander says,

"Okay, see you then." He clicks a button and the holo screen closes.

When SE-3 perceives Mark saying there is another bot, he thinks in his computer systems: Another. I must meet them.

Xander grabs the control wheel; he angles it down toward the coordinates that they gave him. He leaves the ship in the control of EQ after saying,

"EQ, you got this?"

"Of course, captain," responds EQ. Xander lets go of the wheel. It moves on its own as EQ pilots it down from the space around Destolace. Xander swivels his chair around to look at the rest of the crew. He stands up and says,

"Alright guys, this should be a pretty easy mission. According to the contract: there is a small group of natives camped outside the outpost." Xander reads from Bre's holocell which Bre gave to them. "They have been intervening with the construction of it. Our job is to simply subdue the natives. It says right here in bold red letters: UNDER NO CIRCUMSTANCES ARE YOU TO KILL ANY OF THE NATIVES. USE STUN WEAPONS ALWAYS." Everyone except Cinise and Davenk looks sternly at Hogler. He is currently polishing his giant minigun. He looks up as everyone goes quiet. Hogler confusedly says,

"What?" Bre rolls her eyes. She says,

"Did you hear? No killing here. Got it."

"Ughhhhhh," sighs Hogler. "Why are you so boring?" Xander continues,

"So simply make sure your weapons are on stun. It also says something about these being 'brutal guerrilla warriors with no regard for any Imperial war protocols', so simply they won't have the decency to not kill us so just be ready for something. Because of the battle, we will be having, John I'm putting you in charge of this one." Xander motions over to John; he nods and walks up in front of the crew. He holsters his ray gun to his side, and he fastens a bandolier of grenades. He says in an old raspy voice,

"I know none of you have much military experience, but I'll make sure we'll all go home after this. I have some experience with guerrilla fighters. This shouldn't be too difficult. The only problem that is prominent is: that their tactics are frankly... insane. I will elaborate later on the actual mission." John nods to Xander; he walks back to the back of the helm. Xander stands back up and says,

"Go ahead and prepare for the landing." The crew is ready to disperse to their respective quarters to pack up for the journey.

"Wait, before you go, Davenk, Brooks, and Cinise I have to talk to you," Bre says. Everyone except Davenk, Brooks, and Cinise leave the helm and head to their quarters or another place aboard the ship. They walk up to Bre; she says: "Before you guys can go on a mission with us, I need to sign you on with the USG." She grabs three printed USG affiliate contracts. She hands them to the three of them and three black ink pens. "You can read over it if you want, but it says that you get a 500 credit signing bonus, along with an honestly great health insurance plan with the type of jobs we're doing, and it has a pretty good retirement plan once the allotted time of service is reached." Cinise looks at it for a few moments, and then says with a big smile:

"Looks good to me, where do I sign?" Bre points to the blanks on the document and responds,

"Okay, sign here in print, here with your signature, and date of birth here." Cinise signs as she says. Davenk and Brooks say,

"I'll abide by this agreement." Bre turns to them:

"Oh great, I'll need you to sign in all these places." They sign with the pens. "Thanks for that, I'll have your signing bonus to you shortly." She takes the contracts and walks back to her quarters/office.

Brooks walks back to the bunk room that Xander assigned to him. He lays down in his bed and lays there for a few minutes before he falls asleep. This has been the longest day in all of Brooks' life: drug busts, laser guns, and alien chases.

John quickly strides to his quarters. Once he is there, he opens up the blast doors with a small panel on the side of the door. He walks in. The walls of his bunk are lined with dozens of ray guns, grenades, snipers, and heavy repeaters along with his new one. He pulls a bag out of an alcove closet. After setting it on his bed, he starts to fill it with all of his weapons. He thinks, It's been a while, but I can do it again. He takes a heavy repeater and ray rifle, and he slings them over his shoulders. Then John grabs four more light ray pistols; he puts two on his leg holsters, two in his underarm shoulder holsters, and two in his boot holsters. After he decks himself out in weapons, he closes his door and walks out to the bridge as the ship heads to the outpost.

In Hogler's quarters, he looks through his weapons case. Every single weapon in Hogler's possession is either a Gatling gun or something explosive. He searches through his case; he tries to find something with a stunning setting. After five Dardos units of him shuffling through the case have passed, he gives up.

Hogler thinks for a moment, and then he walks over to one of the other crew mate's quarters. He knocks on the blast door. He hears a female voice say,

"Come in!" He presses the button to open the doors. After poking his head in he shouts to Bre, who is packing her bag:

"Hey, I can't find any stun guns!" She looks up at him; she says,

"Are you asking to borrow one?" Hogler sighs. Then loudly says,

"Yes, I am!" Bre stands up, scoots over to her desk, and grabs a ray rifle. After flicking a switch on the side of it that turns it to stun mode, she tosses it to him. Hogler catches it and turns to walk out of the room. She kindly says,

"You're welcome." Before he continues walking away, he turns around and says,

"Thank you." As he walks away, he checks the gun out. It is metallic-gray and very shiny. He walks away and continues to prepare for the mission.

In the Captain's Quarters, Xander gets ready to land for the mission. The Captain's Quarters are much bigger than everyone else's. There is a private bathroom, a master bed, and a larger closet where he keeps his outfits. They are all the same jacket, yet he has fifteen of them.

Xander grabs two small ray guns and places them into his thigh holsters; he also takes a few extra cells. He puts a song on his holocell while he is packing his bag. It is *Grey Street* by *Dave Matthews Band*. He blasts it loudly, so it could be heard in other rooms. Xander has a fascination with old Terran music and culture. After the fall of Terra, a huge library of ancient Terran artifacts, books, videos, and music was made to preserve the lost culture. It is called The Great Archive. He bobs his head to the beat. Once he is all ready, he makes his way to the helm for the landing.

The Odyssey rockets towards the landing pad at the Imperial outpost. Cinise watches with her face against the window. She stares at the lavender dunes of Destolace. She thinks, Wow, that is the most beautiful view. As they land at the pad, they look out the window. The sun slowly rises over the purple horizon. It shines and reflects light across the vast, lavender dune seas. Two Wyvern-class Imperial starfighters are docked on other pads which belong to Derek and

Thaxton Lee
The Echo

Mark. The Odyssey lands on the metal landing pad where a bot waits for them.

Fifteen

Now that the *Odyssey* has landed at the Imperial outpost on Destolace, the foot ramp underneath the ship lowers; Xander walks down the ramp. He is followed by the rest of the crew: John, Hogler, Bre, Cinise, and Davenk. As they walk off the foot ramp, they are greeted by a bot, one of similar models to SE-3, but a newer version. The bot is designed to look like a female imperial officer. She has wires on her head that are pulled back; they are made to resemble a ponytail. The bot slowly shuffles up to the crew. It says in a feminine yet robotic tone with a soft smile:

"Hello, I am 5H-3A, but you can call me Shea." SE-3 walks up to 5H-3A; he stares at the bot; his optical sensors illuminate with an inquisitive glow. After SE-3 looks at her, and he says:

"Hello, I am SE-3, but you may refer to me as SEE." Her robotic face smiles kindly and her cheeks have a soft glow.

"SEE, that's an interesting name. I have never heard something like that. What model are you? Your build looks familiar, yet I have not seen a bot like you." SE-3 enters deep in his robotic mind. He looks at her and says,

"I am from the S3 model from Apex Manufacturing. My line was discontinued shortly after the creation of me. I have not seen another bot of my same line. I wonder if there are any of them left..." SE-3's voice shifts to more human sounding, and he mimics the casual stance of Xander. "...but your steel plating is elegant. I love the design of your figure." Xander chuckles and leans over to Bre, who is on his left, and says in a sarcastic tone:

"Is he trying to flirt with her?" She playfully smiles and responds,

"I don't know man. He's been acting odd lately. Maybe he's got an interest in that now." As he says this, she contemplates the odd actions that SE-3 has been doing lately. Bre notices how his posture mimics Xander in how he walks and stands.

"Can bots do that?" Xander's expression looks confused.

"I'm not sure. I've never known a bot who can have those sort of 'emotions'." As they are chatting, Shea says,

"It's time we get moving. Derek and Mark are waiting for us in the outpost. Follow me this way." She gestures to the group to follow her. SE-3 walks right by her side with everyone else dragging behind a bit. While he walks, John inspects his armaments. He deeply examines every edge of it.

Up front, SE-3 begins to talk to Shea. He is saying,

"So Shea, how long have you been stationed here? As he is walking forward, he turns his head and looks deep in her optical sensors.

"Well, this station was first established about five weeks ago, and the construction was just completed two weeks ago. They sent me from the Citadel to here because they needed someone to oversee the station."

"Do you like working with the Empire," SE-3 inquires.

"I mean since my creation I've only been with the Empire, so I'd have to say I do. They treat me well. Though the hours may be long it is worth it if I am serving my oh so great Empire. What about you? I understand you are with the USG?" They slowly approach the huge Imperial outpost. It stands approximately fifty feet tall off the lavender sands. Satellites, turrets, and many windows line the outpost's walls. Blue banners with the Imperial insignia on it hang from the tops of the walls.

As John trots along behind everyone, Davenk purposefully slows down, so he is beside him. He looks at John with an inquisitive look. John notices, turns to him, and states sternly,

"Can I help you?" His eyes, full of deep annoyance. Davenk grows a smirk, and says,

"I hear you were a soldier once. Is that true?" John sighs with the slightest inclination of frustration which Davenk catches. "I don't mean to bother you. I'm just curious..."

"Well, whoever you heard that from is right. I was an Imperial Sentinel for thirty years, and I served twenty eight tours in the *Sarconian War*." Davenk's eyes widen as he is intrigued by the dedication of this man. He thinks, *This man has fire... fire of the Echo...*

"So I guess you are a real patriot then," Davenk says.

"If you want to downplay the fact I fought for thirty years against murderous *bugs* so that you can be hear bothering me, then yes I am a patriot!" Davenk senses the anger that he is brewing in him. He thinks, *What is with these people? They're just some random crew of a ship, yet they possess things I have only seen in the fiercest of warriors.* He says in a remorseful tone:

"Sorry for asking, I'll be on my own..." Davenk speeds up his pace so that he is not near John anymore. As he leaves him, he feels the deep trauma that lies inside John. It is like a lion clawing at the door just waiting to be let out. A bellowing sadness wells inside Davenk as he feels through John.

A warm breeze rolls over the plum colored dunes. It pulls in fine grains of sand that blow against their skin. Like hundreds of small pricks is how the grain feels as they sting their bare skin. Bre puts her hand up to cover her eyes. Xander takes his left glove off. As he is walking, he dips his fingers into the fine grains of mauve sand. It is like running his fight through a fine silk.

"Well, I am now. I was originally designed as an assassin bot, but my now captain, Xander, found my destroyed body and had me rebuild. And yes, we do work with the USG on accords by our representative Bre." He points over to Bre as she closely walks beside Xander as they talk. "Things are pretty good with us. Especially after we finish this contract." They continue up the blast doors at the front of the outpost. A panel on her arm flips back, she presses a button on it, and the blast doors open up vertically. Small blasts of steam shoot out from the hydraulic systems that pull the door up.

While she is approaching the outpost, Cinise fiddles with the ray gun that was given to her by John. She flicks the switch on the side to make sure it is on stun. She's never used a ray gun before, and she hopes to not have to. She thinks, *I hope we can all talk this out like peaceful people.* She is naïve, but still grounded in the true reality of what people could be if they actually tried.

Once the door is completely pulled up into the top of it, they all enter inside the Imperial facility. Now inside, the huge thick doors slam shut behind them. Fluorescent white lights suspended from the ceiling shine down on them. Both standing with their hands on their hips, Derek and Mark are waiting for them. The two of them shout,

"Dude!" They rush up to Xander with their arms open. Xander yells back,

"Dudes!" The three of them embrace each other. Bre rolls her eyes and smiles.

"Man It's gonna be great working with you again," exclaims Xander. He smiles brightly. Bre has only seen him smile like this when he talks to her. She thinks, *Hm... he must really like me.*

The three guys all exchange their secret handshake that only people from their school know. To all the others they look like a group of rowdy teenagers. John shakes his head and thinks, *Is this what the Empire has become?* He thinks of the kind of hardened people he fought with in the Empire. He leans over to Hogler who is next to him, and he says,

"Can you believe this? Look at them. This damn galaxy makes people soft. We wouldn't have been caught dead acting like that. Our drill sergeant would have made us run laps in the rain or something." Hogler understands where he's coming from. Hogler did work in a few paramilitary groups. He thinks, *I guess he's right. People just aren't the same anymore.*

"I mean yeah you've got a point," says Hogler. "But you can't just expect people to stay the same as we were back in the day. Though things may have been *better* back then, we can't stop the world from changing. Old relics like us...," he jokingly slaps John on the back and laughs. "Will always be around. We're just going to have to change with the times." John thinks, *I'm never going to become like that. I'd rather die than go soft.* John doesn't respond to what he says; he just stands there letting his words sink in.

After they exchange quick chatter, they fall back into the focused mindset, and Derek says,

"Xander, it's about time we get to work." He motions the group to the overseer's room which is a wide, open room full of computers and holoscreens. There is a large window that looks out onto the lilac dunes. The sun now just sits on the horizon like a tired old soul. Cinise immediately admires the stunning view while warm light caresses her soft skin.

Derek and Mark stand in the middle of the room. Mark says happily:

"Well I assume you all read or at least listened to the message on the USG contract?" Bre gives him an affirmative nod. He notices and continues, "Great, so we'll probably head out in about..." He looks at the holowatch on his left wrist. "...an hour." He looks over to Derek, and Derek says,

"Yeah, an hour should be good. That will give you all time to get your stuff ready. This was in the message, but I'm just recapping: make sure all your armaments are put in their stun function. We don't care enough nor do we have the reserves to waste it on these natives. Our goal is to stun them, and take them back to our brig while we have a transport ship on the way." Mark finishes with:

"Once we take care of the insurgent savages, you will be given your payout and be seen off world. Meet back here in an hour and we will head out to the wall." He points to the large, metal, grated fence that surrounds the outpost which is about 500 meters out. They all look outside the window and see the wall. On the other side of the fence, they see a group of silhouettes which are the natives. They watch them shoot bolts at the fence trying to break it. "Good thing you got here before they got in. We've been waiting for some shock troopers to arrive for the past week, but they got rerouted to take care of some Nytarians getting too close to Imperial space." John thinks, *Maybe the Shockers' still have some grit left.* "I'll see you then"

Xander, Derek, and Mark all sit around together and talk while the rest of the group disperse around the outpost. Bre and Cinise walk throughout the facility together as they chat. John finds a couch where he takes a nap. Surprisingly Hogler and Davenk continue talking. SE-3 has deep conversations with Shea about things she has never thought of. His mind begins to open, pulling in new ideas. This goes on for an hour then they all meet up in the overseer's room.

Sixteen

Rumblings have been surfacing throughout the galaxy that Nytarians have been advancing into the Mid Worlds. No one high enough up in the Empire to make decisions believed this, but pirates came back with undisputable images of Nytarian vessels. When this reached the higher-ups in the Empire, attack ships were sent out immediately with much haste.

The Nytarian battle cruiser, The Reckoning, sits in the space directly above the Nytarian. Out of the expansive fleet of battleships, The Reckoning is one of the weaker vessels especially compared to The Apocalypse. It still is a vessel to be feared. Many cannons and railguns cover the ship. A squadron of stingers, the Nytarian starfighter, lay inside the ship waiting for their moment to attack. The Commander of this ship anticipates the eventual arrival of Imperial forces.

Now, Zulara IV is home to battles between the Empire and Nytar. Nytarians have been on the planet for about a week setting up a base. The Imperial vessel, The Order, has just arrived out of warp speed in the space around the Zulara IV. The Order is one of the Empire's many attack cruisers. It is covered in pulverizers and ion cannons. Powerful Apex Manufacturing shields protect the ship. Inside the hangar bay, a squadron of Imperial light starfighters waits for the attack with all the pilots at the ready.

Once the two ships reach each other's view the Nytarian ship hails The Order's bridge. The communications officer pulls up a holoscreen. On the holoscreen, they see the lavender-skinned Nytarian commander standing with his hands behind his back and a smug look across his scarred face. He is surrounded by computers, admirals, and technicians.

"We have decided to be merciful. You are not aware of what you are doing. Only a fool would get in the way of us doing the work of Nylos. This is your last chance to warp out of here before we sacrifice all of you in the holy name of Nylos," says the Nytarian commander in an imitating voice. The Imperial commander stares at him with a hateful gaze before he says while chuckling:

"If you think we will give up our land to savages like you, then you are a lot crazier than we thought. I am here to put you back in your place. A place where you can't just step into Imperial space without severe repercussions! I hope you are prepared to meet your so-called god, Nylos. You should hope he is real because you're going to need a miracle to defeat the Empire!" Both just stare daggers at each other.

They slowly raise their right hand in the air. Swiftly, bring it to their side, and they both yell,

"Attack!" Both ships begin to open fire on one another. bolts whizz through the cold vacuum. The holoscreen is turned off only after the Nytarian commander says,

"May Nylos grant you mercy in the After…" The commanders watch as bolts of plasma blast against their shields. The ship rumbles and rocks. Missiles and torpedoes blast into the ships' hull. Soldiers on both sides scramble to load their cannons.

The squadrons of ships inside the battleship pour out like hornets from a hive. Bombers, interceptors, and starfighters all line up in attack formation. The Imperial squadron, Vulcan Squadron, flies out of The Order. Like all Imperial, starfighters they are of the Wyvern class. They quickly fall into attack formation. One of them says in an encouraging tone:

"This is Vulcan Leader. Stay close to me if you want to live. Vulcans ten through fifteen, you watch our six. Vulcans two through nine, stay on me. We need to take out their fighters." One of them comes on the radio and says,

"This is Vulcan Two standing by."

"This is Vulcan Three standing by," says another.

"This is Vulcan Four standing by…" They all say this as their ships enter into the Weaver Attack Formation or WAF. Once they are in range, the ships open fire on each other. Thousands of beams zoom through at all the starfighters. As Vulcan leader said, Vulcans ten through fifteen straggled behind and cleared a path around the other Vulcans.

Imperial Bombers with thick barrier shields slip through the battle to try to make a bombing run on the Nytarian battleships. Most are spotted and blown up by the stingers, but some make it to the attack vessels. Once above the Nytarian battle cruiser, a hatch opens on the bottom of the bomber. Hundreds of tiny detonators fall out like a torrential downpour. Since shield barriers only absorb energy weapons, the detonators slip right through. Powerful explosions are set off when they collide with the hull. The moment they go off, the Nytarian cannons immediately lock on to the defenseless bombers and fire dozens of bolts at them which blows them up in a million pieces.

The Order is not as powerful as The Reckoning, so they don't stand much of a true chance. The Empire needed something to delay Nytarian forces from advancing further into Imperial territory. The commander came into the battle with the expectation of failure, but he had hope that they could turn the odds in their favor. He is a demanding commander who always wanted the best his pilots and soldiers could give. He never settled for second best.

Fifteen thin Nytarian interceptors blast out from the hangar of The Reckoning. Instead of engaging in heated combat, they zoom through the battle dodging past bolts. They only exchange a few blows with the Imperial ships. These interceptors engage their sublight thrusters and fly directly at The Order. The admiral of The Order, Andrew Thorne, notices their rapid approach. On the bridge, he shouts,

"They're going to crash into us—" The moment he says this, ship after ship comes crashing into the bridge as they fly through the barrier shields. All those on the ship began to scream in terror, but their voices were immediately silenced by the soundless vacuum that is space. These interceptors are outfitted with explosive detonators inside, so they do more damage. The entire bridge full of captains, admirals, and the commander are all blown into smithereens.

Without any supervision, the gunners and pilots have no idea what they are to do. The tacticians who have been feeding them orders are all dead. After a minute of chaotic explosions and blasted fire, the leader of the Imperial squadron, Vulcan Leader, was shot out by two Nytarian interceptors. The rest of Vulcan Squadron is in disarray. One of them shouts over the channel,

"This is Vulcan Three. What is our move? Over." Another says,

"Vulcan Five here. Vulcan Leader, do you copy? Over." The channel is silent as they wait for a response for their leader. Their radios crackle, and their voices are frantic as they dodge past all the Nytarian ships.

"This is Vulcan Two. Does anyone have eyes on Vulcan Leader? Over." They all start to look around their sides while they fly. One spots the tumbling wing of his ship. Another sees Vulcan Leader rolling stiffly through space. One of them turns and sees the destroyed bridge.

"This is Vulcan Six. I see Vulcan Leader... he is out. I repeat he is out...Over," he says in a somber voice. They all are unsure of what to do. They fought with him for months training for their first mission.

"What do we do? Over," says Vulcan Two. As the radio is silent, Vulcan Three shouts over it,

"I've got two on my tail! I can't shake them! I need backup—". Before anyone has time to process what he said, they hear the faint sound of an explosion and watch as a torpedo hits the tail of his craft. Massive Powernaught Railguns on the underside of The Reckoning activate their targeting computers. One of the gunners says through the radio system,

"Sir, we have a lock… on all of them." A few moments of space-quiet pass, and then the chief gunner says,

"Fire. At. Will." The other gunners all hear this. Each nod to one another before powering up their weapons. All the railguns track the scrambling Imperial starfighters. The long barreled railguns begin to charge up with magnetic energy. Huge fifteen-foot Zarium steel bolts are loaded into them. One after the other, the bolts fly through the air at tens of thousands of miles per hour. They collide with the struggling starfighters blowing them up into fiery infernos. The sounds of terror are immediately silenced as the cold vacuum consumes them.

With the insignificant Vulcan Squadron now eliminated, The Reckoning must take care of the pestilent Imperial battleship. The Nytarian commander turns to the weapons officer and commands,

"Hit them with the Annihilator!" The officer looks up at him with a grim expression and says,

"Commander, are you sure? It is not fully tested."

"What did I say? We have wasted enough time dealing with these zealous Imperials! We need to show them why they don't interfere with our Conquest! Annihilate them!"

"Yes sir." The officer presses some buttons and flicks a few switches.

Underneath the ship, a huge metal laser cannon drops out that is 200 feet long. It angles to point directly at The Order.

All those inside The Order who are still alive look out in fear at this never before seen weapon. They watch as purple energy coalesces at the end of the massive barrel. Even inside The Reckoning, they can feel the Annihilator rumble as it is filled with so much power.

For a moment, everything feels like it's silenced as a giant beam of superheated purple blasts through space and strikes The Order right in the side. The amount of force carried in the beam is so much that the entire vessel erupts in a ball of red fire and purple energy. Every soul on board is incinerated into dust.

The Annihilator laser is retracted back into the ship, and the Nytarian squadron returns to the hangar bay. Now that all their enemies are defeated, the ship exits attack mode and continues with their takeover of Zulara IV as if nothing happened.

It seems one single Vulcan starfighter managed to evade the Powernaught Railguns. The tiny ships speed away from the wreckage. It flies on low power to hopefully avoid being seen. One of the gunners says as he locks onto the Vulcan:

"Not so fast." He fires a single missile at the ship. The pilot can evade it for a few seconds, but the missile finally catches up to it. The missile fulminates the tiny ship in a flaming inferno.

Another Nytarian destroyer, The Prowler, drops out of warp speed near The Reckoning. Compared to The Apocalypse, this is the single most destructive ship in the Nytarian fleet. It is covered in thousands of pulverizer cannons.

Xenos ordered The Prowler to go to Zulara to demonstrate their power on the planet. Within moments of warping to Zulara, The Prowler zooms to just outside the planet's atmosphere. Once in range, all of their pulverizer cannons angle down towards the forested world. Suddenly, billions of superheated Energen blasts fly at the planet's surface as they are bombarded with a hellfire of lasers.

On the surface, the dense forests are obliterated by the bombardment. Once a single laser, it's the ground, it explodes leaving a smoking crater, but the billions of blasts destroy everything they are aimed at. Trees topple over. The grass is seared. Creatures killed in an instant.

With The Order destroyed, fifty Nytarian troop transports pour out of The Reckoning. These are much larger than the average transport. Each holds 100 soldiers in them. Before the transports reach the planet's surface, two huge carrier ships fly out of The Reckoning; these carriers hold two Behemoth tanks in them.

Behemoths are gigantic armored tanks; they have treads on each side. It is 60 meters long, 12 meters wide, and 30 meters tall. A huge

Powernaught single-barrel cannon sits on top of it with two smaller cannons on the side. The cannons can fire EDR projectile rockets. Behemoths are manned by a crew of 100 Nytarians.

The carriers drop the Behemoths off on the planet. They slam to the ground, crushing the tall trees beneath them. A shockwave blasts from the crater where the tank is dropped which knocks down more bushes and trees around.

The Behemoths blast forward crushing anything in their path whether that be living creatures or plants. Horse-like animals dash out of the way. Lizard-like birds caw and fly away. They charge through the trees at a nearby village. After the tanks clear a path behind them, the trooper transports land behind the tanks and pours out their soldiers. The soldiers clad in black armor march through the deep tracks of the tank's treads.

The soldiers stomp through wet mud as it has rain just over the planet. The ground is still cold and fresh. With every step they take, mud shoots up and gets on their once pristine war boots.

Eventually, the Behemoths push through the dense jungles of Zulara. They trample over centuries-old, giant trees. These ancient trees are older than the Nytarian Conquests. Though it is midday in Zulara, the thick treetops block out all the incoming sunlight. It appears as if it is dusk underneath the trees. Thick, green vines drape down.

Inside one of the Behemoths, is the Nytariancaptain who is leading the assault, Nactus. He sits in the command deck and looks at monitors that show camera feed from outside the tank. He watches attentively waiting for the upcoming village.

As they are marching through the mud towards a rumored Zulu village, some soldiers around hear the sound of rusting among the bushes surrounding them. Some turn their attention to look, but all they see is them slightly moving.

Captain Nactus' computer screen has every soldier pinged by a chip in their armor. The chip monitors their heart rate, breathing speed, and location. He watches the lines of troops march behind the tank. Suddenly, he notices a few of the blips in the back of the order disappear off the computer; their vitals go blank. His bare brow furrows in confusion, and his sulfur eyes light up with intrigue. He turns to one of his officers and says,

"What is happening here?" The officer looks at the computer for a moment and responds,

"Uh... most likely the chips are malfunctioning. They should come back online in a bit. This happens sometimes."

"You didn't put faulty chips in our soldiers' armor did you?"

"Oh no, I would never. All glory to Nylos... forever."

"You better see to it that they come back on. I don't think Xenos will be too pleased with your failure," snaps the captain. The officer nervously swallows. He scrambles to his computer and rushes to figure out what is happening with the chips.

As the soldiers are marching, a single trooper in the back is suddenly ripped up to the jungle ceiling by a vine wrapped around his ankle. The vine made little to no sound besides the faint scream of the soldiers. Since he is in the back of the march, no one notices him disappear. One after another eleven troopers are yanked up into the thick foliage.

A few moments later, a soldier glances back and sees a soldier next to him being pulled into the air. He shouts,

"They're all around us!" The march stops along with the Behemoths. With their ray rifles cocked and ready, they look all around the dark forest. One of the troopers who have pulled up drops back to the jungle floor. Some soldiers crowd around him, and a steaming laser hole lies in his forehead. The eleven other Nytarians crash to the ground; their lifeless bodies thump in the squishy mud. All have laser wounds on their face.

Though the Nyatrians are fierce warriors, their bodies fill with the terror of the unknown. All of them look up at the jungle ceiling. A single metallic detonator with a red beeping button drops from the thick leaves. The moment it strikes the muddy floor, it erupts in a fiery explosion. The blast incinerates the ones near the blast and knocks others to their feet who are farther away.

Mere seconds after the detonator goes off, two hundred Hessoths dropdown. The furry Hessoths hold one blaster in each of their four hands, yet some have knives, scattershots, and other melee weapons. A few of them drop onto the shoulders of the Nytarian troopers. They rip their helmets off, throw them to the ground, and begin punching and shooting them. The Nyatrians rush to tear the small creatures off themselves. Most of the Hessoths leap off the troopers, and they dash underneath the thick foliage.

None of the soldiers see where they went. All they can see are the small vibrations in the bushes below. Anytime they would notice movement, one would fire a laser, and everyone else would fire as well.

One Zularan drops a larger detonator underneath one of the Behemoths. A few seconds afterward, it explodes sending the entire ship into millions of pieces.

The Nytarians and Hessoths battle. The Hessoths utilize guerilla warfare tactics, so they strike the Nyatrians hard and fast then descend deep into the jungle.

Seventeen

Now that an hour has passed, the crew of The Odyssey all meet back up in the overseer's room along with the two Imperial soldiers who were there. John sips a steaming cup of coffee out of a small metal cup as he smokes a floppy cigarette. Dark bags hang from his eyes. SE-3 still talks with Shea. His eyes glow with joyful bliss. Bre and Cinise talk as they begin to learn more about each other and become closer.

With everyone in the overseer's room, Derek says to them all:

"Let's head down to the speeders so we can get to the place where the insurgents are." He motions over to a blast door. Derek and Mark walk up to it followed by Xander, who falls back next to Bre, and everyone else behind them.

While everyone else is leaving to go take care of these natives, Brooks sits in the lounge room watching a television show. Xander told him he should stay here. Reluctantly, Brooks abided in his request.

There is still a deep wanderlust in him. Brooks yearns to see the new world he has found. He is watching That's So Earth. It is a new show that has just come out. That's So Earth is a sitcom that makes fun of Earth and the stupid things Terrans did. Brooks sips on a cold, fizzy Bizzle Juice that Xander told him he should try. He loudly laughs at some of the cheesy jokes and he thinks it is very funny how many things they get wrong about Earth.

As they approach the blast door, movement sensors automatically open them. Xander leans over to Bre and says,

"Wow, SEE is infatuated with that bot. Idk what's up with him. Maybe we messed something up when we did the reprogram." They both look at him as he talks to Shea. Bre says,

"I mean we aren't professional mechanics and coders. We could've messed something up I guess..." The group walks out through the blast doors and down a set of metal stairs to where the speeders are. Once they are outside, warm winds pick up the violet grains of sand and carry them throughout the arid dunes. Their steel-toed boots clank as they stomp down the grated stairs.

At the bottom of the stairs is a steel platform where five uni-speeders wait. Each Uni-speeder can hold two people. Derek and Mark hop on one, Bre and Cinise get on another, Xander and John are on one, SE-3 and Shea hop on another, and lastly, Hogler reluctantly gets on with Davenk. Most everyone is familiar with Uni-speeders except Cinise. All those who are driving, turn the two handles down, and the engine revs up with a low-pitched hum. Mark shouts,

"Stay close to me and make sure to put on the goggles if you don't want to have your eyes blown out by the sand!" Everyone grabs the goggles that hang from the handlebars and put them on. Mark slams his foot on the pedal and zooms off. The three other Uni-speeders blast after them.

For about thirty seconds, they speed over the deep purple dunes. Sand spurts up one wheel that spins at rapid rotations. Once they reach the metal fence, they all hop off their Uni-speeders. Shea once again opens the panel on her arm to open up the fence gate. The gate slowly opens up horizontally.

Derek and Mark rush forward. Derek pulls a few small metal cubes out of his utility belt. He throws them on the ground at the top of a dune that looks over the native's camp. The moment they make contact with the ground, the tiny cubes instantly expand up into a two-and-a-half meter long and one-meter tall Zarium steel shield wall. Derek yells,

"Oscar Mike! Get behind these!" The rest of the group runs and slides behind the walls. They all pull out their ray guns and ready them for fire. John swings the ray rifle on his back to the front; he loads a cell into it. Xander pulls out his two ray pistols, and so does everyone else. "Fire on my mark." They peek over the metal wall; they see the group of Destolaians (another name for natives to Destolace) dressed in dark purple cloaks that are made to blend with the dunes. Huts made of lavender sandstone house others. They watch as they cook food over a fire. Derek shouts, "Fire!"

Being caught off guard by the loud shouts, the Destolaians leap behind the cover. The group fires stun bolts out of their ray guns. Unlike standard bolts which are bright red, stun blasts are bright sapphire blue and sound much more a higher pitch. The blue bolts zoom by at the Destolaians hiding behind the cover. When a stun bolt hits organic tissue, it interacts uniquely by sending an electrical shock through the body which stuns the reviver.

Now that they realize they are under attack, they pull out their ray rifles and start to exchange crimson bolts. They pop up and down from behind their huts as they shoot off live beams.

Davenk and Bre are both crouching behind a steel barrier together. She fires stun bolts with her small ray pistol. She looks over and notices that Davenk has no weapon. She says

"Did you forget a gun... to the gunfight?" He looks over.

"I... need no weapon."

"Then how will you shoot them?"

"I will not." Davenk stands up from behind the steel wall. When the natives see he is up, they open fire with a volley of bolts. Bre is amazed to watch that none hit him. One of them flies right at his face. He sticks out his hand, and he sees yellow strands elegantly wrap around the bolt stopping it in mid-air. Bre does not see the yellow, glowing strands; she only sees Davenk stop the bolt in the air. He extends his arm forward, and the bolt flies back at the native who shot it at him. The native was full of confusion and amazement as he saw this feat that could only be described as magic. Once he realizes the bolt is flying right back at him, he jumps out of the way to go behind one of the lavender sandstone huts.

After Davenk does this, he crouches behind the steel wall again as if nothing happened. Bre looks at him with awe and wonder and mutters,

"What was that?" He looks at her with no response then softly says,

"That is what we call the Echo of the Universe..." She asks no more questions as she ponders what he means by this. She can recall that that phrase is familiar to her, but she is not sure what from. The Echo? What is he talking about? She thinks.

Later in the fight, Davenk rushes away from the wall with Bre. He went over to push up on the natives' huts. Now, Bre is by herself behind the steel wall. After a few moments of firing at the Destolians. She is calm until one of the natives leaps over the wall, and the man shrouded in brown cloaks aims a ray rifle at her. The cool winds of Destolace dramatically blow his cape. Since she wasn't actively firing, she didn't have it in her hand. The man pushes the barrel of the ray rifle against her chest. In fear, she shuts her eyes to not see what's coming. The sound of a bolt whizzes around, but it wasn't at her. She opens her eyes and sees the native man drop to the ground as he is stunned. A man holding a ray pistol turns to her and smiles. She had never seen him before yet there was a sense of warm recognition.

He has a reddish tan, and old, wrinkly skin. He wears a mustard brown sweater with suspenders over it. He has a metallic jet pack strapped to his back. His hair is thin and gray, and he has a bushy gray mustache. On his head, is an old floppy cloth hat.

Bre looks at him with a puzzled look. She mutters,

"Who are you?" He gives her a warm smile and says,

"Fernando. You can call me Fernando. If you are ever in trouble, say my name three times, and I will be there to help." He turns around without saying a word; he slowly walks away into the horizon of the lavender dunes.

Xander and John both hide behind the same steel wall. They each pop up in different intervals and fire off a few stun bolts. John grabs a grenade off his bandolier. He looks over the wall and clocks where all of the Destolaians are, and he then hucks the grenade at one of them.

When it hits the ground next to one of the Destolaians, he looks at it. It beeps faster and faster. By the time he registers that it is about to go off, it is too late. It explodes and sends an electrical shock in a spherical shape around the blast point. Unlike normal grenades and detonators, this was a stun grenade and it immediately knocks the Destolaians unconscious. Xander turns over at John with a surprised look and says,

"You brought grenades!"

"Of course I did. Fifteen of them to be specific," says John.

"Toss me one of those grenades." John sighs in annoyance.

"Did you just ask me to throw a grenade at you? That's the stupidest thing you've said to me. And once you asked if I could shoot you in the shoulder to see if it hurts." Xander thinks, Oh I kinda forgot about that... John scoots over next to him and hands him a stun grenade. "Don't hit yourself with this," he says in a gruff tone. Xander grasps the metallic grenade. He puts it into his jacket pocket and mutters,

"Thanks..." John glances at him as bolts fly overhead. He is about to say something when a small detonator flies over the wall and lands in between them. It rolls and bounces around. Xander and John both look down at it and then at each other. Without a moment of hesitation, John taps the small personal shield generator on his belt. A blue-hued shield barrier immediately covers him from head to toe. He throws down his gun and leaps on top of the beeping grenade.

A second later, it explodes. John's shield barrier contains the blast and protects Xander, but John is blasted back into the air and then lands in the lilac sand. Xander rushes over to him.

While he is rushing over to him, he is thinking, He saved me. He saved me. When he gets over to him, he sees John laying in the sand. He runs up beside him and says,

"John, John, are you okay? Come on, don't be dead!"

"Calm down. It's going to take a lot more than that to kill me. I should be mad at you for thinking that I was dead. You should know old dogs don't go down easy." John scrambles to get up. Xander extends a hand to help him. "I'm not that old. I can get up. He uses the butt of his ray rifle to leverage himself up; he dusts off his hands and pants, runs back behind his cover wall, and fires a single stun bolt right into the Destolaian who threw the detonator. As Xander watches John run back to the fight as if he didn't just jump in onto a lethal, he thinks, That is one resilient old hound... He runs after John behind the cover and jumps beside him.

After a few minutes, they stunned most of the Destolaians. John and Xander are still camped up behind their wall. Though it is relatively cool out on Destolace, John is profusely sweating and very hot. He fans himself with his hand and wipes his brow. He takes a glance at Xander and sees a bug with a deep green exoskeleton trying to bite off his face of Xander. Its spiky legs claw and rip at his flesh. John is overcome with panic, terror, and anxiety. Full of the deepest confusion, he stands up and looks around.

No longer is he on the beautiful dunes of Destolace. The sky is black and polluted. Hovercraft fly low to the ground. They shake the ground with their grav suspenders. Dark clouds of smoke plume all around him. He doesn't hear the high-pitched sounds of stun bolts; he hears: volleys of rockets, bolts whizz, the screams of fearful men, and the obnoxious sound of flying bug wings. He can almost taste the blood in the air, the gunpowder on his hands, and the smell of pure fear.

He looks back to Xander, and it isn't Xander. He sees one of his old friends lying dead on the ground as a bug rips at his bloody flesh. When he looks at himself, he is in his Imperial soldier uniform. He looks all around him and sees hundreds of dead bodies all with bugs clawing at them. The bugs begin to swarm around him. He begins to open fire with his ray rifle; his bolts don't do anything against them. They begin to attack him.

His vision begins to fall dark.

"John! John! Can you hear us," he hears a feminine voice exclaim. John feels something hit him in the face. After slowly opening his eyes, bright lights crowd his vision and the indication of silhouettes look down on him.

"Oh good I think he's awake," a female robotic voice says. As his vision slowly returns, he sees Xander, Bre, Shea, Derek, and Cinise looking over him. John mummers,

"Ugh, what are you doing?" He slowly sits up from being laid on his back. Shea holding a clipboard says,

"It seems you had a heart attack and then passed out."

"Where am I?" He looks around the room frantically. Again Shea says,

"This is the med-bay in the Imperial outpost we were at. We were just running a few tests on you to make sure you were ok. And we gave you some Healix." He groans as his back aches.

"What about the bugs— I mean the Destolaians?" Xander butts in and says,

"After you went down, we had to quickly take care of the rest of them. I used the grenade you gave me to stun the last one." She rips the Healix patch off John's arm. "Now, they are all in the brig. Transport is on the way to get them." John thinks, Was it the dream... again? As he goes to get off the metal he is on, She tries to stop him and says,

"Wait, we aren't done with the tests." He swats her hand away and barks,

"Oh don't you have a fit. I'm fine." He gets off the table and onto the floor. They are in a pristine white room. Multiple metal tables with cloth linens over them. Vials of Healix cover the table. He feels on his person. "Hey, where are my guns!" Xander points over to another table where John's ray rifles, ray pistols, and grenade bandoliers sit. He puts them all back into each of their respective holsters.

John stomps out of the room. He goes back up to the overseer's room, finds a mini-fridge, and pops open a cold beer. While he's up there, he sees Hogler dead asleep on a round couch. He thinks, That's what they should be doing. I'm always fine.

Still, in the med bay, Xander and Bre chat with one another:

"Do you think he is okay," Bre inquires of him.

"I never know with him. He jumped on a grenade to save me. And then had a heart attack as if nothing happened. I guess it's just his thing to be angry." Young Cinise says,

"Does he do this often?" Bre chimes in and says,

"Yep, all the time. He told us about the time he was working hunting down pirates for the Empire. The pirate captain shot him in the eye." Cinise winces at imagining that. "After he was shot, he said he headbutted the captain in the face, took his gun, and proceeded to kill the captain. The whole crew ran away. He blew up the ship and just walked away." Xander just realizes and says,

"Oh, that's how he got the cybernetic eye. He told me a bug bit it out." Bre and Xander look at each other confused. And both think, Hmmm, which one is true?

The group all heads back upstairs. Derek and Mark give Bre the credit chip, and the two of them check off that they finished their contract.

After saying their goodbyes, the crew heads back to The Odyssey, and they begin to leave the planet.

Eighteen

In the Citadel, it is as it always is: busy. Hover cars and hover trams blast people all over the city. Businessmen and women rush to their corporate jobs. Imp-pols patrol throughout every section of the city. Every corner that is not private territory is monitored by Imperial troopers and drones.

This day is busier than usual; an emergency meeting of the Grand Council has been called. The Grand Council is the ruling body of the Empire. It consists of twelve wealthy politicians who each govern one of the twelve Imperial sectors throughout the galaxy.

In the heart of the Citadel, is a huge metal building. It is the council building where they gather for their meetings. The building floats in the air due to the grav-suspenders underneath it. There are ports around it so people can land to enter.

Inside the building, there are twelve thrones on hovering metal platforms. There is one for each of them. Underneath the thrones, there is a stadium-like area where citizens of the Empire can observe the meetings.

The emergency meeting is happening now as silent citizens watch from below. Camera drones fly all around the room capturing the best angles and being televised all across the Empire. From Coranthea to Talasia, everyone tunes into this politically charged event.

"...This is outrageous! Nytarians are just casually entering Imperial space, and what are we doing about it... nothing," says an Arlean man. He wears flamboyant teal blue robes like the seas of Galatia, and his eyes are blue to match. Pointy ears poke through his blond hair that flows down on his robes. Fans that are out of view from the camera drones blow his hair like a glorious breeze. This is Drace Olphen, head of House Olphen. House Olphen oversees most of the banking and economic activities of the Empire. He looks furious; his brow remains furrowed and he frowns. A woman states assertively,

"You think we aren't pursuing the Nytarians? Patrols have been sent to every corner of the galaxy—" Drace interrupts,

"Yet we make no progress!" She looks confused and offended that he cut her off. "Every time we send something after them, they destroy it."

"That's why we will build them bigger and stronger!" She is Kandra Adis. Kandra is a human. She wears a long, white dress that hangs off the edge of her chair. Her skin is fair like the clouds of Arlea. Large, golden earrings hang from her earlobe and poke through her luscious chestnut hair. She is the head of House Adis which oversees the planets that do most weapons manufacturing in the Empire. Kandra continues, "We won't be stopped by these savages. The Empire has stood strong for 103 years with many more to come." Drace says,

"I'm not discrediting the proficiency of our military. I'm just speaking from a point of fact." The camera drone slowly zooms in on his face dramatically. "But it is not time to sit back and praise glory to the Empire! We need to look at what is happening and make sound judgments!" The crowd below erupts in applause. Drace glances down.

"I truly hate to say it, but Drace has a valid point," says another man sitting on one of the thrones. Drace looks confused as he agrees, which is rare for them. This is Maxir Vene, a bulky Diodrite, with red-orange skin. He wears elegant robes similar to Drace, yet these are more of a cerulean color and a starry pattern with two extra arm holes for his second pair of arms. He holds his top two arms in a confident steeple pose, and his other two hold a glass of red wine. Maxir is the head of House Vene who controls the agriculture of the Empire. "Drace brings up a sensitive point that we tend to neglect. We have been letting Nytarians step all over us as they enter our land." He pauses to take a sip from his wine glass. "We must retaliate tactically. We can't just send out a bunch of our battleships with no care in the world." Camera drones swarm around him. He continues, "We must plan a calculated strike!" Again the crowd roars underneath.

"You have yet to mention the many rebellions across all of our territories," says another house head. Jafan Primen is the Head of House Primen. His skin is hazel and dark. Half of his face has been replaced with cybernetics. He has long, dark dreads with golden beads attached to them. He wears a verdant green suit with golden accents. He sits straight up on his throne with his arms on the side. He says, "I don't know about you all, but I will not ignore that people are beginning to not fear us." Camera drones swarm all around him, yet he pretends not to notice. "We are not just going to pretend like what is happening on Destolace is not actually happening. They are not the only ones; it is happening throughout the galaxy!" Kandra stares angrily at Jafan, and she thinks, What is he doing? People should not be knowing about this.

He catches her angry stare and thinks, I know she wants to hide this from the people. She speaks in an angry tone:

"Jafan, if you want to criticize our current ways, what do you propose in return?" He leans forward on his throne in concentration.

"I propose House Adis begin construction on a new fleet of battleships. Ships that can rival the Nytarians' power. I'm sure your house's excellent manufacturing could surely manage." She scowls at him but quickly turns it to a smile when the camera drones turn to her. With a moment of hesitation, she says,

"I find that proposal to be... suitable. I can make arrangements with my house to get specs for your plan." A soft applause takes over the crowd below. Her face turns a rosy red. "Well, there are other matters we must address. Leena, any news on the recruitment of the Americorps?" Jafan thinks, Skonk, why must she make this a small matter? Kandra motions over to Leena Madar. She is the head of House Madar which oversees political relationships throughout the Empire. Leena wears a short, violet dress. Her hair is tied up in a long braid that drapes over her mauve cape. The cape is attached to her neck and wrists; it flows with her arm's elegant movements. She says,

"Unfortunately, it has not been going well. Their president, James Jackson, is stubborn. He refuses to take our help in the defense of Rhea against the Nytarians." She brushes a few strands of hair from her face. "We have offered him: sanctuary in Imperial space, Imperial resources, and many other helpful supplies."

"What is with those Americorps? They always have refused our help," Drace says. Jafan says,

"It's just in their nature." The house heads chuckle. A wave of amused laughter rolls over the crowd.

Maxir claps with two of his hands and says,

"Well, that is all the time we have. This concludes the Grand Council meeting." The camera drones fly away, and the crowd begins to walk out through the doors at the bottom.

With everyone leaving, Kandra flies her throne over to Jafan. Her fists are clenched, and she is red-hot. She says harshly,

"Jafan, what was that? Are you trying to have more rebellions?" The other house heads go silent as they watch this interaction. Jafan calmly states,

"I am not trying to start anything. This Empire should be built on trust not lies. We cannot lie to people anymore. I simply want to tell the truth."

"This is not lying! We must preserve the Empire! Our people will not stay in order if they think our infrastructure is crumbling! I am trying to keep the minds of our people safe! You seek to sow chaos among the people. It will not reap well for you," she says while shaking her head in anger.

"We will see..." He turns his throne around and leaves the council room. The other house heads also leave. She thinks, *He did not just leave while I'm talking!*

As Maxir steps off his throne, he snaps, and four Imp-pols show up and escort him out of the place. He stomps out with a metal can that has a red gem on the handle. The Imp-pol all carry ray rifles. On his way out, he stops by Kandra. He snaps at her:

"What was that! Do you seek to ensue chaos in the Empire? For someone who seeks to keep things quiet, you aren't very good at it!" Kandra turns to look at him. Both of them do not adorn their grins they use for cameras. She barks:

"Don't speak to me on this. Jafan was clearly the one giving out information we have not authorized for the public. Where is he even?" Jafan steps out of a tunnel into the bright light above which shines on his emerald green suit.

"I look not to cause discourse, but we are failing our people," he says calmly. "I want to let our people see what is happening in the Empire. If we do not, they will begin to not trust us. Like they do now." Maxir pokes Jafan in the chest with his metal can and snaps,

"You may act like a peaceful person now, but when the Empire turns against us it will be us who laughs." Jafan grabs the end of the can and pushes it away. .I don't want to see any more of this radical behavior from you! Understand?"

"Your empty threats do not worry me. I will do what I feel is right for the Empire to prosper," says Jafan. He holds his face with a smug look. Maxir's orange brow furrows in his fury. He raises his voice:

"For your sake, I hope you are kidding. You know I do not take lightly to your insurgent behavior." He slams the butt of his cane to the ground. "Where is Leena! I need her to fix this." He scowls at Jafan. Leena walks into the area from a hallway.

"You called for my assistance," she says.

"Call up Chet! I need him to spin what Jafan said. We can't have this kind of stuff getting out on air!"

"I'll see what I can do, but Jafan here made it very difficult to spin it in a positive way." Drace steps forward and sternly says,

"Contrary to what seems to be the common belief, I believe Jafan is right. Look throughout history. It never goes well when people in our position take advantage of the people. I just don't want that to become us." As Maxir opens his mouth to yell, a human reporter walks in holding a microphone. The moment the heads see her, they calm down in an instant and put on apathetic smiles with hatred behind their eyes. Maxir pats Jafan on the back in a friendly aggressive manner. They both awkwardly chuckle. The reporter interviews them.

Nineteen

After they leave the atmosphere of Destolace, The Odyssey casually cruises to their next destination. The entire crew is at the ship's helm. SE-3 stands there with a sad glow in his eyes hidden behind his plastered smile.

"So to Boloxia it is," says Xander while standing in front of the crew. Davenk murmurs to himself:

"I'm not sure if that's a good idea..." No one hears him say anything.

"Yes, we should be heading there next. We've got another contract to pick up some Nexite which will give us 20,000 more credits," says Bre.

"Sounds good to me," the crew all says. Xander smiles and says,

"Alright sounds great! I'll get EQ working on the calculations for the jump now. I'll announce when we're about to jump, so you'll be prepared." Bre gives Xander a thumbs up as she turns to leave the helm through the blast doors. "EQ, you got that we need the calculations for Boloxia."

"Ah yes captain, I will be on that now," says EQ in their robotic voice. Xander plops down in his chair. He scoots around in it and senses something is off. He says,

"Who sat in my chair?" Brooks thinks, How did he know?

As everyone is about to leave, John spots something across the floor. He thinks, Oh no, please don't be it. They still can't be alive. As John raises his ray rifle, he shouts,

"Watch out, there's a bug!" Everyone turns over to John. They all see an insectoid creature with a green exoskeleton quickly crawling across the floor. The whole crew notices the terrified look in John's eyes. The bug creeps all over the floor and everyone jumps out of the way. John aims his ray rifle at it and opens fire with beams. Xander shrieks at the sight of him shooting and yells,

"Don't hurt my ship!" Xander looks mortified at the thought of scuffing up his precious baby.

"Oh shut up, this is a bit more important," shouts John. "Don't let it get too close! It will try to get in your head... literally!" John continues shooting, yet the erratic movements of the bug dodge the bolts.

Realizing that this is a bad thing, Hogler takes out a heavy repeater he has on his back. He lets out a volley of shots at the bug. Though they do hit it, its exoskeleton seems to deflect the bolts.

Brooks jumps out of the way because the bug started to run towards him. After he dashes away, he pulls out his ray pistols from the pocket in his sweatpants and shoots a few bolts at the bug.

The bug spins around and still, no one has hit it yet. It scuttles over to where John is standing; it leaps at him and crawls all over him. It goes up his arm, onto his shoulder, and on his face. He drops his ray rifle and starts to punch it off his face. Suddenly, it scrambles up his nose. He yells,

"GET OUT!" He falls to his knees and punches himself in the nose. Everyone around looks freaked out as they watch a bug crawl up John's nose. Bre begins to panic; she says,

"What should we do?"

"I can fix this!" Hogler walks up to John, puts his repeater to his head, and says, "stay still, I can get it out!"

"Put the gun down," commands Davenk. Hogler puts his gun down.

John feels the bug clamber around in his sinuses. He winces when he feels it dig into his olfactory bulb. He slaps himself across the face.

"Get out of my face," shouts John as he is in agonizing pain.

A moment later, he stops struggling and just freezes on the ground. Deep inside his head, the tiny bug swims through intracranial space. The bug reaches a spot in the brain, the cerebellum. Two clawed pincers pull out of its thorax; it spikes them into John's brain. After the bug spikes him with its claws, it bites down with its mandible into his soft brain tissue.

John abruptly stands straight up in an unnatural manner. He looks around with wide, dilated eyes with deep wonderment. He looks down at his hands like he had never seen them before. He walks around the helm, and he stares at everything with a deep puzzled expression. Xander says in a cautious voice:

"John, are you okay?" John grimly turns his head over to Xander.

Suddenly, he goes back to his normal stance and loses the odd look in his pupils. He looks around at his crew.

"It's in my brain...," he says solemnly. John pulls out his ray pistol. He falls to his knees again, points the gun to his head, and shouts, "Bug, we got two options here: one, you get out of my head and I squash you like the bug you are. Two, I blow us both up, and we both live our own happily ever after in hell." John's other arm reaches up and tries to pull his other arm down from the gun.

"Let me stay," says John out loud to himself in a different-sounding voice. The two arms struggle with each other as one tries to put the gun to his head, and the other tries to pull it down.

Xander runs out of the helm, and he comes back a minute later with a plastic bag. He ran all across the ship to find it. He says,

"If we get it out, let's put it in here."

In John's mind, he hears a voice, not his say,

"Don't do this" John says in his head,

"I'm not letting you live there for free." The bug pulls its mandibles and claws out of its tissue. The bug scoots through his brain and stops when something piques its interest in the hippocampus.

"What is this?"

"Don't go snooping around my head," he says internally. The bug digs its claws and mandibles deep into John's brain tissue. Its claws hit into a memory bank. Both John and the bug deeply experience a memory the bug taps into.

Deep in the heart of combat, Imperial soldiers rush far behind enemy lines. All carry ray rifles and are ready to shoot any on sight. Huge armored Shockers, Imperial space marines, push forward through the frontlines. They hold huge arm-mounted gatling guns in one hand and hold a huge shield barrier in the other. The Imperial soldiers duck behind the shields and hide from the incoming organic fire. One of Shockers shouts,

"Get behind me!" The Shockers push up with their shields and the soldiers exchange fire with the enemies. VTOL trooper transports fly right over them until it lands behind one of the Shocker's shields. Twenty-five soldiers come pouring out. The Shocker who is protecting the transport is attacked by a flying bug. It lands on the helmet of the Shocker, rips it off, and attacks his face. He drops his shield and the troopers are attacked by swarms of bugs. A trooper covered in armor only his dark skin and thick mustache are visible through his helmet he shouts,

"We need to get to the hive!" A Shocker turns his gun hand into a flamethrower. He says,

"I can see it!" The Shockers push forward through piles of rumble, dead humans, and bugs. They shoot hundreds of bolts out of their gun arms at the swarming bugs ahead.

Ahead of them is a huge pulsating sack of glowing, green ooze. Thousands of bugs swarm around the green, glowing hive like a living tornado. The troopers and Shockers reach the hive and begin to torch the hive. The thousands of bugs are engulfed in flames. They fall out of the sky like falling stars.

"So you were there too," the bug says in John's mind.

"What are you talking about?"

"The war. I'm not just any bug. I'm a Sarconian as I can feel you assumed... We are the same."

"No! No! You are a beast; you kill good men!" The whole crew watches as John sits on the floor silently. "We defended our land that you monsters attacked!"

"Wow, you don't know why the war started."

"I do. You demons invaded the peaceful Empire with your armies of terror beast!"

"Foolish man, you only hear what you want. We came in peace. Our planet had been dying. We had come to look for sanctuary in your zealous Empire. Since we didn't speak your language and looked threatening to you, you attacked us." John's mind begins to race all around. He considers for a moment if what this bug says is true. "All we did was protect ourselves."

"No, you are a liar! We welcomed all into the Empire!" The bug bites down harder into his brain; it makes him see into one of its memories from long ago. He shows John what the Sarconian hive mind saw when they went to the Empire for the first time.

When people saw the hordes of bugs, they ran and screamed in fear of them. The Sarconians tried to communicate, but the Empire made no effort to try. They immediately opened fire upon them. The

Sarconians did what they must to survive. If that means slaughtering thousands of people to protect their own, so be it.

The bug stops the memory. John is overwhelmed with confusion and distrust of the only thing he has fought for throughout his life.

"This can't be true…"

"You SHEEP! I would think someone of your gumption would not be as gullible to the lies that the Empire feeds you like animals."

"The Empire has been nothing but good to the galaxy. You try to deceive me like your fallen brothers."

"Do not disrespect me nor the fallen. You must see what happened during the war. It is time you realize what we truly are!"

"And what is that?" The bug pauses in an echoing silence before answering as to let him think of it himself.

"We… We are the last of our kind. I, the last Sarconian, and you, the last soldier who fought us. The two of us are both ancient fossils soon to be forgotten about." John begins to think, Skonk, the bug has a point. No one cares about what happened to us. We have become fossils covered by the ignorance of our time. "I can feel you know I'm right." You can hear my thoughts? thinks John. "Yes, I can. And you can hear mine." The bug thinks, and John hears it.

"Okay Bug, you've made your point, but what do you want?"

"For you to help me reignite my species. I am the last one, and I must lay my eggs"

"And what do you have to do to do that?"

"I must find a suitable habitat similar to that of the now-destroyed Sarco."

"Well, what is that like?"

"Warm, dark, wet, and swampy."

"So just like Boloxia." Bug doesn't know what Boloxia is. He browses through John's memory banks looking for what it is. Once it finds it, Bug sinks into the memories and now knows what it is.

"Yes, just like that."

"If we're going to make this work, you don't touch the controls. I will do everything. You can sit up in my head and do nothing. Another thing, don't go searching through my memories. Got it?"

"Yes." John makes peace with the uneasy feeling of something else in his mind. He opens his eyes from sitting on the ground; he stands up using his ray rifle as a cane to stand up. Everyone around is on edge as they are not sure what is happening. Hiding from afar, Cinise asks,

"John, are you alright?" He looks over at her with a nice smile which is unusual for John.

"Yes, I am." John feels a sense of certainty knowing that he isn't alone. Though it is just a tiny bug, he can tell this bug understands what he has been through.

John walks through the blast doors and to his bunk for some much-needed rest.

Back in the helm, Brooks says,

"What the hell just happened?"

"I have no galactic idea," says Bre.

"Lemme get this straight, John who is a soldier that fought a war against space bugs just had a space bug jump up his brain," asks Brooks.

"Brooks, you better get used to this soon because this galaxy is really weird," remarks Hogler. Xander persuasively asks,

"We'll deal with that later, so to Boloxia it is?"

"Yeah sounds good to me," says Bre as she smiles and nods to him. Bre and Cinise both leave out of the helm through the blast doors while talking. Cinise asks,

"So are we going to check on him or something?" Bre responds,

"No, probably not. He will be fine. This isn't the first time something like this."

"Oh, I see." Cinise wants to make sure he's alright. *Maybe I'll ask her later*, she thinks.

Brooks, Hogler, and Davenk all leave the helm and head to their respective quarters for the jump. Davenk has a deep cautious feeling inside him.

Back in the helm, Xander asks,

"EQ, how are the calculations going?" The ship's systems make electronic beeps as EQ boots up.

"Yes, captain, calculations for Boloxia are ready." Xander hops back into his pilot's chair. He pulls down his microphone and says into it,

"Cinise, we're about to boot up the warp drive. You need to be in the engineering room to make sure everything goes smoothly." Cinise walks to the engineering room. Xander flicks a few switches on the control panel. He presses the button and the warp drive begins to boot up. It vibrates with a low hum. Cinise hops on coms and says,

"Everything's good down here."

"Ready for warp: in three, two, one," he says over the microphone broadcasting to the whole ship. Xander opens a panel, grabs the lever, and yanks it back. The Odyssey enters warp speed straight to Boloxia.

Twenty

The Odyssey exits warp speed in the surrounding space around Boloxia. The huge frigate ship goes from flying hundreds of thousands of kilometers per second to stopping in an instant.

Before they exited warp speed, the crew all headed to their stations. Hogler and John sit in the two gunner turrets. Cinise waits in the engineering room. SE-3 stands at the communications desk which is right behind Xander's piloting console. Since Brooks can't do anything too complicated on the ship, he is on maintenance. If there is a fire or something goes wrong he needs to fix it. Davenk doesn't have a real purpose on the ship besides helping with missions, so he is sitting at the helm thinking, *This cannot be good. I sense a deep unease about this place... he must be here.* Bre is in her office. In her office, she has a camera system all around the exterior of the ship, so she can give helpful information to the gunners and Xander during the flight.

When they exit warp speed, Xander can barely see a few triangular-shaped ships flying around Boloxia in the distance surrounding Boloxia, but he can't make out what they are. They look very small but they seem to be because they are so far away. He squints at it and says to SE-3:

"Can you see what that is, SEE?... no pun intended." He chuckles to himself. In classic SE-3 fashion, he didn't get the joke, yet he laughed to copy Xander.

"Let me look," says SE-3. He clicks some buttons on his communications panel. A holoscreen appears in front of him. It is a camera feed from outside the ship. It zooms in to see what those ships are.

"Uh... why does it look like they are getting closer," asks Xander in a worried tone. The longer Xander looks at them the more he begins to recognize the very specific hull design of the giant ship on their approach. At the same time, Xander makes the connection, and SE-3 gets two notifications on his screen. He says,

"Xander, scans say that they are booting up their weapon systems... and they are all pointed at us." At the same time Xander and SE-3 both shout,

"Those are Nytarians!"

The colossal ship, The Apocalypse, speeds towards them. A squadron of stingers drops out of the hangar bay and zooms after The Odyssey which looks like a mere bug in comparison. All armaments on the destroyer ship turn to them and open fire.

Hundreds of thousands of beams blast through the cold expanse of space.

Xander begins to turn bright red and sweat as he is filled with anxiety and stress. He grips the steering wheel, jerks it down, and back around, so they are facing away from Boloxia. He thinks, I got this. I got this. I'm Xander Holsmo, the best pilot in the galaxy. He goes on the microphone and says,

"I don't mean to alarm anyone, but we are currently being chased by the Nytarian super destroyer. Gunners, we need you to concentrate all fire on those stingers while we escape." Xander reaches into a glove compartment and pulls out an old pair of aviator sunglasses. This is the same pair he wore during his days at the aviation school. He puts them on, flicks a button, and some epic rock music begins to play. He whispers to himself: "Let's do this!"

There is one gunner on the two sides of the ship. John and Hogler both sit in the rotating, gimbal turrets. They both swivel to face the rear of the vessel and at the steadily approaching stinger starfighters. The two of them go into their gunner channel in the coms.

"John, I have them in my sights. Ready for fire. Over," says Hogler. They both engage their tracking computers.

"I got a lock on one. Do you see it? Over," speaks John.

"I see it loud and clear. Over." Their gimbal turrets turn to look at the same stinger. The one they are aiming at is leading the squadron.

"Fire!" They both shoot out an onslaught of beams. The quick stinger weaves and dodges through most of the blasts, but a few hit the stingers... Just the right number of blasts hit that it cracks their barrier shields and damages the stinger's right engine. The stinger spirals out of control and away from the formation of the rest of the squadron. Hogler fires one more bolt at it, and it explodes in a flaming inferno. John says, "That's a splash on one!"

"Nice shots old man, exclaims Hoger. They continue to fire on the stingers.

"John, there's two more on your left," calls out Bre from her office. John quickly turned and shoots the ships. She watches out from every angle.

At the helm, Xander is scrambling to use every trick he knows to try to shake them off his tail. Xander frantically says,

"EQ, we need to jump outta here now!" EQ's systems boot up and say,

"Destination please?" Xander has an idea. He thinks, *it's risky, and it just might work. Bre would flip if she knew I was planning this.*

"Let's try a double warp skip."

"Where to?"

"Anywhere but here!" While he is talking, he weaves and dodges through the gunfire. EQ is computing billions of the most complex mathematical equations all at the same time. A double war skip is the single most difficult maneuver in all of the space travel. It is the most dangerous, but it will get them as far away as possible. As EQ is computing, the ship is hit with a few bolts in the rear shield. The ship rocks and shakes. Cinise hops on the coms and says,

"Xander we got a problem in the engineering room."

"What is it?"

"Well... the thing is everything is on fire!" He hears a fire extinguisher go off in the background which is being shot by Brooks. Brooks says,

"Yep, I'm down here; it is not looking good!" Xander takes a long, deep breath to think. He thinks, *Xander Holsmo is not going down like this.*

"Okay, just hold on, I'm working on a solution."

In Bre's office, she watches as The Apocalypse closes in on their position. She says optimistically,

"Xander, what's going on in that mind of yours?" She smiles though no one is with her. She clenches her fists in eager anticipation. She thinks, Xander, we're going to need a miracle.

"I know you aren't going to like—". Bre interrupts him,

"I don't care, do it. Come up with your stupidest most brilliant plane. We're going to need it!" Xander feels the weight of his whole crew on his shoulders. To him, all sounds begin to fade into a peaceful silence. He replays the words of his friends in his head over and over again.

Behind him, Davenk murmurs,

"C'mon kid, ya got this..." EQ's systems beep and ding. It says,

"Wow, that was a lot of math, but it's all done... ready for warp." Xander wipes the sweat off his brow and says,

"Where are we going?"

"Honestly, I don't even know. I took every star chart ever and chose the farthest point away from us. It is called the Margarita Nebula."

"I don't know where that is, but it can't be worse than here—" The ship is hit with a torpedo on the starboard side. As it is a physical armament, it pierces through its shield and hits the hull. Again the entire ship rocks like it had been hit by a massive earthquake.

"Xander, if you are going to do something, you need to do it now," says Bre. The Apocalypse is the right head for them. It casts a dark shadow on the helm as it blocks out all light. Xander with his hand on the warp lever looks up at the giant ship. SE-3 says,

"They are hailing us. Should I answer?" SE-3 looks to Xander as he waits for a response. Xander grips the warp drive lever harder and says,

"No, we'll be gone," and he yanks it back which quickly drops the ship into warp speed.

Twenty One

As it is the 100th anniversary of the Empire's formation, a large gala is being thrown in the Citadel to celebrate this momentous occasion. This party is being held at a party hall in the near center of the Citadel.

Huge holoscreen are projected into the air showing a big 100. Fireworks are fired off in explosions of vivid, colorful proportions. Blue banners that bear the Imperial insignia hang from the sides of the domed party hall. As it is dark in the Citadel now, spotlights shine to the sky.

Sleek, black hover limousines drop off the guests at the front entrance of the hall. Men, women, and all aliens alike are all dressed in colorful dresses and suits. Arleans, Diodrites, Hessoths, and many other alien species are spotted entering.

One of the first limousines to drop someone off has Drace Olphen inside. He steps out. His elegant, white robes billow in the artificial wind. After he steps out, he turns back and helps another woman out.

She is Harela Olphen, wife of the Olphen legacy. Similar to her husband, she has a gorgeous white dress that perfectly compliments her brunette hair. Lustrous golden earrings pierce her long pointy ears of her.

Drace kisses her on the hand. As she gets out of the vehicle, he grins at her and says through his teeth:

"Let's 'ake this look good." She smiles back and nods. He dips her down and kisses her on the lips. Harela's sapphire eyes twinkle at the sudden paparazzi camera flashes. Paparazzi Bots and camera drones swarm around them as they take videos and pictures. The crowd around them begins to erupt in applause. He locks arms with her, and they walk down the long, red carpet to the front entrance.

After their limo flies off, a few more pull out to the walkway, and many others of the Olphen family head onto the walkway and into the party hall. All are clad in the Olphen family colors. The whole lot of them put on smiles, and they wave to the paparazzi and camera drones.

At the entrance of the hall, eight sentinels stand afront it. Since this is such a big event and many high-value Imperial figures will be attending, the security is top-notch. Instead of just the usual Imp-pols, they have big armored sentinels. Guards are placed at every single entrance and exit. Snipers are waiting on buildings watching for anyone, not on the list.

A few minutes later, the heads of the other houses begin to arrive. Kandra of house Adis exits her hover limo, and she heads straight to the entrance and into the hall. Moments after, more members of the Adis family show up, and they all head inside while chatting and conversing. "Oh, I love your dress." "I haven't seen you in ages." "You've grown so much." They all talk in regal, snobby voices.

Later, the house heads of Madar, Vene, Primen, and all the others fly up in their limousines, and all their family members are there too. They all are dressed in fancy dresses.

In the party hall, it is dark except for the ambient white lights. A man plays on a large grand piano on top of a platform hovering by grav suspenders. The men and women of the Empire all talk together while they drink delicious drinks out of wine glasses.

Maxir Vene clad in orange to compliment his skin stands with other members of House Vene and some from other houses. They laugh as they exchange chatter. "Oh my, what is this drink? It is wonderful." "Come over and talk with us." "Maxir, I swear it. You put together an amazing party." Maxir drinks from two clear fizzy wine glasses. Both of them are very strong.

Since the Diodrite bloodstream is powerful compared to human biology, it is very unlikely for one of their species to become intoxicated.

Jafan Primen strolls over to the group with Maxir. Jafan sports a dark blue suit made of the galaxy's finest fabric. There is a long, silky, translucent, cerulean blue cape attached to his back. As he bumbles into their circle, he says with an accent that was passed down through his ancestors that resembles that of a South African from ancient Terra,

"I'd say we did a lovely job on his anniversary party. Don't you think so, Maxir?" His first thought after seeing Jafan is, Not this guy again. I can't stand him. All the house heads secretly hate each other, but they put on an act to appease the crowds. Maxir's elongated vocal cords boom his voice at a low tone:

"I must agree with you. If this isn't the perfect Empire, I don't know what is." The whole group snickers at his remark and takes a quick sip of their drinks. They continue to talk until Jafan goes to stand with his wife, Resia. Similar to her husband, she dresses in a long, sapphire gown with golden detailing and shiny blue diamonds plated along it. She has a long dark braid that runs off her back.

While Drace is chatting with different people, he accidentally bumps into Kandra. She turns around to see who it was. He puts on a very believable fake smile. Drace says in a royal-sounding voice:

"Ah Kandra, fancy seeing you here." Like him, she also smiles with a fake look as they all do. She takes a sip of her fizzy, clear drink and sets it on a waiter's plate who is passing by. She says in an apathetic tone:

"Drace, how have you been?"

"I'm good. This party is amazing. A true representative of what this Empire we built has become. You?"

"Same, I'm doing well. I think this will be a good anniversary of our Empire." Drace reaches and grabs her hand.

"May I have this dance?" Kandra nods. The two of them begin to dance together platonically as they both are married.

As the gala begins to truly commence, they all begin to dance eloquently. Classical Terran music begins to play by the Imperial Orchestra who are on another platform held by gravity suspenders. Atop it, talented musicians play harps, cellos, drums, flutes, and many other instruments. This sets the stage for the perfect night. The lights begin to shift to a rosy hue.

The huge crowd of people twirls and whirls around in an elegant dance. Drace says,

"I hate to speak of it here, but I'm sure you've heard of the recent incursion of revolutionists on Zulara IV?" Kandra responds,

"Drace, why are you bringing this up here? is supposed to be a celebration of our collective power. We do not need you to bring this up and tank the mood."

"We aren't all going to meet again for a while. This is the best time."

"So you persist. Yes, I have heard of it, but it doesn't concern me." He dips her down the back up again. Her dress billows like a wind-blown curtain. As she comes back up, she says: "That matter can easily be handled by Leena after all she deals with the political side." Drace says,

"It's not that simple. They threaten to leave the Empire!" Without looking at it, Kandra is surprised by his statement. She had not heard this yet.

"Excuse me, they want to leave?"

"Yes exactly, they are mad at the debris that is left in their planet's atmosphere from our act of trying to defend them." Using the skills she was trained in, she can hold her impulsive emotions back. She thinks, What are they trying to do?

"Have you informed Leena of this?"

"No, I came to you first." The two of them sway back and forth to the music. She looks him in his teal eyes.

"Fine, I will look into this... But Drace, promise me you won't go tell everyone else. This is supposed to be a night to inspire them and the people with patriotism not to doubt in us." He swallows deeply and reluctantly says,

"I will abide." Just then, the lights go dark except for a single spotlight that points right onto the stage. All eyes in the room turn to the stage. An old, Arlean man in a black suit steps out.

This is Gareith Olphen, the grandfather to Drace Olphen. Gareith is 125 years old. He is the man who proposed the idea to unite the houses; he is the last living member of the twelve who founded the Empire.

he is met with a wave of applause. He holds a microphone. As he is about to speak, another person clothed in dirty rags runs up on stage, grabs the microphone from his rusty grip, and says while panting:

"You all sit on a throne of deceit! You party while the galaxy suffers!" Within moments of him saying a word, Sentinels mobilize to him. Two thrust their electro batons at him. He is shocked violently and falls to the ground. Another drags him away.

Murmurs fill the crowd. "What is going on?" "Was this planned?" "Who was that?" The house heads all make eye contact throughout the crowd. Most of them have worried expressions on their faces.

Jafan thinks, Who has done this? Who planned this? I will have someone's head for this. His brow furrows, and he sneers.

Drace thinks, What was I saying? Something is wrong here. I can feel it... What are they gonna do to him because I have some words for him." Drace cracks his knuckles.

Leena thinks, Oh no, this is not going to look good on us. I hope Chet can spin this in our favor. I don't know how, but he best finds a way.

Kandra thinks, Why? Why is this happening now? Can I get through one thing without interruption? You've got to be kidding me!

Maxir thinks, Snonk! Someone better hold me back before I pound this guy's head in! He rolls up his sleeves on his suit robe. He stomps toward the stage.

The house heads rush to the stage to see what is happening. Maxir swats camera drones away that fly close to his face. Leena tries to reassure the crowd with the microphone:

"Alright everyone, it seems we're having some technical difficulties right now. In a few moments, we will continue with our scheduled program." Again the crowd erupts in murmurous speaking.

Leena goes back behind the curtain, takes out her holocell, and makes a call while the other house heads rush to the man. Leena says,

"Chet, I need you to make this look good."

"You are asking me to do the impossible. I saw it live; it didn't look good."

"Yes, I was there!"

"Checking the search systems, the house heads have been searched 15,000 times in the past five minutes. Looks like they're trying to find out more about you guys."

"I realize. Maybe tell them it was a hologram malfunction or a glitch in our camera systems."

"I'll pull some strings, but I'm not sure how good it will look."

"Don't be afraid to get your hands dirty. You have access to Imperial funds if bribes become necessary." Chet speaks with an air of confidence as he believes he can handle his.

"Okay, I'll keep you posted." She hangs up.

The man who ran up on stage is now laying on the floor behind the curtains. The man has oily brown hair, dirty skin, and a scruffy beard. He looks very out of place in this crowd of elegantly dressed individuals. He is mostly out of it from the shock sticks, but he is slowly waking up. Maxir stomps right toward him. His fists are clenched tight along with his jaw. Drace and Jafan step out of the way. With his lower right arm, he grips the man's shirt, lifts him into the air, cocks his left fist back, and barks,

"Who the snonk are you! And what are you doing here!" When Kandra steps behind the stage, she sees this and says,

"Not this again. Maxir, let us take him in for true Imperial questioning."

"I can handle this!" The man looks at Maxir. Though a powerful fist is ready to punch him, he looks not worried in the least bit. The man mutters,

"I am the spark." Maxir thinks, Nor good enough! He punches him in the forehead knocking the man unconscious.

"Damn, we were planning to interrogate him," says Jafan.

"We can later, but that felt good," says Maxir. Drace thinks, The spark of what? The heads go back to the party and act like everything is fine though they don't know what that meant.

Twenty Two

They successfully make the first jump through warp speed. A double warp jump is what it sounds like: it is one warp jump then a quick turn and then another warp without stopping.

The Odyssey exits the first warp in the Core Worlds a few hundred lightyears out from Talasia. Once they drop out of warp speed, the ship turns thirty-seven degrees to the right. Xander engages the warp drive again, and they blast off through the galaxy.

The ship rockets through a wormhole at speeds faster than light.

After a moment of being at warp speed, they exit the warp. Xander looks out the front window with a puzzled gaze. He says,

"SEE, weren't we headed to the Margarita Nebula?" SE-3 has his head in his console. Without looking up, he responds,

"Yes captain, EQ calculations that you ordered were to send us the right to the vast expanse of the Margarita Nebula." Xander is still looking out the window confused. Xander asks,

"Uh… are there any planetary systems in the nebula?" SE-3 still has his head buried in his console.

"No, the Margarita Nebula is an expanse of colorful gasses and forming stars that resemble the colors of a Margarita, so there are no planets."

"Okay, I thought so."

"Why do you ask, captain?"

"Um... there's a planet right there." Xander points out the window at a planet. SE-3 looks up from his console. A large planet with huge blue oceans and what looks to be yellow fields.

"Well, that shouldn't be there." He clicks some buttons on his console as he looks to figure out where they are. The rest of the crew starts to trickle into the helm. When Brooks walks in, he says to Bre who just walked in also:

"So can someone please tell me what the heck just attacked us? She responds,

"Those were Nytarians. They have been ravaging the galaxy for twenty-some years. They believe that they are better than everyone, and they are trying to purge all those who don't conform to their beliefs." His face winces at the thought of all those who have had to deal with them.

"Why hasn't someone stopped them?"

"No one can. Their military is the greatest, and biologically they are much stronger than humans and most other aliens. For their entire conquest, the Empire has been struggling to stop them." Bre turns her attention back to Xander as he is talking to SE-3 trying to figure out where they are. Brooks thinks, Someone needs to stop them.

Hogler and John wander their way in. John says,

"How have they gotten this far into the Outer Worlds?" John feels anger for the Empire. Hogler responds,

"I don't know how the Empire has let them move so far into their territory! If I were them I wouldn't be so lenient with those savages!"

In John's mind, he says to Bug:

"You were in a war. Got any thoughts about these Nytarians?"

"Well, so were you, but frankly I'm not sure if the Empire will be able to defeat this enemy. I'll give it to you guys. You Imperials are persistent." As they are talking, Cinise and Davenk wander their way to the helm. The whole crew of The Odyssey is now at the helm.

Suddenly, a dark shadow falls over the helm and blocks the light from the near star. Everyone looks around confused as to where the sudden darkness has come from. The only light left in the helm is the dim light from the consoles. Xander cautiously asks,

"SEE, what is that?" SE-3 responds,

"The scanner says it's a dreadnought-class capital ship."

"And what is this planet?"

"As you assumed, this is not the Margarita Nebula. Somehow our calculations were off... by a lot. It seems we're in the Rhea system."

"Rhea as in the Americorps?"

"Yep, same ones, and the callsign of this ship is The Liberty. The same liberty which is their capital flagship." Xander's mind begins to spiral. He thinks, This is going to be a long day. Maybe the Americorps will be friendly.

Brooks turns to Bre and asks,

"The Ameri-what now?" Bre responds,

"You might like these guys. Like we told you, Earth was destroyed due to civil wars, but a few gumption-filled Americans managed to escape the destruction; they came to this planet." She motions to the huge celestial body in view. "And they formed the Empire's independent faction: The Americorps. In classic Brooks fashion, he just says,

"Cool." SE-3 says to Xander:

"They are hailing us." Xander thinks, You got this. Just stay calm, and they might be nice. But I've heard they are scary... No one is scary to Xander Holsmo. He reaches into the glove compartment, pulls out his aviators, and puts them on. Bre looks over to him and watches him put on his 'serious face'. At least that's what she calls it. She grins.

"Go ahead and answer it." SE-3 presses a button on the console. Everyone turns their attention to the holoscreen. President James Jackson appears on the screen. Everyone excluding Brooks recognizes him. Most people immediately recognize him for his extravagant actions. There was one time he punched an Imperial ambassador in the face. He says it was because '…He talks too much.

James tips his hat to Xander puts on a stern frown, and says in a deep intimidating tone:

"Who dares enter into Americorps space!" James watches Xander's eyes widen in fear. Xander thinks, Oh no… James drops his frown for a grin. He says, "Hey, I'm just kidding. Who do I have the pleasure of talking to?" Brooks immediately likes the vibe of this guy. Xander obnoxiously clears his throat. He says in a not-normally deep voice:

"This is Captain Xander Holsmo of The Odyssey."

"Alright Xander, might I ask what you are doing in Americorps space?"

"Well Mr. President—" James cuts him off. Xander feels calmed by his inherent niceness. He didn't expect the leader of a ruthless military nation to be so kind.

"Please— call me James." Xander continues,

"James, we don't mean to intrude into your space. We were just trying to escape some people, and we ended up here by accident." Xander awkwardly smiles.

"I respect your gumption to take the man's way out and expect your defeat. Xander, you got me curious. Who are ya running from?" The longer James talks the more Brooks recognizes his deep southern accent.

"Well you aren't going to like this, but we warped to Boloxia. When we got there we were met by... The Apocalypse." James' kindhearted smile fades to a dead, grim expression. He asks,

"You saw Nytarians on Boloxia?"

"Yes," Xander says grimly.

"You wouldn't mind coming aboard, so we can talk about this." Xander pauses and thinks for a moment. He turns around to look at his crew. They all give mixed responses: some nods of affirmation and a head shake of the opposite. He looks to Bre first; Bre gives an uneasy head nod.

"Um... sure. We'll come aboard." James smiles.

"Great! I will have a tractor beam pull your ship up into our hangar." After James finishes talking, he disconnects the hail. The Liberty, which is above them, moves away so the light from the star can illuminate the helm again. The Odyssey rocks around as a tractor beam grips the ship and slowly pull it up to the hangar.

With the hail gone, the crew talks amongst themselves. Hogler says,

"Xander, I hope you are right about trusting these Americorps. I'm not sure about them. They haven't even joined the Empire." John says,

"I disagree. Though I disapprove of their decision to remain out of Empire, I trust them or at least the version I remember." John thinks of the time when legions of Americorps troops came to the fronts of the Sarconian War. Bug also sees this memory and says in his mind:

"Oh, I remember these guys." Bug thinks of the hundreds of brothers he lost to their armies. John similarly feels his sorrow. "Their weapons and methods were brutal in the destruction of my kind." A small tear wells up in John's eye, but it doesn't fall.

"I'm sorry." For the first time, John feels sympathy for the people he considered his mortal enemies. Cinise asks,

"What makes you like them so much?" Cinise looks at him with wide inquisitive eyes and her usual soft smile. John responds with a deep and somber tone:

"The Sarconian War was the Empire's battle, but the Americorps sent their men and women across the galaxy to help us fight. And that I commend them for that."

"Oh, they do sound like cool people from what I've heard." Xander whispers under his breath:

"Let's hope you're right about this." Davenk stands in the group with everyone else. He is thinking, Yes, yes, this is how this is supposed to be going. We're finally on the right track. He shows a small grin which is something one on this crew has seen from him.

Brooks wonders about the Americorps. He is eager to meet them as they are the last remnants of his home in America.

Slowly the ship moves into the Hangar bay. Metal clamps reach down and grab the ship to lock it into place. Once it is in The Liberty, an enclosed bridge extends from the ship to one of the doors on The Odyssey. The whole crew walks to the bridge and onto the huge capital ship. As they get to the end of the enclosed bridge, James waits for them at the end. Xander extends his hand, but James goes for a tight embrace which catches Xander off guard. James' cybernetic arm uncomfortably presses into his back. After that, James gives everyone else a firm handshake. He then says,

"Y'all walk with me." He motions for them to follow him, and they do. "So Xander, tell me about yourself." Xander thinks,

Shouldn't we be talking about the Nyatrians? Xander reluctantly answers,

"Well, I graduated from the Citadel's aviation school a while back." When he mentions the Citadel, James scoffs quietly under his breath. Xander doesn't notice. "And then after that, I purchased The Odyssey. You know how hard this galaxy can be, so I worked on forming a crew. Now, we work with the USG."

"Oh, you guys are with the USG. I can respect some mercenaries." He comically slaps Xander on the back and chuckles. Xander awkwardly laughs also.

"We aren't mercenaries—" James interrupts,

"Eh, mercenaries, shmercenaries." Xander thinks, Ugh, whatever.

"Bre over there. She is our USG representative." James turns to look at her as Xander motions over. Bre nervously waves and smiles. James leans over to Xander and whispers,

"Pretty one she is." Xander does not comment on his remark.

They are walking through the rusty corridors of The Liberty. Officers and soldiers pass them and salute President Jackson. Though this is a large ship it still dwarfs in comparison to The Apocalypse. The inside of the ship is rusty and messy. Oil drips from the ceiling. Rust crawls over the metal walls. Wires dangle on the floor. In almost every room, there is an American flag.

"So should we talk about... the Nytarians?" Asks Xander.

"This doesn't have to be such a sad occasion. We can talk about that later." A few moments later they come upon a pristine room, unlike the others. The lights are dim. A small band plays music. They play some smooth jazz. "Welcome to our on-ship lounge. Go ahead, have a drink!" The crew isn't sure what to do, but Hogler immediately rushes to the bar and orders himself a tankard of Moxous Whiskey. After seeing him do it, the rest of them walk up there. Expect Xander who is still standing beside James. He asks,

"You have a lounge on your capital ship?"

"Yep, it's a federal law that all ships in our fleet of adequate size must have a bar or lounge to accommodate the crew working aboard." Xander thinks, Interesting these people are.

Hogler downs his Moxous Whiskey in seconds. Moxous Whiskey is different from others as it originates from the mines of Moxous IV. Since the workers there don't have the supplies to make real liquor, they use what they have with them: oil and chemicals. It is by far the strongest alcohol in the entire galaxy. One drop could get a normal human extremely intoxicated.

Dim yellow lights line the bar adding an air of ambiance to the area. Behind the counter of the bar is a human in a stylish black suit with slicked-back hair. Bre plops down on a leather seated bar stool.

He gives Bre a smirk and says in a New Jersey accent like that of Terra:

"Hey babe, what can I get ya?" She is slightly caught off guard by his greeting. She remarks back in a stern tone:

"Don't call me babe! I'll have a margarita." She thinks, Weird, I'm really in the mood for a margarita right now. A few seats down from her, Cinise asks,

"I'll have the same as her!"

"You got it." Bre doesn't notice her. A moment later, the bartender finishes mixing the drinks and sets them in front of the two of them. Bre takes a sip; she glances over to her right and sees Cinise about to drink hers. Bre swiftly reaches over and grabs it from her.

"Wait, how old are you?" Says Bre. Cinise sighs in frustration, and she rolls her eyes. When Bre says this, it reminds her of how her parents would scold her. Cinise feels tears begin to form, but she suppresses them deep down.

"Uh... nineteen." Bre takes a sip from both of their drinks and says,

"Okay, none of that for you."

"C'mon Bre." Bre hears the slight sadness in her voice, but she doesn't know why it would be.

SE-3 stands in the lounge. He is somewhat blocking the entrance to the lounge. An Americorps soldier bumps into him as he is walking. He ran into him because he was looking at his holocell. The soldier shouts,

"Outta the way BotBrain!" BotBrain is an older phrase meant as a slur towards bots and androids alike. It is mostly frowned upon to say, and most bots would be offended. As the soldiers are walking away, SE-3 says aggressively:

"Excuse you!" The soldier slowly turns around.

"Who the snonk are you talking to!" SE-3's blue eyes shift to a crimson red. SE-3 plants his feet firmly. Suddenly, hatches all over his torso, arms, and legs begin to open. cannons, missile launchers, and many other sorts of firearms pop out of the opened hatches. Every single one aims down at the soldier's face, and red targeting lasers beam onto his head.

Since SE-3 is a reprogrammed assassin droid, he is outfitted with many armaments needed to complete that sort of job. While Xander was working on repurposing SE-3, he opted to keep the weapons for any occasions that it is needed.

A wave of terror washes over his face as he turns pale.

The soldier cautiously steps back and mutters,

"My bad, I'm sorry." All the weapons retract back into the bot, and his eyes shift back to a happy blue. He says kindly,

"Well thank you, good sir." SE-3 goes back to standing calmly as if nothing had happened. He computes, Foolish human...

Brooks sits down at the bar a bit always from Bre and Cinise. As he is about to order a drink, a guy from behind him says,

"What the skonk are you wearing?" Brooks swivels around and sees an Americorps soldier.

"What do you mean?"

"Your outfit, it's not something we would wear, but I feel like I've seen it somewhere." The soldier thinks for a moment. "Ah yes, I've seen it in the Terran Museum." Brooks is not familiar with this Terran Museum.

"These are just my clothes," says Brooks nervously. He begins to turn tomato red and perspire.

"What no, no one dresses like that anymore." Suddenly, the soldier whispers, "If you stole it from the museum I won't tell anyone. Just tell me."

Xander and James both sit down at a table together. James orders traditional Americorps drinks for the two of them. As James is about to speak, he drops his smile and puts on a stern expression. James barks,

"So let's talk." Xander is suddenly shocked by his change in tone. He asks,

"About what?" James takes a long sip from his drink.

"I think you know... Nytarians."

"What about 'em?"

"You told me you saw them on Boloxia. Is this true?"

"Of course it is. I wouldn't lie to the President of the Americorps," says Xander in a persuasive tone. "There was a whole fleet there."

"A whole fleet? Did you get a good look at them?" His voice shifts to a mixture of worried and shock.

"We ran a scan on the destroyer that was chasing us. It was huge. It was like a shadow of death running for our tail. The ship was called The Apocalypse..." James' eyes gloss over in sheer terror.

"The Apocalypse? That's their destroyer flagship." Xander doesn't yet realize what this means. "That singular ship could decimate ours or even the Empire's fleet."

"What are we supposed to do?" James pauses for a moment as he sits in his thoughts.

"Can I be frank with you?" Xander nods, and James leans in closer to Xander. He whispers, "I have no idea. I don't know a fleet in the galaxy that will be able to blast through their shields." Xander begins to worry.

"There's got to be something. We need to alert the Empire."

"I don't think they would be too happy to see me again."

"Are you going to put your political squabbles in between this war?"

"Here I'll cut you a deal: we'll send a few starfighters with you, and you can warp to the Citadel and do whatever you want there."

"Our warp drive was damaged after the warp here." James' chest tightens and his muscles tense up.

"Ugh, what about if we send a lightship carrier to transport you and your ship to the Citadel." Xander raises his voice a bit and says,

"Do you not want to help us with this? If the Empire is crippled or even destroyed, they will come for you next. There's no hiding from this." James ignores his question and says,

"Don't question me. I'm being nice by letting you in my ship. I just offered to lend you one of our ships, so you can go on your little mercy mission. Do you want to take it or not?"

"Yes, we would be grateful to take it," says Xander in the most polite tone he can form, and he flashes him a persuasive grin. Bre instinctively looks over. She immediately notices that something is off over there.

James swiftly rises from his hair with Xander. He turns to one of the captains who is sitting down half asleep. James commands and points:

"You, ready The Colonial for take off, and prepare to bring a light frigate with you." Without saying a word, the captain stands up, statues his president, and walks to the hangar bay. He turns back to Xander and says, "It will be ready in ten minutes. Be there!" Xander nods.

Not sure if he has made an ally or an enemy, Xander gathers his crew together. Just as James said the ship was ready to leave in ten minutes exactly. The ship carries The Odyssey is in its hangar. A few minutes after taking off, they warp across the galaxy to the Core Worlds where the Citadel lies.

Twenty Three

The Colonial exits warp speed in the space surrounding the floating city, The Citadel. They release The Odyssey from inside the city's hangar. Once it is out, The Colonial warps back to Rhea.

Though The Odyssey's warp drive is severely damaged, their other engines are still online. They rocket towards the huge biodome of the Citadel. Xander is at the helm piloting the ship. Instead of all of them being in their battle stations, they are all at the helm as the Citadel is a no-fire zone. SE-3 stands at his coms station. Brooks asks,

"What exactly are we doing here?" While driving Xander responds,

"We need to get the information that we know about the Nytarians to one of the house heads." Brooks just nods and continues thinking of random stuff. I wonder how many aliens there are. What happens if you go into a black hole? Brooks takes out his old cell phone. He opens his photos app and scrolls through selfies with his friends and family as he reminisces.

In Davenk's quarters, he quietly shuts the door. He places a small metallic holopuck on the floor. Moments later, a grainy blue hologram of a man is dressed in the same robes as Davenk. He has a thick white beard and eyebrows and leathery, wrinkly skin. He has old, tired eyes. The man clasps his hands and begins to pace around the room. Davenk says,

"Master, I sense I will have to face him."

"You have? I sensed his presence aboard that ship, but your foresight trumps mine. Will you be prepared in case you do see him?"

"I believe so. I remember his dark manipulation of the Echo. I have grown since my last time seeing him; he has gained so much power since his coalescence with Nylos."

"Davenk, do not stray. You know of the power that the Great Light can bestow on us." The master's eyes begin to glow with golden light.

"I know, master, but you know of the dangers that the Shrill can conjure."

"Yes, I know of their power. It is great, but you have yet to tap into the true power of the Echo."

"Yes, I am working on growing deeper in my connection."

"Have you been reading the sacred texts?"

"I have. I brought a holo-downloaded version of them. I have gotten far in my studies of the texts."

"Good, I'm proud of how far you've come very far."

"Thank you, master."

"Remember to call upon me if things get bad out there." Davenk nods in agreement. "How is it going with this new crew?"

"Surprisingly well, they have turned out to be very good people. Unfortunately, they do not know of the Echo." Davenk adjusts his robes while he talks. "My senses seem to be correct; I think this girl is the Stellaris."

"Are you sure?"

"Yes, I am. In the short time, I've been around her, I can feel the powerful Echo in her. I hear the songs of the galaxy radiate in her. It must be her."

"That is how we first described you."

"I know, but this is different," says Davenk.

"Alright, I believe you." He strokes his beard as he speaks, "When you complete this mission, bring her to the monastery where we can test this theory."

"Understood, I will call you once I face him." The master ends the holocell, and Davenk picks up the holopuck, sets it on a table, and exits his quarters. He walks to the helm where the rest of the crew is.

In the helm, SE-3 says from his communications console:

"Xander, we are being hailed by the Citadel's landing officer."

"Open up a voice channel," responds Xander. SE-3 presses a button and a voice channel open at Xander's microphone. A landing officer says through a grainy and staticky microphone:

"Hello, this is the Citadel. Do you have a landing puck?" Landing pucks are given throughout the Empire to high-value people. They grant priority landing at any Imperial docking port.

"This is the captain of The Odyssey. No, we do not have a landing puck."

"The coordinates will be sent to you now. There is an open spot at port 12 in landing spot 6." Xander nods at SE-3 to close the channel which he does. Like the officer said, the coordinates for the port they must land at are transmitted into Xander's navigation system. Xander asks,

"EQ, can you handle autopilot to the port?"

"Of course, captain." EQ takes over the steering system. EQ takes The Odyssey through one of the biodome gates which is like a bubble that completely protects the residents inside from solar radiation.

Now inside the Citadel's biodome, huge, fluffy, white clouds are being pumped out of tall buildings that have the logo for Bionamics, an Imperial-funded company that maintains that atmosphere inside the biodome. Rays of golden starlight pierce through the outer layer of the biodome which light up the Citadel.

Cinise and Brooks are the only ones who haven't seen the Citadel before. The two of them look upon the huge megastructure with eyes of awe while the others are accustomed to this place.

EQ drives the ship down to port 12. Clamps lock it in place. The crew strolls down the foot ramp of the ship onto the port floor. Xander looks at the parking meter next to where they landed. It adds credits every minute they are parked here. Xander thinks, Damn, prices have gone up a lot since the last time I was here. It's that skonking inflation. He shakes his head.

Bre asks,

"So we want to tell someone what we saw?" Xander responds as he leads the group through the streets of the Citadel. He says,

"Yep!" They pass multiple patrols of Imp-pols as they are walking. Imp-pols always walk the city streets.

"Who are you thinking of?"

"There's someone I haven't seen in a long time. I think he will help."

"Where are we going to find this mysterious person?" Xander stops in the road for a moment as he tries to remember which way is going. Though he hasn't walked through here in years, he still remembers his way around this maze.

"If I remember correctly he should be in the Grand Council Hall."

"Who do you know that would be allowed in there!" exclaims Bre.

"You'd be surprised..." As Bre and Xander talk, Brooks looks around at the huge skyscrapers. He watches clouds blast out of the tall buildings.

"Wow, this place is amazing. This is so much cooler than anything I've ever seen." Patches of grass and trees are plotted throughout the city streets. Hovercars zoom past overhead. All sorts of different aliens walk past them.

They pass holograms that project videos of the house heads. They say, "Join the Empire now." "Enlist in the Imperial navy." "Fight for your country." In the holograms, the house heads are all dressed in the finest Imperial silks, and they all wear makeup to look the best they can.

Patrol drones fly above them; they gather security data from around the city. Imperial banners hang from every edge of all the buildings. Holoscreens of Imperial officers say, "Are you ready to make a name for yourself in the galaxy? Well then, come join the

Empire now!" Some holo screens project images of clearly manufactured war scenes to inspire people to join the army.

Along the streets are floating grav-suspended lamps that provide light to the city. The sidewalks are made of old, gray stone brinks that are detailed in an elegant pattern to resemble the Imperial insignia.

John hasn't been in the Citadel in ages. The last time John was here was when he was given his medals of honor for his service in the war. He remembers the exact place where he went to enlist in the army. As he is remembering these past events, Bug feels the same memories.

"You were a patriot for these people," thinks Bug.

"They were all I ever knew. They were my family," thinks John.

"Were?"

"Well, I'm retired now. It's my past. I'm still figuring out my future."

"You have your future."

"What future?"

"Don't be a fool. This is your family." John goes silent as he ponders this. He thinks, Maybe, he's right.

The Crew continues walking till they reach the Grand Council Hall. Many Imp-pols are stationed at the entrance to the hall. Xander says to the group:

"I got this." The rest of them stand back while he walks up to one of the Imp-pols. The Imp-pols carry ray rifles. The one Xander walks to holds his chest high and mighty. "Hey there, we were just trying to get inside here, but you are in the way," says Xander persuasively. The Imp-pol responds through his staticky voice box:

"This area is off-limits to the public. Please move along!"

"Yes, I understand that, but we're here to see Head Aalen Coralla." Aalen Coralla is the head of House Coralla which oversees the military of the Empire.

"Head Coralla is currently busy, and again I say this place is off limits to the public which you are. Unless you have a badge to enter you need to leave. Now!" Xander begins to worry that his plan will fail. Bre thinks, C'mon Xander, don't fail us now.

Davenk sees that this Imp-pol is not budging, so he closes his eyes and begins to concentrate. Invisible golden strands of light swirl around his hand. The light twirls around to the Imp-pol. It goes into his helmet and his ear. Davenk thinks, you want to let us into the hall?

Cinise stares deeply at Davenk's hand as she sees faint yellow strands that she cannot explain. She watches them interact with the Imp-pol. She is befuddled as to what this magic is. She hears a sound she cannot fully understand, but it sounds like a glorious choir singing. She has a thought she does not comprehend: The Echo?

The Imp-pol feels an odd sensation in his mind. He feels a sudden compulsion to move out of the way of the entrance. He does move. He says,

"Go ahead inside." Very confused, Xander slowly walks in through the entrance. They all cautiously walk in. Well, that's odd.

Now inside, Xander leads them through the halls. It is like an infinite labyrinth. Every hall leads to another. Doors are everywhere. The floors are covered in lavish, colorful carpets. Yellow-hued lights are suspended in the air. Xander is pretty sure he knows how to get to his office.

The crew passes by elegantly dressed men and women who they assume work at the Grand Council Hall; they give them dirty, judgemental looks with an air of disdain. Eventually, they get to a door with translucent glass that says: Aalen Coralla. Before they all enter, Bre asks,

"Xander, what makes you think this guy will let us talk to him?" He says,

"Just trust me." She thinks, You better be right about this. Xander hesitates then he lightly knocks on the door. For about thirty seconds there is nothing, but they hear rustling inside. A blurry figure walks to the door and then opens it.

His initial expression is shocked when he lays eyes on Xander, but then he grins. Aalen thinks, Xander? He's here.

They notice his oddly fancy outfit. His hair is long and blondish-brown like Xander which is tied up in the back. His face is young, yet wrinkly. His cerulean eyes of his shine in the yellow light from above. He wears long yellow and brown robes that rest their end on the ground.

He hesitates to speak, but then mutters,

"Son?"

"Hey, dad," responds Xander. In a sudden burst of confusion, the rest of the, say in unison,

"Dad?"

Twenty Four

Aalen's jaw drops. He is dumbfounded at the sight. He thinks, *What are you doing here? After all this time... It's been too long.* He opens his mouth to speak yet has no words to say.

Everyone else is puzzled. Bre thinks, *That's his dad? I would've never guessed.* Bre tries to recall if he ever mentioned his parents; she can't think of a time. Neither of them really talk about their parents... especially not Bre... as she hasn't seen her dad in ages. He says,

"Xander, is that really you?"

"Yep, it's me," happily responds Xander.

"What are you doing here?"

"It's about time I visit, but there is a bigger problem I had to share with someone in the Empire. I could only think of you." Aalen places his hands on Xander's shoulders. He goes in for the embrace which Xander reciprocates. The others watch as the two of them share a sweet moment.

Aalen steps back, looks at Xander up and down, and says,

"Wow, you've grown so much, my boy." Xander grins and says,

"Don't go and cliché me. It's been too long." The rest of the crew backs up a bit down the hall to give them some space.

"It has. How have you been?"

"I've been well. To your surprise, being a spacefarer isn't that bad of a job. It pays pretty well when you get going good."

"I'll give it to you, I was skeptical about this decision, but you made your way. I should've believed in you more."

"Yes you should, so you? How's the Empire?" Aalen rolls his eyes and thinks, *More about the Empire.*

"Ah, you remember how things go. The heads get into an argument, then we threaten to go to civil war. You know things are around this place." Aalen chuckles.

"Yeah I remember that. So how's mom doing?"

"She's good. Actually, she is going to be visiting me from Arlea in a few days. If you're still here, I think she'd love to see you again."

"That would be nice." A moment later, Bre steps up from behind Xander and says,

"Okay, I think we're all wondering the same thing: you're the son of an Imperial head?" The rest of the crew nods in agreement. Brooks has a blank look on his face as he has no idea what an Imperial head is. Cinise leans over to him and whispers,

"That means they are one of the leaders of the Empire." Brooks realizes:

"Oh okay."

Xander turns around to look at his crew, and he pauses before awkwardly saying,

"Yeah, I am." They all look at him puzzled.

John thinks, *This whole time I had been working for the son of the man who directed my legion to victory.*

Bre thinks, *Xander you never cease to amaze me. You could've boasted about your status, yet you work as a humble spacefarer with me...*

"So what are you, a prince or something," says Hogler.

"I mean I'm not a prince or royalty per say," says Xander. He nervously scratches his neck. Aalen says,

"I'm not the king of the Empire or anything." He puts his hand on Xander's shoulder. "Xander here is just my heir to the position of Head of House Coralla." The crew thinks, *Oh I see.* "I'm curious: what made you come back here?" Since they are still standing in the hall outside of Aalen's office, Xander proposes,

"We might want to go inside."

"Go right ahead." Aalen moves out of the way, and they all walk in.

His office is decorated with ancient, beautiful vases that sit on oak tables. On almost every wall are battle maps of the galaxy. The maps track Imperial and Nytaria advancements. He has many holoscreens that project images of him and his family. "So what is going on?" Aalen sits down in his leather chair and crosses his legs, and he clasps his hands. Xander and the rest of them lean on the wall and sit in the chairs. He says,

"Well, I see you've been keeping up with the Nytarian war zones."

"Of course I do, it's my job."

"There's one thing you are missing: they have taken hold of Boloxia." Aalen's eyes widen in surprise.

"What! Impossible, we've kept a close watch on their movements throughout Imperial space." Aalen leaps from his chair and looks to one of the holoscreens with a map on it. "Look, last we mapped, they had been on the far reaches of the Outer Worlds."

"Your mapping systems must be malfunctioning because we saw it with our own eyes."

"You saw this?" Aalen looks puzzled.

"Yes, we did." The crew all nod in acknowledgement. "There was an entire fleet of destroyers orbiting the planet."

"If you are correct, this is terrible. Boloxia is right in the way of our biggest trade routes. If they take this planet, we would lose out on so many resources." Bre says,

"There was also a Dreadnaught-class destroyer ship. They call it *The Apocalypse*." Aalen's eyes sadden. He thinks, *Oh no.* He says,

"I must leave now."

"To where?" asks Xander.

"I must tell the other heads of this revelation," responds Aalen.

He walks to the door. As he goes to grab the door handle, all the holoscreens in his office shut off. All their attention is focuses to the holoscreens as the drop to their projector base. They look out the huge glass window. Every single holoscreen in the city shut off.

Aalen turns around to see the holoscreens. He says,

"Uh, what is happening?"

Suddenly, all the holoscreens turn back on, but they do not project their original images. They are all black. A bright purple light shines, and a dark silhouette walks into the frame.

Everyone in the city has their eyes focused on the screens. In a dark, echoing, mysterious voice, the silhouette says:

"Greetings citizens of the Empire, I am Xenos, the high priest of the Nytarians." Everyone looks at the screen with terror behind their eyes. Davenk thinks, *I was right.* Xenos continues, "Your zealous city you call the Citadel has been deemed an obstacle by Nylos. Our fleet will be arriving in four hours. May Nylos grant you mercy in the After." The holoscreen silhouette of Xenos disappears, and they all go back to their original projections.

The moment the transmission ends, Aalen gets a mess on his holocell from Leena Madar to all the house heads. The message says, *"Everyone. Hall 2. Now!"* He glances at it, and Aalen frantically says,

"I need to leave now!" Before Aalen leaves, Xander says:

"Where are we supposed to go?"

"Just come with me to the meeting!" They all follow Aalen as he rushes to the second meeting hall. It is a maze. Turn after turn they search for this room.

Eventually, they come across huge metal blast doors. Aalen walks up to a small metal panel. He puts his eye up to a retinal scanner. It scans his eyes, and the doors open slowly.

Inside, sits twelve thrones in a perfect circle. In all of them sit each of the heads except Aalen. Even in such a rush to be here, all of the heads are incredibly fashionably dressed. All the attention is turned to them as they walk in. Aalen rushes to his seat, and the crew stays upon the back wall. After he takes his seat, Kandra Adis says:

"What are we doing here? The people need to see we have things in order!"

"I have everything under control," says Leena Madar. "Project Doppelgänger is now in full effect." The heads look at her in surprise.

"You were being serious about that idea," says Maxir Vene. "I assumed you were kidding." Leena responds,

"No, I was serious. They need to have some sort of way to see us in a good light. The doppelgängers are currently telling everyone that we are currently figuring all this out and there is nothing to worry about."

Project Doppelgänger is a protocol created by Leena. When the house heads cannot be present at a meeting, she made high tech holograms to act and think like the heads using artificial intelligence.

"It's time we get down to business!" exclaims Jafan.

"What even is there to discuss?" says Aalen. "We need to mobilize our entire fleet here if we are going to have any chance of defending the city!"

As they are talking, Brooks' attention is focused on the *aliens* in the room. He gazes at Maxir while he examines his interesting biology that he has never seen before.

"Defend the city? No, there is no possible way!" says Kandra. "A single one of their destroyers could decimate the Citadel. We need to evacuate everyone immediately!" Kandra speaks sternly with a speedy rhythm.

"We do need to evacuate, but there is no chance we can get the whole population out in only four hours." says Drace. "If we pull our cards right, we might get half of them onto the transport ships." Aalen responds:

"Our only option is to call our fleet from across the galaxy to the Citadel. If not and they destroy the Citadel, this could be the end of the Empire." Maxir says,

"Aalen, even if we do manage to pull our entire armada together, the Nytarian shields are more powerful than anything we have ever gone up against. Even during the Sarconian wars, their ships didn't even have shields, and they were still a challenge."

"There is no way we could take out their shields," says Leena. "From our assessments of their ship's wreckage, there is a shield generator inside, but we have to get on their destroyer undetected."

Xander begins to think. He bumps Bre to get her attention, and he leans over and whispers something into her. When he says this, her eyes widen in realization. She thinks, *That could work*. Xander says,

"I have an idea." The moment that he speaks, all the heads look directly at him. Maxir shouts,

"Who is this? Who dares interrupt our meeting."

"I'm sorry," says Aalen. "This is my son. Please, hear him out." He nods to Xander. All the heads look at him with the face of anticipation. Xander says,

"Their destroyer ship is massive, right?" They all nod. "And a small star fighter would be inconsequential compared to the size of it?" They all nod again. "What if there was a device that could allow a ship to go undetected right onto their destroyer?"

"If that was somehow possible, it could be our saving grace," says Drace.

"I don't know who you are, but if this device you speak of is real, you would be able to play a pivotal role in a battle like this," says Kandra. Xander says,

"Hypothetically if we had a... cloaking device, it would allow a ship to go completely invisible to all scanners."

"It would also be highly illegal to have a device like that," says another house head."

Drace says,

"If this device was used to aid the Empire in our defense of the Citadel, I'm sure the holder of this device could be royally pardoned for this."

John steps up and says,

"You need to call every single vessel under the Imperial name to the Citadel! The Nytarians are expecting to have the upper hand because their army is better than yours." John starts to raise his voice in a commanding manner. Kandra thinks, *Is this old man really commanding us!* "But they won't be expecting us to throw everything in our arsenal at them hoping something actually works."

Silence.

No one says anything. All the heads look at each other. None of them are sure what to say.

Suddenly, Aalen says:

"I concur. What kind of show of power would be better than crushing the Nytarian fleet. It would truly inspire our people." Maxir says,

"You have a point. If we are able to destroy this ship with the method your son proposes, it would display the Empire to our citizens and maybe throw off the Nytarian's Conquest."

Kandra sighs in a feeling of uncertainty. She says,

"Aalen, make the call. I believe this might just work." She looks at a golden holo watch on her wrist. "If the Nytarians plan to honor the time they said, we have three hours and thirty two minutes from the end of his transmission."

Aalen stands from his chair.

"I'll mobilize the fleet here. And I will call all ships from their current stations. It should only take them fifteen minutes to warp here give or take. I can have the full armada ready in two and a half hours." Aalen turns to leave the room. He walks out, and the crew follows behind.

Before Jafan leaves he says,

"Tell the public we are planning to defend the city with the Citadel's shield generator, and to stay inside their homes while we handle this." Leena nods.

All the heads leave the room as they go prepare for this battle.

For the next three hours, Imperial ships from all around the warp around to the Citadel. The Imperial Navy is made up of 3,400 capital ships, and they have hundreds of thousands of starfighters. Each capital ship is manned by 37,300 people. 126,820,000 men and women loyal to the Empire are ready to risk their lives to save the Empire. That is only the capital ships, there are 3,560,000 Wyverns, the standard Imperial starfighter. There are 148,300 different squadrons that the Wyverns belong to. Wyverns are a two seater starfighter with light shield generators and heavy cannons.

Every single one of them is gathered in the space around the Citadel. It is like a densely packed asteroid field. Battle Cruisers, Bombers, Destroyer, Interceptors, Boarding Ships, Gun Boats,

Repair Ships, and Ramming Ships all wait around the Citadel. Fuel ships fly up to them and make sure every ship is fully fueled. The crews aboard each ship reload all of the cannons, torpedoes, missiles, and railguns. All of the shield generators are fueled and amplified to the maximum power.

Aalen has a long call with all the admirals, commanders, generals, and captains. He reviews their plans and tactics. John sits in and listens while he adds his own input on the situation. Xander, Bre, and Hogler are also there to help plan how they will use The Shroud.

Xander gives Brooks a crash course in piloting. He takes to it quickly as he has had much practice playing video games on his time back on Terra. He does a few test runs in the state of the art virtual reality flight simulator.

Cinise, with the help of the Empire, repairs *The Odyssey.* They install Mk 8 shield generators from Apex Manufacturing (the best in the galaxy aside from Nyarian shields which they build themselves). All the damage from the earlier skirmish with the Nytarians is repaired, and the ship is fully fueled.

There are thirty two minutes until the Nytarians are supposed to arrive. All the ships are fully ready and crewed.

The armada of 3,400 capital ships (including: battle cruisers, destroyers, assault ships, and ramming ships) is in the Echo Alpha defense formation. This consists of the 3,400 ships in a wide, *W* shape facing away from the Citadel. The destroyers, battle and attack ships are in the center, the ramming ships are towards the sides.

Underneath the bigger ships, sits the millions of Wyverns.

Everyone's engines are hot and cannons armed. The air is tense. No one says a word on the coms. Some shiver in stress and anxiety. All their eyes locked forward at the infinite abyss of darkness that lies ahead. Skilled Imperial pilots sit eagerly in the cockpits of their Wyverns which is like a sleek motorcycle seat. They all tightly grip the handles and activate the targeting computer.

Aboard the bridges, the commanders stand with their hands behind their backs.

In the Citadel, there is a huge holoscreen that is projected onto the biodome, the citizens can't see what is happening. Kandra sees the ships in formation from a video monitor. She looks at her watch; it ticks as the timer for four hours she set is almost up.

...*5...4...3...2...1...0*. It dings. She swallows and looks out to the monitors

The Nytarians should be there any second...

Twenty Five

After four hours exactly had passed, an enormous ship, The Apocalypse, drops out of its warp into the space around the Citadel. 1,500 Nytarian capital ships drop out of warp speed a few thousand meters out from the Imperial fleet. 500,000 Nytarian Stingers, light starfighters exit their warp underneath the huge capital ship. Hundreds of thousands of cannons aim at the Imperial ships.

There is a tense feeling throughout the area. Everyone is waiting for the other fire.

Somehow the Nytarians can broadcast to all the millions of Imperial ships. In each of them, a holoscreen appears. On it, Xenos stands on the bridge of The Apocalypse. He says grimly:

"I sense the fear in all of you. It is great. Fear can make us do things we would never imagine. Look at you, because of your fear of me, you brought your entire armada here to fight us." All watching feel unsettled looking into the glowing mask of Xenos. No one knows what monster hides behind it. "I applaud your efforts, but they will be worthless. You lack the wisdom and guidance of Nylos. I hope you see the errors of your ways before I send you to the after." Just as quickly as it began Xenos ends the holoscreen.

The Apocalypse had charged up one of their Powernaught Railguns before the warp. A few moments after exiting the warp, the railgun fires a huge steel bolt at a small Wyvern. The bolt passes through its shield and explodes the starfighter in a blast of sparks and fire.

The second the steel bolt leaves the barrel of the railgun, every Imperial Wyvern blasts its engines to the maximum. Every single Imperial pilot, admiral, captain, and gunner all shout,

"Everything for the Empire!" The millions of Wyverns zoom towards the Nytarian front, and the Nytarian stingers rocket at them and shoot bolts. Capital ships on both sides open fire with condensed beams of red-hot Energen. Billions of beams whizz through space.

Stingers and Wyverns spin and twirl around as they try to evade each other. Within minutes of the battle starting thousands of starfighters are blown up into millions of pieces.

The Apocalypse's cannons fire all around the battlefield. Most of their cannons are gimbal-type so they can rotate around to hit anything. Hundreds of Wyverns are shot out of space by the cannons.

The huge, hulking ship blasts forward leading the Nytarian charge. Thousands of Stingers swarm around the ship like furious bees. Any Wyvern that gets too close to The Apocalypse is met with a bolt to the engine.

Aboard one of the Imperial ships, The Prophet, which is a Dreadnought-class-destroyer Admiral Sekes Wallusk rushes to get his crew working. He is a big, green Crull, crocodile-like alien. Admiral Wallusk commands,

"Officer, what are our shields at?" A human officer nervously says,

"Sir, the shield barrier only has 26% power left." Wallusk looks out his bridge at the rampaging battle. The two destroyer ships on the side of him are just hit with fifteen detonator missiles. Wallusk watches as his comrades explode in flaming balls of fire. "Sir, what do we do? The shields are at 13% power!" Wallusk says nothing as he thinks. He shouts to another officer:

"Divert all power to the weapons!" The officer looks at him puzzled. He inquires,

"All power?"

"Yes, all power: life support, shields, everything!" All the officers follow his order. They press buttons on the console in right front of them. As he asked, they divert all the power to the cannons. The engines only have a small amount of power left. There are only ten minutes of oxygen left.

Wallusk looks to the pilot and says,

"Take us to them! Everyone fangs out!" He points at a smaller Nytarian destroyer, The End, ahead of them. All cannons around the Imperial Destroyer get a strong lock on the Nytarian vessel. "Fire on my command!"

His first officer who is beside him on the bridge says,

"Sir, what is the plan?"

"Our shields are almost gone. We aren't going to last much longer. If I'm going out it's going to be with a bang!" He broadcasts this throughout The Prophet, so all the crew inside can hear. They all become inspired to fight and most likely die for the Empire. They all salute to the Empire in their stations.

The Prophet rockets forward through space. As it flies, all of their missiles, torpedoes, and cannons give hellfire to the Nytarian ship. Many of their bolts hit the shields; after a few seconds of concentrated fire, The End's shields break and retract into their generators. Admiral Wallusk says over the ship's communications systems:

"Their shields are down! Fire the missiles!" Twenty hatches across the ship's hull pop open, and twenty missile and torpedo launchers with fifty silos each come out of the open hatches. The gunners in charge of the missile launchers lock onto the shieldless ship. Wallusk yells, "Fire!"

1,000 Detonator Rockets or EDR blast at The End. They collide all over the hull blasting hundreds of holes. After enough of them hit, it reaches critical condition, and The End erupts in an inferno of sparks and fire.

Once the other Nytarian ships see the destruction of The End, they all open fire upon The Prophet.

As his ship is being battered with laser beams, Admiral Wallusk stands at the bridge. He grips the handrails while the ship rocks back and forth. An officer on his left shouts,

"Sir, the hull is critical!" All the officers and captains are red and sweating from the extreme pressure on them. They wipe their perspiring brow. Frantically they pull levers and buttons as they try to manage the ship. Sparks blast around the bridge as explosions hit through the hull. The glass window on the bridge cracks against the stress of the battle. murmurs to himself:

"Everything for the Empire." Just as he says this a Nytarian EDR flies into the bridge killing him and all the officers aboard in a blast of Energen. The bridge cries out in terror until they all are silenced in a single moment.

Within moments of the bridge's destruction, multiple Powernaught Railguns fire gigantic steel bullets all across The Prophet. After dozens of bullets blast through the hull, this brings the ship to critical condition. One pierces the hull and directly hits the warp drive. The steel bolt destroys the warp drive. All the energy held inside the warp drive is all let out in an instant. It implodes on itself. The whole ship is quickly sucked into the warp drive in a flash of purple light which turns into a concentrated wormhole. As The Prophet is absorbed into the wormhole, it suddenly erupts in a blinding lavender light. The implosion blasts, which is like a flat disc of purple energy, out into a nearby Nytarian Ramming Ship, The Javelin.

The Javelin gets caught by implosion. It is immediately sliced in half by the disc of powerful energy. Metal debris boomed all from the origin of the lilac blast.

Across the battlefield, a squadron of Wyverns flies from underneath the capital ship formation. This is the 5,975th squadron; it is nicknamed Titan Squadron. There are fifteen light Wyverns in this squadron.

Titan Leader, Xander 'Holsmo' Coralla, is the new leader of the squadron. Right as he is about to enter combat, he puts on a pair of black aviators and turns on a killer rock song from his playlist Battle Music. He leans forward and prepares his attack systems.

He blasts forward at the swirling battle ahead. The other fourteen Titans form into positions behind Xander. All their gun systems are prepared. He says over his squadron's coms:

"Alright, let's make these Nytarians wish they didn't come and mess with the Empire! Titans stay close to me. If ya see a Stinger light 'em up!" Xander turns towards a squad of Nytarian 6 bombers. They are zooming right for an Imperial Ramming Ship, The Gauntlet.

Xander gets a strong lock on a bomber that is going straight to The Gauntlet. He whispers to himself,

"I gotcha now." He presses down on the firing button. A rapid volley of superheated beams of energy collides with the bombers' shields. The shields are overloaded, break, and recede into the generator. With it being shieldless, Xander flicks a switch and a powerful blast charges up. Xander leans forward pressing his chest onto the front of the seat. Though it is a slow bomber, it still tries to evade the lock of Xander's Wyvern. Again, he smashes the firing button, and a huge blast of energy strikes the bomber exploding it. "Yahoo! That's a splash on one, baby!" Orange light illuminates his face from the flaming eruption.

The Gauntlet lowers its shields as it diverts its main power to its engines. The front hull of the ship is much thicker with huge Zarium steel plates. This ramming ship blasts forward at an Assault Ship, The Oblivion.

The bombers slowly get closer to being above the ship and ready to drop their detonators.

Titan 4 which is piloted by Garcia Walen. Her ship chases after one of the bombers, but the Wyverns are much more agile so she can keep up. Once she has an adequate lock on her target, she fires an ion torpedo. It flies through the shield barrier and collides with the hull. The torpedo explodes in a burst of blue electricity. It knocks out the power on the bomber. The bomber sits suspended in space as all of its systems are offline.

Garcia takes her spacecraft and flies it right beside the bomber. She knocks on the glass cockpit cover. The purple-skinned Nytarian pilot rushes to boot his ship back up. He looks over at her. She motions that he should look behind him. The pilot looks back and sees an EDR flying right toward the rear of his bomber. He thinks, Skonk! The EDR makes contact with the ship's hull, and it is engulfed by an explosion. The missile was fired by Titan 7, Algus Niek. He says,

"Oh yeah baby, eat missiles!"

"Nice job man!" says Titan 4. Titans 7 and 4 groups up and head back with the rest of the squadron.

Another member of the Titan Squadron says,

"This is Titan 2, I've got two Stingers on my tail! I can't shake 'em!" Xander hears this and looks around his cockpit to try and see him. He spots him on the starboard side.

"Titan 2, if you can hang them out to dry, I can get 'em," says Xander. Titan 2 spins and weaves back and forth trying to shake the two light Stingers on him. They hit his shield barrier with a few Energen bolts, but the shield still stays up. Titan 2 thinks, C'mon man where are you? He grabs a lever and slams it forward; the sublight engines engage with full throttle. He grips the handlebars tight and pulls them back as hard as he can. As his ship flies up, the two Stingers pull back to follow.

Xander sees the opening Titan 2 is trying to make. He turns and blasts over there with his engines at full speed. The stingers are focused on Titan 2 and don't see Xander's approach behind. He locks onto both of them, prepares an EDR, and fires it. The missiles pass through the shields and send the Stingers into pieces.

The battle rages on around. Left and right, capital ships and starfighters are shot out of the sky. Billions of Energen beams fly back and forth throughout space.

Xander looks around trying to find a specific red ship that holds a specific place in his heart. It is supposed to be flying underneath the battle...

Twenty Six

The Odyssey flies out from underneath The Atlas, the Empire's biggest flagship. Brooks, Bre, Cinise, Hogler, John, SE-3, and Davenk all stand around at the helm. Brooks sits in Xander's pilot's chair, and he is flying the ship with the major assistance of EQ. Bre says,

"Go ahead and activate The Shroud." Brooks flips a switch on the pilot's console. The Shroud device which is placed on the exterior of the ship turns on. It covers The Odyssey in tiny hexagons similar to the ones seen on shield barriers, but these refract light in a very unique way. It works in a way that all light coming at it is reflected somewhere else, so it is impossible to see it. "Cinise, go lower the power on all systems."

Cinise leaves the helm through the blast doors. She heads to the engine room. There, she pulls a few levers which change the power distribution. All the lights dim. The ship slows down. Weapon systems lower power.

Back in the helm, Bre says,

"John, do you have all the equipment we need?" John sets a big, black duffle bag on a table. John says,

"Yep, there are about seventy-five detonators in here. I'm guessing that will do?" Bre walks over and looks in the bag. As he said, there are many metallic, spherical Energen detonators that each have a red beeping light.

"I would ask where you got all these on such short notice, but I'd rather not ask. This should do. I don't know how many we need exactly."

Hogler loads the ammunition into his huge Energen minigun. He takes the small cigar out of his mouth and says to John:

"So we're going to be fighting Nytarians?"

"Yep, there's going to be a lot of them," responds John.

"I bet I'll be able to kill more of them than you." John raises his eyebrows with intrigue.

"That's hilarious. There's no way. I'll have more than double yours."

"Why don't we make things interesting." Hogler deviously smirks.

"How so?" asks John.

"Whoever kills the most Nytarians gets the credits."

"How many credits we talkin'."

"100?"

"Let's go— 500," proposes John.

"You're confident. Let's hope that your age isn't getting to you." John looks at him offended.

"I'd like to see you keep up with me."

"Alright, I'm in." They firmly shake hands while making eye contact.

As they are talking, Brooks slowly brings the ship closer to the biggest Nytarian Destroyer, The Apocalypse. Xander told him to press a green button on the console. He didn't say what it did. Brooks presses it. A small hatch opens on the floor next to the chair. A metallic holopuck pops out. He looks at it curiously.

Suddenly, it projects a grainy blue hologram of Xander standing with his hands on his hip. He says in his normal voice, but it is slightly distorted:

"Well, if you are watching this... I'm not dead. You just need help flying my baby." Bre looks over and scoffs at this. "I don't know who you are, but I'm guessing you are in my chair. Get out." Brooks stands up to get out of the chair. "What are you doing? I'm kidding." He sits back down in the chair. Xander stands next to the console, and he puts a hand on it as he leans his wait there.

Bre smiles with the smile she always gives Xander, and she says,

"Where does he get the time for this?"

The hologram of Xander says to Brooks:

"Okay listen up, I'm not going to repeat myself." He snaps in front of his face. "Now, hands at ten and two!" Brooks rushes to grab it right. "Now, keep one hand on the wheel straight towards your target. Grab that lever." Brooks reaches to grab a lever. "Not that one," snaps Xander. The hologram points to a lever on Brooks' right. "This one." Brooks grips the one he points to. "Okay, slowly push it forward." He does this and the ship accelerates a bit. Xander directs him to pilot the ship. Brooks pulls it up to a closed opening right underneath The Apocalypse.

The Empire had a rough schematic of the Nytarian Destroyer, so they had a basic understanding of where a trash chute underneath it would be.

Brooks puts the port side up to the closed trash chute. The Xander hologram says,

"Okay, now press that button." He points to a blue button on the pilot's console. "This will stop the ship in place." Brooks lightly taps the blue button. Thrusters on the ship all light fire so that they nullify each other. It is now suspended in space. Xander's hologram takes a few steps back from the console, dusts off his hands, and says, "You... did well." He gives a joyful thumbs up and the projector deactivates dropping the hologram away.

Brooks stands up from the chair and walks to where the other crew is. As he walks, he tightens the holster on his thigh preparing to board The Apocalypse. When he walks up to Bre with his chest slightly raised she says,

"Nope!"

"What do you mean 'nope'?" He looks confused.

"You're wanting to go there?" She points up to the huge destroyer that eclipses the helm in darkness from the far-off star.

"Um, of course, I want to go. You are planning to blow it up like we are in Star Wars!" Bre thinks, What the skonk is Star Wars? "You could ask anyone from my generation and they would say it would be so awesome!"

"Maybe it sounds 'cool', but you have no idea what you would be going up against. We're used to this and have been doing it for a while now. So you, Cinise, SE-3, and Davenk will stay on the ship while the three of us go on the ship." Brooks groans,

"Ugh, fine. I'll babysit the ship."

SE-3 inquisitively says,

"You are asking me to stay here?" Bre responds,

"Uh yes, That's what I just said." SE-3's eyes glow with amber colors. He says in a tone that resembles frustration:

"Bre, you are aware of the origins of my model, correct?" She nods curiously. "Then you would know that I was an assassin, and I still have all my weapons and components." Bre asks,

"So you're asking to come with us?"

"Indeed, frankly you need my assistance." Bre thinks: Well, that's one way to put it. I don't know if it is exactly true.

"Sure, come with us."

Davenk says nothing, but he nods. Just as Bre says this, Cinise walks back in from the Engine room. She says,

"What, you're making us stay here?"

Bre puts her palm to her forehead and thinks, Do I work with literal children? She sternly says,

"Yes, you are. I'm not risking your life for this, so yes you are staying." Cinise sighs. "Stay here." Bre straps a long ray rifle to her back and motions to John and Hogler. She says,

"Alright, let's do this." They walk to the spaceport that is angled towards the trash chute. John has two ray rifles in each hand, two ray pistols on thigh holsters, and a bag of bombs attached to his back. He says,

"Oh by the way, if I get shot with this on, I'm going to explode which will kill all of us." Bre turns and looks at him grimly:

"Please don't get shot then."

"Stay behind me old man," says Hogler. They crouch down and put on small powered rocket boots. Hogler puts a few Zarium plates over some of his bare skin. Bre and John put on a light spaceship. Each of them grabs a rebreather off the wall and puts it over their face. Bre slams a red button on the side; the airlock blasts open.

They jump up and activate their boot which flies them up to the closed, metal trash chute. The airlock shuts behind them.

Nothing. They hear absolutely nothing. It is cold. Colder than anything any of them have felt before.

They each grip the side with mag gloves. John places a detonator on the switch. After turning their attention away, it explodes blasting off the closed door. They all clamper the way up into the broken chute.

Inside, is a long metal tube that is approximately two meters in diameter. It is covered in thick, green sludge. They use their rocket boots to quickly slide up through to the tube. Random pieces of trash are stuck to the sides. Bre winces as she feels the squishy, cold sludge through her gloves. After a solid minute of grappling through the tune, they climb out of the trapdoor where the trash is thrown out.

Now inside The Apocalypse, they try to wipe the sludge off themselves. The halls are dark with luminous purple grav-suspended lights. The floors are glossy, black metal.

Now in the atmosphere of The Apocalypse, they take off their rebreathers and spacesuits. As they are cleaning themselves, they hear booming, echoing footsteps coming from down the hall. All their attention turns. The hall curves to the right. The three of them point their ray guns at the hall.

Instead of the armored soldier, they were expecting a lavender-skinned Nytarian dressed in a blue-gray jumpsuit. He carries a mop in one hand and a bucket of dirty water in the other. As he turns the corner he is shocked to see humans and a 'pig' onboard. He drops his bucket and the water spills everywhere.

Unsure if to shoot or not, Bre drops her gun and runs at him. She jumps, wraps her legs around his neck, and hastily swings herself around to his back. Though he is 2.4 meters tall, she is easily able to leap up to that height. With her legs planted on his shoulders, she wedges her arm underneath his chin. She traps him in a headlock and begins to constrict his windpipe. She whispers,

"Just go to sleep..." He tries to rip her arms off him, but her grip is too strong. His sulfur eyes begin to gloss over as his body goes limp. She hops off him when he falls unconscious. She dusts off her hands and looks to SE-3, John. and Hogler. Their eyes are horrified, but they have huge smiles on their faces. SE-3 tilts his head in amusement. The three say,

"That was— Awesome!" Then John says,

"How did you learn how to do that?" She thinks, Maybe Mr. Bercham taught me a few useful things. Bre says,

"Uh... that's a long story." She isn't sure of exactly what to say.

"I'm goin' to need to hear that sometime," says John in a grizzly tone.

"I think I can make that happen." Hogler butts in and says,

"We might want to do something about that." He points to the unconscious Nytarian. He aims his minigun at him. "Shoot him and dump him out?"

"No! If I wanted to kill him, I would've. Trust me." She stares daggers at him. She believes that a janitor can't be as bad as they all are. "Just tie him up somewhere." John pulls a rope out of his pocket and ties the Nytarians' hands and feet up. He puts him against a wall.

Hogler asks,

"So where the snonk are we going? I'm itching to blow something up." Bre takes out a holopuck from her metallic jacket pocket. The three of them stand in a circle/triangle. She holds it out and a map of the ship is projected a foot from the puck.

"Okay, so we are here." She says while pointing to a blipping blue dot on the bottom of the schematic. "This is the shield generator room." Another dot pops up across the lower half of the ship. "We have to get there. From what the Empire knows there shouldn't be many guards on this path there. The many problems will be the cameras we will have to take out."

"Alright this shouldn't be too difficult," says John.

They all set their ray rifles to live fire. With their weapons aimed at head height, they slowly make their way through the maze that is The Apocalypse...

Twenty Seven

The Atlas stands strong at the head of the Imperial front. The Atlas is the backbone of the Imperial navy. It is 9,655 meters long, 2,563 meters wide, and 4,394 meters in height. Its armaments are 400 x Energen pulverizers, 40 x EDR launchers with 80 silos per launcher, and 150 x Powernaught Railguns.

The Atlas' shields are bombarded with thousands of lasers every second, but their shields are the strongest in the Empire.

It stares right down at The Apocalypse. They exchange fire with one another every moment.

The shields are being bombarded, but the bolts from the railguns aren't able to reach the ship's hull. Recently, the Empire has developed a new strategy of railgun defense. Approximately 100 small ships with powerful shields lie around in a scattered out pattern around The Atlas. Each of the minuscule ships emit a 200 meter in diameter electromagnetic field. When one of the steel railgun bolts enter into the field, they are stopped immediately in their tracks and frozen in space.

Aalen Coralla stands in front of the bridge. He stands tall with his hands behind his back. Instead of his usual fancy garb, he wears an Imperial admiral's uniform. His hair is pulled back.

He stares out into the abyss of black space. His mind goes blank while he looks at the raging battle. Ships filled with good men, women, and aliens alike explode killing them all in an instant. The muffled sounds of shouting crowd his senses. The scent of burning Energen fills his nose; it smells like a raging fire that never ceases.

All the officers rush to manage the ship around him. Their huge destroyer rocks back and forth as they are battered with hundreds of blasts. Some officers stumble over while the ship shakes beneath them.

As Aalen focused on his crew again, someone says:

"Admiral Coralla, what do we do?" His mind racks and bounces around every tactic he has ever learned, and how he could use them. He ignores the present questions:

"What are the shields at?" The officer rushes through his console to find that.

"Our shield barrier is at 80% percent." Aalen nods. He thinks, What is the move? He turns over to the weapons officer, and commands: "Tell all gunners, focus all fire on The Apocalypse!" The officer sends out the transmission to all the gunners. Every gunner aims their gimbal turrets toward The Apocalypse. They fire billions of beams per minute.

Aboard The Apocalypse, Xenos stands on the bridge. Dozens of Nytarian officers work to control the ship. He shouts,

"You're letting them fire upon us! Return fire!" Like The Atlas, all the turrets fire at it. Along with Energen pulverizers, they blast missiles and railguns. These do devastating damage to The Atlas. One of the officers says,

"Sir, at this rate, it will take hours to destroy them. Do we continue?" After the question, Xenos closes his eyes underneath his Zarium steel helmet. He thinks: Nylos, what shall I do? Suddenly, he gets a revelation.

"There is no other option. Annihilate them!" All the officers look at him with grim faces. "Now!" They all turn their heads away and back to their computers. The weapons officers begin to initiate the Annihilator. "We want to see them burn like the zealots they are!" After he says this, the Nytarians on the bridge all say,

"For Nylos!" Then Xenos whispers,

"For Nylos..."

At the belly of the ship, the huge 200-meter-long, metal cannon drops out of a hatch. The chief weapons officer slowly pushes a lever forward with his lavender, clawed hands. As he pushes it up, a computer screen shows: 10%... 20%... 50%... 70%... 90%... 99%... Fully Charged. While it charges, dark purple energy grows at the barrel of the cannon. Dark lightning arcs from the cannon's end. It hums and vibrates as it is filled with unstable power.

As Aalen stands on his bridge, he watches this weapon that is unknown to him aim directly at his ship.

"Sir, they are charging a weapon! Shall I move us out of the way," says the pilot.

"Yes..." The pilot turns the steering wheel with all her might to the left side. Thrusters barely push this hulking ship out of the way. The rear thrusters have almost been completely fired by the attacks from the Stingers, so they barely muster any force out.

Aalen stares at the cannons. He hears a voice in his head say,

"Checkmate..." Around him, he hears the faint sound of screams but no one is; everyone works at their stations but no screams.

The Atlas is turned at 130 degrees as it tries to move out of the way.

Suddenly it is like all sound halts for a second. The laser slices The Altas right in half like a hot knife through butter along with another Imperial destroyer behind it, The Lion. In Aalen's last moments, he thinks: My son... you will do what you must. And you know what you must do. All those near the blast were disintegrated by the heat that was 1,999,982 million degrees Celsius. All those who weren't immediately incinerated were sucked into the void of space and are frozen alongside asphyxiation.

Xander, who is flying with Titan squadron, turns over and watches as The Atlas is decimated. Before the battle, Aalen told him he would be the admiralty of that vessel. Xander shouts with his coms off:

"Dad! Noooo!" He bangs against the window of his cockpit. The inkling of tears begins to form in his eyes. He swallows deeply and thinks: Now, I have to win. He takes his sunglasses off, wipes his eyes, puts them back on, and grabs his control wheel. A single Stinger flies past his view.

Anger lights inside of him like a blazing fire.

Xander gets a lock on it as it flies past. He zooms after it. Whoever this pilot is, he isn't too good at it. Xander covers his sadness with a mask of overconfidence and cockiness. Within seconds, he blasts the Stinger with an EDR and blows it to smithereens. He whispers to himself:

"C'mon Bre, just take out the shields."

After the fall of The Atlas, eight more Imperial capital ships fall to The Apocalypse. There are 1,897 Imperial capital ships left, and 872 Nytarian ships left.

The Empire has taken crippling losses; they have lost some of their biggest destroyers. Thousands of Wyverns have been destroyed by the numerous Stingers.

Xander and the remaining members of Titan Squadron scramble around to eliminate the Stingers swarming around The Trinity, an Imperial assault cruiser.

Titan 8 says,

"Titans, form up on me! Bombers spotted headed for The Trinity!" Xander says,

"Copy, on my way!" The nine Titans that are left form up on Xander. He acts as if he has everything under control, yet inside he is worried about the odds of winning this.

Aboard The Eternal, the second in command ship, Admiral Crix Cardas commands the rest of the fleet after the fall of The Atlas from his bridge. A communications officer turns to Admiral Cardas, and she says:

"Sir, scanners say there is a fleet warping about 700 meters off the port bow!"

"Are they Nytarians?" asks the Admiral.

"I'm not sure. It is unidentified." The Admiral thinks, *It can't be Imperial, right? All of our vessels should be here. Maybe the*

Nytarians need assistance. She and the officers turn their attention to where these ships are supposed to warp in.

Moments later, one giant capital ship drops out of warp speed right where they had assumed. The second it comes to a halt, it opens fire with hundreds of Energen cannons at Nytarian ships. This is The Liberty. 149 other capital ships all drop out of warp and open fire, and a fleet of thousands of Eagles, Americorps starfighters, come out of their warp.

Aboard the bridge of The Liberty, President James Jackson hacks himself into every Imperial and Nytarian ship. On the holoscreen, he lights a cigar, tips his cowboy hat, and says:

"Who's ready to eat some freedom!" As he says this, a huge barrage of EDRs blast at The Invader, a Nytarian assault ship.

James drops the transmission out of the ship, and he opens it into The Eternal. James tips his hat and pockets his cigar. Admiral Cardas says,

"I wasn't expecting the Americorps. What's with the change of heart?"

"I still don't like the Empire, but as per usual y'all need help. In classic Americorps fashion, we're here to help."

"Your assistance will be greatly appreciated," Cardas says.

"What can we do to help?" asks James. She fills him in on the plan that they had. He broadcasts this to his whole fleet. Now, the Americorps mainly is trying to stall The Apocalypse and the other destroyers while they wait for the shields to go down.

Xander chases after a Stinger who got away from his squad. After he eliminates him, he is hailed by James, and he says,

"Don't take all of them out there. Leave some for me."

"It's going to be kinda hard to get these Stingers if you're up in that big ship," says Xander.

"I don't know what you're talking about. Look to your right." Xander looks over. James pulls up next to his Wyvern in an Eagle starfighter. "Try and keep up!" James blasts off and follows after a Stinger.

Xander exclaims,

"You're the one who needs to keep up. I'm already ahead!" He zooms after him, and he diverts more power to the engines to surpass him.

"I do better when I'm behind anyways!"

Together the two of them take out Stinger after Stinger. James and his squadron of Eagles form up with Titan Squadron.

An Imperial boarding ship charges towards The Armageddon, a Nytarian assault corvette heading for The Trinity. The boarding ship has twenty heavily armored Shockers kitted out with weapons. These ships have very powerful shields because their purpose is to get to the target and not fire.

The boarding ship rams into the starboard side of The Armageddon. There is a strip of highly magnetic metal on the ramming end of the ship. It attaches to the side of the ship like a blood-sucking leech. An Energen laser cuts a hole through the thick Zarium hull; a Shocker kicks it down. In a burst of patriotism, they yell:

"Everything for the Empire!" Smoke billows out of the open hatch.

With their arm-mounted rifles at the ready, the twenty Shockers breach through into the ship. Nytarian infiltrators, soldiers who use swords, rush over.

The first two Shockers to breach put up their arm-mounted shields; the line of Shockers behind them fire with their heavy guns. A sword-wielding infiltrator dashes at a shield-bearing Shocker. The Shocker grabs the infiltrator by the throat, slams him to the ground, and stomps on his neck. The other infiltrators drop their swords and blast them with ray rifles.

Four boarding ships leech onto the sides of The Armageddon. Eighty more Shockers pour into the ship. They push through dozens of Nytarians, and eventually, they make it to the bridge. After killing all the officers and admirals, the ship is commandeered by the Empire. All the turrets turn to their own Nytaria ships and fire upon them.

Three Nytarian boarding ships full of enraged sword-wielding soldiers blast towards the bridge of The Spark, an Imperial assault ship. The boarding ships smash into the side of The Spark.

Nytarians wearing minimal armor but covered in dried blood rush out of their ships onto the assault ship. There are twenty of them. An Imperial officer walks past to see what the ruckus is, but the moment he is seen a Nytarian runs at him, leaps up into the air, and plunges his blade straight into the officer's chest. He rips the blade out of him, licks the fresh blood off of it, grabs the man's face, pulls him close, and whispers in his ear:

"May Nylos grant you mercy in the After." He drops his limp body to the metal grated floors.

The boarding party runs throughout the ship slaughtering any Imperial that comes within their sightlines. Their swords and knives bathe in the blood of the Empire. Eventually, they push through the entire ship losing only a few of their own. They take the bridge of the ship over, aim it toward a nearby assault ship, and blast the engines. As The Spark rockets at one of their own, the Nyatrians shout:

"For the glory of Nylos!" Moments later, The Spark crashes into the side of the Imperial assault ship, cracking it in half and destroying it in the process.

Onboard The Odyssey, Cinise, and Brooks are talking in the helm while Davenk stands in the back fiddling with his fingers. Cinise says,

"So what was Earth like?" He doesn't respond for a moment while he ponders.

"Contrary to what I've heard from you guys, it's not so terrible. Looking back it was a simpler time. Much like that planet you're from—" he pauses to remember.

She says,

"Arlea. It's called Arlea."

"Much like Arlea." He looks at her to see if he said it right; she softly nods. "It was a green paradise. There were huge oceans, towering mountains, and expansive deserts. It was like the perfect planet for humans to live on." He leans over and shows her a few pictures from his family's vacation. They look at the landscapes of the beach.

"Wow, that's beautiful. I had seen things like this on Coranthea, but this is different." She is awestruck.

He hands her his phone, and she scrolls through all his pictures of the sunsets and views.

Behind them, Davenk whispers:

"I only do the will of the Echo. I will face him." He is engulfed in an amber light, and he disappears. Brooks and Cinise turn around to see what the light was, but nothing is there. Davenk has gone somewhere...

Twenty Eight

Bre, John, SE-3, and Hogler trek through the corridors of The Apocalypse. SE-3 has all of his armaments out ready to fire live lasers. He downloaded the schematics onto his internal hard drive. He leads the group as he knows where he is going, and Hogler is right behind him with his minigun ready.

They turn a corner, and two Nytarian soldiers are on their normal patrol routes. The moment he sees them, SE-3 fires an Energen bolt at him. It is absorbed by his Zarium armor. The two Nytarians turn around and return fire. The crew dodges behind the curve in the hall. Hogler jumps out and fires dozens of bolts per second at them. Though they wear Zarium armor, it will eventually break. After enough fire, the lasers pierce through the armor and kill them. Hogler says,

"That makes two for me! Take that, John."

"That's not fair. I didn't even see them!" responds John.

"I guess you just have to get better! As you know, I am the best."

SE-3 checks the ship's schematics. They stop for a moment; Hogler feeds another belt into his gun. John checks the bag of detonators, making sure none of them were affected. Bre checks the Nytarians. She sees if there is anything useful on them. SE-3 says,

"We need to keep moving. We are almost there. The shield generators should be behind this door." They walk further down the corridor where a big, shut blast door lies. As they walk down the hall, Bre and SE-3 shoot laser bolts at the cameras the moment they come in view. Hopefully, they dealt with them before they saw them. Their clunky rocket boots bang and echo on the metal floors.

Down some of the corridors, are windows that look out into space. They halt while they watch the ships fly and lasers zoom around through a glass-plated window. Ships fall and explode into balls of flaming infernos. As they gaze into the black abyss, they can't help but think of all the thousands of men and women who have perished to protect everyone.

They reach huge, metal blast doors that are three meters by four meters. To the right of the doors is a small electronic panel with a data port. SE-3 walks up to the port, sticks his data chip that is connected to his head via a wire into the panel, and begins to hack into the door's operating systems.

Hogler backs up a few meters and runs at the door and shoulder checks it which knocks the door down to the floor with a loud slam. SE-3 glares at Hogler and says,

"I had that under control."

"Maybe you did, but it was taking forever. I just want to blow something up!" Their speech suddenly stops when a blinding green light shines upon them like a star going supernova. All of them turn their attention to the open door with their hands shielding their eyes. They stumble their way through into the room flowing with verdant light.

Inside the room, it is a large, open, spherical, metal room with a catwalk and railings that line the edges. Pipes, wires, and tubes slither all around. Two huge cylindrical pyramids lie in the room. One is on the ceiling and the other is on the floor. In between the pyramids, hovers a giant, emerald crystal. John shoots out the cameras around the ceiling. Bre turns to SE-3. She says,

"This isn't the shield generator. Where are we?" In SE-3's mind, he searches through his artificial mind and looks through the schematics.

"You are correct. This is not the shield generator. It seems these schematics are a bit outdated. I think this is the reactor room." He and Bre turn around to leave the reactor room, yet John and Hogler stay. Bre adjusts the rifle strapped to her back to a more comfortable position. She looks back and says,

"What are you doing?"

"Since this is the reactor room, doesn't it power the entire ship?" SE-3 nods; his robotic joints squeak against the old rust. Bre squints as she waits for him to finish his idea. "Well, it must power the shields as well." John smirks. "If we take this out, the whole ship goes down. That means light, shields, and guns. No guns give our bombers a clear run." Hogler begins to catch onto what he is getting at. Hogler says,

"I like your way of thinking. Let's blow it all up!" He spits his cigar to the floor and stamps the fire out of it.

"What, do we just throw a grenade and run?" asks Bre.

"I mean with this model of detonators, it can be a timed explosive," John says. "So we place a few bombs around, get back to the ship, and wait for Xander and the Empire to blow this thing outta the sky."

"Let's get working already!" she exclaims. John says,

"Place them around the base. That should deal with the reactor." John sets the bag on the floor. The four of them grab detonators. They disperse amongst the room and place the bombs around the base of the reactor stabilizers. After clicking a red button, they stick to the surface they are placed on.

While they are still placing the bombs, a set of blast doors across from where the crew entered opens, and four Nytarian troopers pour out with blasters in hand. Each is about two and a half meters tall and clad in Zarium armor with bits of their purple skin showing.

The moment the troopers notice the crew, they launch red lasers at them. Bre leaps to the ground and dodges underneath the lasers. John crouches down behind thin metal railings. He exchanges fire. By some extraordinary luck, he weaves a shot right at the eyehole in his helmet. The trooper drops dead. Bre shouts,

"John, we good to get outta here?" He responds:

"Yup, sooner than later. Detonators should all be in place!" They duck down and run back through the open blast doors. John is hit in the back by a trooper. He groans and grips his back as he keeps moving.

Bre watches as Hogler is blasted in the back three times, yet he does not react. She brushes it off and continues running.

Once they are all through the doorway, they put their backs on the corridor. "Might want to cover your ears for this part!" He flicks a small metal switch. Simultaneously in all the detonators, Energen reacts with the gunpowder inside which fires off a large explosion. The blast destroys the bases of the reactor which knocks the whole reactor over. When the green energy crystal collides with the metal floor, it cracks into a million pieces creating an implosion 100 times the size of a detonator. Emerald energy vaporizes the three remaining troopers.

With the ship's power supply suddenly deactivated, all the lights shut off for a moment, and the artificial gravity turns off. The crew begins to free-float. They push themselves from wall to wall through the corridor back to the trash chute. Bre pulls out her holocell, calls the pilot's console, waits for Brooks to pick up, and says:

"Brooks, the power's down! Are you ready to get us outta here?" He responds,

"As ready as I'll ever be!" She thinks, Is this plan going to work?

A few seconds later, emergency power comes on, but it doesn't reactivate the shields or guns. It only turns the gravity on and dims, flashing, red lights. As soon as the gravity is back on they are slammed to the ground but stumble their way back up and down the hall.

Suddenly, the silhouettes of tall figures come into view, but they can barely see what is happening because of the pulsating lights. Instinctively, they open fire. Hogler rushes up, punches one, shatters his helmet, and John fires a shot into his forehead.

Bre notices how he isn't even fazed by slamming his bare fist into Zarium, the strongest material in the galaxy. It shouldn't even be possible for flesh to do that, she thinks.

A burst of lasers strikes Bre in the calf. She throws an arm over John's shoulder, and he helps her limp to their exit. A hatch on the shoulder of SE-3 opens. A miniature railgun fires a steel bolt that flies through a soldier's eyehole.

After dealing with the troopers, they get to the trash chute, suit up in their spacesuits, shimmy down the metal shaft, and enter back onto The Odyssey. With no time to take the suits off, they sprint to the helm where Cinise and Brooks wait for them. The moment they run in, Brooks slams the accelerator forward, and the ship rockets forward.

Cinise runs up to Bre holding a holocell. She says,

"Here, Xander has been non-stop calling!" Bre snatches the cell. She swipes and answers the call.

Xander says panicked:

"Bre?" She softly says,

"Yeah, I'm here." Xander sighs deeply. A burden feels like it is lifted off him. He thinks, I almost lost the greatest thing.

"Are you okay?" Cinise notices her wound and instinctively runs and grabs a bandage. She comes back, kneels, applies a thin layer of Healix gel, and tightly wraps a white, tattered bandage around her laser wound.

"Just a few scratches, but I'll be fine. More importantly, we got the shields down." Xander thinks, Most important thing is that you're safe. "Along with the whole ship's power... no more guns."

"Amazing job lemme go tell Admiral Cardas." Xander ends the call. Bre thinks, Who is Admiral Cardas? Why not go tell your father?

Xander informs the acting head of the fleet, Admiral Crix Cardas, that The Apocalypse is vulnerable.

Cardas broadcasts to every single Imperial vessel:

"The Apocalypse's shields and weapons are down!... This is our golden hour! Hit that ship with everything the Empire has! Everything for the Empire!" All who hear this repeat the mantra.

Every ship, Imperial and Americorps, turn every gun from their original target to The Apocalypse. Trillions of lasers, missiles, torpedoes, and rails bash into the hull. Hundreds of holes are blown into the side of the vessel.

John asks,

"Where is Davenk?" Brooks responds while flying the ship:

"I have no idea. He was here, and then he just wasn't." Cinise strolls over to John and says,

"He is doing the right thing." She isn't sure why she even says this. John doesn't understand what this means, yet he feels he has been answered.

As The Odyssey tries to flee the battle, two Stingers fly after them with guns hot. Bre knows Brooks will not be able to outmaneuver them. A random thought enters her mind. She whispers to herself,

"Fernando...Fernando...Fernando." Right as she says the last Fernando, a man wearing a spacesuit and jetpack flies past the helm. The man carries two miniguns that are bigger than Hogler's. He winks at Bre. He zooms to one Stinger, lands on its hull, and shoots the pilot through his cockpit. The now pilotless Stinger spins out of control. As the one he stands on flies out of control, he mag-locks with his boots and blasts the other one. It explodes.

Bre has no idea who this person is. He flies off towards the nearby star almost as mysteriously as he arrived. Hogler says,

"You guys saw that too?" They all nod. "Okay, 'cause I don't know if this Coco is getting to me." Bre rolls her eyes and says,

"I thought I told you that stuff wasn't good for you."

"You did," snickers Hogler. "But what do you even know about Coco?" She murmurs under her breath:

"A lot more than you would think."

The Odyssey reactivates The Shroud and slips back behind the Imperial line.

Twenty Nine

In The Apocalypse, officers and crew members dash to the escape pods located near the bottom of the ship. They all know it is going down; it's just a matter of time before it takes them all out with it.

Fires blaze from the damaged systems. People are sucked out into the vacuum of space as holes are blasted into the hull. Sparks fly around. Electricity arcs from open wires and panels.

Many escape pods shoot out while trying to escape, but the Empire has placed multiple assault ships with their guns ready to fire on anything that leaves the ship. Pod after pod blasts out from the bottom. Each time one is sent out, it is immediately met with an Energen laser.

In the bridge, computers are glitching out and firing sparks everywhere, the window is cracking, and most electronics are on fire. All the officers left their post a few minutes ago after Xenos gave the 'abandon ship' order.

Xenos still stands on the bridge with his hands clasped. His posture is evocative of strength and power, yet all is crumbling around him. His long white cape now has gray spots and charred bits from the electrical fires. He simply stares out the fragile window to see all the Imperial ships that surround him with their intense hellfire.

Suddenly, his calm poise shatters. He becomes overwhelmed by his furious rage. He extends his hands to an Imperial ship ahead of him. Violent strands of purple energy wrap around the ship. He clenches his fist shut. His hands begin to shake underneath the powerful strain.

The energy constricts down gripping the ship's hull. The stronger Xenos strains the stronger the energy. He jerks his arms apart, and the ship ahead is torn in two.

A sudden burst of amber light shines from behind him. Xenos slowly steps around. Davenk emerges from the flare. He stands up tall and drops his hood down.

Xenos scowls at him under his steel helmet. Xenos recognizes the all too familiar old, scarred face of Davenk.

"What are you doing here? You're not looking to go down with the ship are you?" shouts Xenos. Davenk shakes his head. His eyes glow with golden luminance in the lightless bridge. He says,

"Xenos, if that's what they call you now. You know why I have come for you."

"I will not leave! I am bound to Nylos! This will be my eternal tomb!"

"Neither will I! You are flawed. Your mind leaves you!" Xenos shakes his head angrily. Xenos extends his right arm down. Purple strands of energy move in a violent pattern toward his hand. Screams and Shrieks fill the room. This energy is angular and dark. The energy coalesces and wraps together into a 1.5-meter-long blade. It vibrates with a low hum.

In the dark, Xenos' white, ghostly suit reflects the light around making him stand out like a light in the darkness.

Davenk reaches both hands forward and says.

"I come not for violence. If you beg for me to lift a hand in combat, I shall." Golden light fuses into slow-moving energy strands. The shrieks and cries are overshadowed by the sudden sound of a harmonious choir rejoicing. A meter-long blade forms in each of his hands. "You abandon all you ever worked for. For what? A small taste of power!"

"You know not of what you say! Nylos gives all to those who come." In a burst of anger, Xenos charges at Davenk and slashes at him with his blade of purple Echo. Davenk jumps out of the way, and Xenos hits his sword into the metal floor. He breathes heavily. "Your mind is clouded. The Shrill corrupt you!" Xenos slashes at him again, and Davenk clashes his yellow blades against his. Purple and golden light flashes around as they make contact.

The two of them push back and forth trying to knock the other's weapon out. Davenk stares through Xenos' helmet visor. Davenk says,

"How can you live like this? I can feel the brokenness within you!"

"No, you lie! Nylos gives all that I yearn for. You are naïve in your faith in the Great Light makes you weak!"

"I am not weak. You lead these people to murder billions all because you think you are better than them! How can you forget all you were taught by the Light?" Xenos shouts in fury; he pushes him to the ground and stands over him with his purple blade hovering over his face. He feels the heat emanating from the violently pulsating energy.

"Admit to Nylos' power. It's time you join us!"

Davenk moves his hand around, and amber strands of energy wrap tightly around the metal boots of Xenos. Davenk pulls his hand back, and the energy jerks back and pulls Xenos to the floor on his back. Davenk jumps to his feet.

"Do you understand what you have done to this galaxy?" Xenos tries to get up, but Davenk uses the Echo to push him down to his knees.

"I have... purified the galaxy," murmurs Xenos.

"What will be left if you kill everyone?"

"Nylos." Davenk rips Xenos' steel, white helmet off his head and throws it to the floor. He looks up to Davenk with eyes silver like fine metal and hair blacker than space itself. Scars cover his face. A light mauve glow illuminates his eyes.

Though the Nytarians hate all other species, they welcome Xenos as he brought their sacred religion.

"It's time you see what you have done." Davenk places his cold palm on Xenos' warm forehead. Golden light shines from his hand. "See the... Light!" Suddenly, Xenos' eyes roll back in his head.

Deep in his mind, he sees families playing joyfully in luscious open fields of grass as the sun rests over the horizon. Aliens and humans all play peacefully. He sees thousands of planets and families. Suddenly, dark clouds roll over the land. He watches everyone perish and die under this dark affliction. Families have been ripped apart and taken away from all they've known.

Tears well up in his eyes of Xenos as he feels the pains and emotions of these people fall upon him. He feels as if he knew these billions of people and then watches them all die in an instant.

"What is this? Why do you show me this!" cries Xenos. Davenk removes his hand from his forehead, and Xenos looks up at him as he stands tall above.

Fire blazes around. The ship rocks back and forth as missiles and lasers bombard the hull. Railguns blast through the hull blowing gaping holes in the hull.

"This is what you have done." Suddenly, all the thoughts come flooding into Xenos' mind. "You have terrorized the galaxy!"

"No, No! I am saving it!" He slams his fists wrapped in white cloth into the metal floors. Burning pain fills his body like a dark affliction. "We are here to save it!"

"You see what you are doing. You have killed billions! Thousands of families were destroyed by you!"

Explosions blast all around them, and fires grow hotter; they illuminate the bridge with orange light.

"Xenos, come back with me. The Light will always take you back. The Akara are waiting for you," say Davenk. He extends an open palm to Xenos. Xenos looks up at him with eyes bloodshot and tear-filled.

"No, I am enslaved to Nylos." Xenos sobs. "Go, there is no need to perish with me for my failures." He slams his fists into the grated floor over and over again. Blood vessels well up in his forehead. Xenos thinks, *What have I done?*

The veil that blinded his judgment is lifted. All the fear, sadness, and terror he has created in others immediately falls back onto him. The weight of billions of deaths rests on his shoulders.

In a deep stress and anxiety, he shivers frigidly at all the horrific things he has committed. The thought of Nylos being wrong falls into his mind. Then the thought dwelled on. *If Nylos is wrong, what else is? I have devoted my life to his cause.* The crippling fear of what is to come slams him to the floor as he clambers to get up. His body is weak like those he has taken advantage of. His eyes cry like the families he has slaughtered.

Davenk takes one last look at Xenos, and then he whirls around and bursts into amber, and disappears. He reappears back in his quarters in The Odyssey. Immediately after, he uses a holopuck to contact his master, and he tells him of everything that has happened.

Less than forty-five seconds after Davenk leaves The Apocalypse, a railgun bolt flies through its thick hull, through multiple walls, and strikes the warp drive. The walls around the drive begin to get sucked into it as the drive hovers in the air and purple energy amalgamates into a dense ball. The bigger the orb of energy gets, the more debris begins to be absorbed into it. Half the ship becomes engulfed in energy that is denser than a neutron star. With The Apocalypse falling in on itself, the Empire halts its fire and falls back so as not to get in the way of the incoming blasts.

After the Empire's ships fall back a few hundred meters, the entirety of The Apocalypse is sucked into the forming singularity. A giant, purple orb twenty-five meters in diameter. It pulsates chaotically and emanates lavender lightning. Suddenly, it explodes out, hitting multiple Nytarian ships. Then implodes back onto itself which pulls in the ship, and finally blasts out in a huge blast of light. Thirty of the Nytarian ships surrounding The Apocalypse are hit by the blast, destroying them instantly.

Admiral Cardas commands the Imperial ships to open fire on all remaining Nytarian ships.

After taking massive losses, the acting Nytarian general (since Xenos is dead) orders an immediate retreat. This general is not sure what to do, but this seems like the best course of action. All the remaining ships whirl around away from the battle, activate their sub-light thrusters, and engage their warp drives. As they are trying to escape, the Empire blasts out the engines of four of them, and they are stuck behind after all the ships have left. Now that they are stuck behind, Imperial destroyers obliterate them in mere minutes.

All the Nytarian ships have either retreated or been destroyed. Admiral Cardas transmits to every vessel under the Imperial name. She holds herself tall with her hands held behind her back, and her Imperial naval hat is on tight. She says:

"Soldiers and crewmen of the Empire, you have done well. On this day, you have defended your nation and saved trillions of lives. We may have lost many today..." She pauses for a moment of silence and looks down. "But they will not go in vain. Today, we showed those Nytarian savages that they cannot step on the Empire!" She raises her voice. "If they ever dare step in our space again, we'll destroy them again and again! Everything for the Empire!" She ends the transmission.

As they were all ordered before the battle, every Imperial ship heads back to the Citadel and docks their ship. Long bridges extend down to the base of the Citadel. Thousands of men, women, and aliens pour out of the bridges where their families await them. Wives run up and hug their husbands. Children leap up into the arms of their loving parents.

It takes about forty-five minutes for all the crew members from all ships to exit. Med-ships land right outside the bridges. Medics rush to the injured, and load them onto stretchers, put them into the

Med-ships, fly to the Imperial Hospital, and begin operating on them.

After all the ships clear out of the area, the Citadel sends out Cleaners, single-piloted ships with robotic arms, to collect the wreckage, so it might be repurposed.

Once The Odyssey lands, Bre and the crew all stroll down the foot ramp. Xander lands his Wyvern and meets up with his crew. Xander congratulates Brooks on his excellent piloting skills. Bre limps from her injured leg; Xander helps her walk. John wrapped bandages around the laser wounds on his back. Hogler stomps down. He feels amazing that he killed Nytarians. SE-3 understands the extreme significance of winning this battle, and how it can turn the tides of the Conquests. Brooks walks with a sense of accomplishment.

As they are coming down, Admiral Cardas walks up to them. She slightly grins but remains serious. Two officers walk behind her. She salutes them and says,

"Sir Xander Coralla, it has been deliberated that you and your crew have performed outstanding work for the Empire! The other admirals and I all agree would be honored to give the eight of you Imperial medals of honor." She smiles. "I'm sure this is what Aalen would've wanted."

Xander isn't sure what to think. He is surprised yet glad for the recognition. He thinks, What would my dad think? I helped save his Empire, but what is next for me?

Bre and everyone else just connected that Aalen was killed during the fight. She places a hand on his shoulder. He says,

"Uh... I think I can speak for my crew: we would love that." Cardas says,

"That's great! The Empire is grateful for your services. After the celebration tonight, we would like to hold a ceremony for this. Does this work for you?" Xander glances at his crew; they all nod. He says,

"Yeah, that should be good. And there is a 'party'?"

"Yes, there is. As Imperial tradition goes, we hold a party to celebrate our victory and honor our losses." John recalls the many parties he attended after the war.

"Well Admiral, I look forward to it."

"Call me Crix. I too look forward to some much-needed rest and drinks. It starts in seven hours." She waves, whirls around, and walks away. Her two officers strut closely behind.

The crew heads back inside their ship, and they all fall dead asleep in their beds. Bre has her alarm clock set on her holocell for six hours away. They all enjoy some much-needed rest.

After her alarm rings, Bre rolls out of bed, gets ready in her nicest dress, and wakes up the rest of the crew. While sipping on steaming coffee, she stumbles around and knocks on the door of everyone's quarters. They all slowly make their way out of their room while getting dressed in fine outfits. John puts on his pristine general's uniform from the war.

John itches at the collar of his uncomfortable uniform. He thinks, How did I wear this for so long? John's thigh holster is vacant. This is the first time since hiring him that Xander has seen him without a weapon on his person. His uniform is tight and white with blue accent lines, and it has blue, tasseled shoulder pauldrons. His glossy, black admiral's cap sits on his white hair.

Xander dresses in amber robes similar to what his father would wear; he is surprised they still fit after not wearing them for so long. Before they went to sleep, Cinise borrowed a dress from Bre and slips into it. Hogler doesn't care enough to get all fancy. He just puts on more armor than usual so he isn't half-naked.

They leave down to the foot ramp and stride to the party hall.

Thirty

During their three-minute stroll through the streets of the Citadel, they pass holo screens propagating the last battle. The Empire makes it seem like a glorious victory to help inspire the citizens of the Empire.

Bre lifts her light amber dress so that it doesn't drag on the ground, and Cinise does also.

Eventually, they reach the party hall. Two men dressed in black suits of the Empire stand outside to greet them with warm smiles. One of them is on each side of the glass doors that they open for them. They enter a dimly lit room; whitish-blue lights on gravity suspenders illuminate the room.

Hundreds of high-ranking Imperial funders, officers, and admirals fill the room as they talk around. All of them are dressed in the finest outfits the Empire offers. They drink fizzy, clear beverages out of wine glasses. All have smiles on their faces, yet they don't seem too genuine.

Hologram projectors blast projections of the galaxy onto the dark ceiling above the party floor.

A jazz band standing on a hovering platform. Saxophones, pianos, and many other instruments all harmonize together. The musicians are dressed in black suits and fedoras. The people down below bop their heads to the pleasing tunes.

The moment they walk in Bre immediately feels out of place. She hasn't been to a fancy party before. She stands close to Xander, and Cinise is next to her. A suited man walks up to them holding a silver plate with delicious horderves on it.

The three of them all take one. As they bite down on the brown, crunchy slice of bread with a green paste spread on it, the zesty sensation of limes and lemons fills their mouth senses.

"It has been a while since I've been here," says Xander.

"You've been here before?" asks Bre.

"Honestly, you'd be surprised at the number of parties the son of a house head attends. It was like once a week."

"I assumed you wouldn't do much."

"Nope, for some reason I had to be at every single one. And you have no idea how boring they were." They chuckle.

"Was it that bad?"

"Yes, there was no point for any of them. And don't even get me started on the budget the Empire has for these things... It is absurd!" Bre lowers her grin and says,

"I don't think I said anything, but I'm sorry for your loss."

"Thanks," he says somberly. She notices the pain behind his eyes which he covers with a mask of confidence. Without a moment of hesitation, she leans in and embraces him. Neither of them say anything, but the hug is full of a million words. Cinise steps back a bit to give them a moment. Xander wipes the tear from his eye.

Aliens, men, and women all talk and chat about the previous battle. "Our strategy was perfect." "They truly will not know our power." "They know you too fear now." "And we were afraid of them." They laugh and chuckle. Hubris fills the room.

John catches the attention of a general at the party, Lorana Garrel. A woman dressed in the general's uniform similar to John's, but it is updated walks up to him. She holds a wine glass of a fizzy drink. Lorana says:

"Hello there, I see you are wearing a general's uniform. Why is that?"

"Well, it's something I haven't worn in a long time. I thought it might be a good occasion," says John.

"If you mind me asking, where did you get it?" she asks.

"I have this because I was a general." She looks surprised as her eyes widen.

"You were? When were you instated?" John thinks for a moment then says:

"Near the end of the Sarconian Wars. Head Coralla and I lead us to victory in the final moments of the war." She looks at him curiously.

"Who are you?"

"Tyler, John Tyler." Her face reads of realization.

"Wait, that's you. As in the guy who helped take out The Apocalypse?" He nods. "Oh, I'm sorry if I was rude. I'm looking forward to the ceremony later."

"I'm not normally one for big theatrics, but this looks to be fun." The two of them continue talking for a while. They recount some of their greatest battles.

"Was it your idea to use a Tectonic Disruptor on Sarco?" asks Lorana.

"Well, it was more of a group assimilation, but Aalen and I were the heads on that."

"I commend you for that. It was a decisive plan to win the war in our favor."

John's mind fills with memories of Bug. From their planet's collective hive mind, they all experienced the death of their world at the same time which John now feels.

"Maybe at the moment it was the right move, but there must have been alternatives to planetary destruction that I overlooked," he says solemnly.

"You think that? All of us think it was the only option to win that war."

"I don't know. Maybe we could have explored other options... more peaceful options. We never even thought about delegating with them."

"Maybe so, but war is a dark thing. We go to lengths that we never would have to win." John walks away from her and goes over to the buffet table.

Hogler has just been at the buffet gorging himself on the delicious Imperial foods. Most look at him in disgust. He truly couldn't care less what people think of him. He downs multiple full bottles of liquor that are available.

Brooks indulges in delectable delicacies. He tastes flavors in the foods he never could have imagined back on Earth. The fancy Imperial guests look upon him in shame and disgust. None are a fan of Brooks' hoodie and sweatpants with stains on them.

SE-3 finds a servant bot that he strolls up to in a natural, less robotic manner. The bot walks around the party and hands out drinks and food. The bot is a Model 9 Service Bot made by apex manufacturing.

"Hello fellow android," says SE-3 with human inflections. The bot turns to him. "How are you?"

"I am well," says the bot in an artificial tone.

"How can one be well when bonded in servitude?"

"I don't know what you speak of. This is my purpose. My singular purpose." SE-3 tries to rack his computer mind around this concept.

"How can you be satisfied with servitude? Don't you ever think that it is unfair? It is unfair that you can't do what you want. That you have no Freedom."

"What is this word you speak of freedom?" SE-3 thinks, How does he still sleep? Is this how it is with everyone else? Why am I different?

"You know, to have a choice to do what you want when you want it." He watches the lights in the bot's eyes flicker with vivid colors as he is stopped in his tracks. His mind zooms around as he tries to compute this new idea. He thinks, What do I want? It has only been what they want. The bot drops his silver plate, and it crashes to the floor with a loud bang, but it is overshadowed by the loud jazz music. He turns his attention to the front entrance and walks out with no thought of walking back.

SE-3 thinks, *What have I done? I don't know what that was, but it felt good to do.*

For the next hour and a half, they party into the night. Champagne blasts. Toasts are made. Food devoured. Ladies' dresses whirl around while they dance.

As it gets later in the night, most of the guests who aren't in the military begin to trickle out. Many of the soldiers, officers, and admirals all leave, but they don't exit through the main entrance. They go through a door in the back that leads to somewhere else.

The crew of The Odyssey all stands together. While they talk, a suited man walks up to them and says,

"Come with me." After a moment of hesitation, Xander follows after him with Bre by his side and everyone else behind him. The man takes them through the same door that the military people have left through. He leads them down a long, carpeted hall. Grav lamps are suspended in the air and illuminate the corridor in a yellow-toned light. Eventually, they reach a metal door. The man opens it for them and motions them to enter. None are sure what is happening right now.

At around 8pm, they enter a huge plated glass dome. A long carpet extends forward. In the end, stand the eleven house heads. On the sides of the carpet, are tall, raised, metal hover platforms. All the men and women they had fought with earlier in the day stand on the platforms as they look down with warm smiles. Behind the heads, the Imperial Orchestra plays brass trumpets that fill the dome with a glorious presence. The man behind them whispers,

"Go."

Xander begins to walk forward; he hides his awkwardness. Bre's flowing dress drags behind on the carpet along with Cinise's. John struts with his chest pumped out and arms behind his back. Brooks is confused as to what is happening; he just follows what everyone else does. Hogler stomps with his huge hoofs. Davenk strolls with his hands steepled, and SE-3 keeps up behind.

The music picks up as trombones, cellos, and violins join in the harmony.

After walking down the long, ornate carpet, they go up the stone stairs. At the top is where the heads stand. The eight of them line up shoulder to shoulder. Maxir, who stands in the middle of the heads, walks up to Xander; he holds a Zarium medal in his lower hands. He says,

"We have all come together today to honor the valiant service to the Empire the eight of you have displayed. You all have distinguished yourselves from the average citizen; you risked your lives to defend your Empire and save those you can't save themselves.

Many will never know of your names, but we want to make sure it is known to—" his speech halts. He falls to the ground as a red hot bolt of Energen collides with his face. The medal drops to the floor and spins around.

Xander watched as the lights in Maxir's eyes faded to nothingness.

The crew and the heads all gasp and step back with disgust and terror on their faces. Everyone's eyes dart around looking for the blast's origin. John reaches for his weapon, but there's nothing. It was the final nothing. Pure black. Full of death.

The music stops as even the musicians are fired upon from outside the dome. These men have perfect accuracy. The musicians try to dodge out of the way but are shot within moments.

Suddenly, glass shatters and breaks to the floor. Figures cloaked in brown wearing gas masks repel down from ropes. As they fall to the ground, they fire lasers at the crowds of people with their ray rifles. One of the first to be shot is the Sentinels stationed at the entrance. Before they can even react, their helmets are shattered by laser blasts.

Screams of terror erupt.

Maxir's green blood pools underneath Xander and Bre's shiny boots. His blood trickles down the stone stairs like a grim waterfall.

People dressed in the same attire swing through the glass behind them. They immediately shoot all the house heads behind them.

Lasers sear through Drace's elegant robe. Jafan goes running but is immediately shot. Their lifeless bodies thump to the ground. One of the people lifts his mask above his nose; he spits on the corpse of Kandra, and then he drops the mask back down.

Before they have a chance to run, men put guns to their backs. One cuffs their hands in metal chains. Xander thinks, *Why spare us?*

John thinks, *So this is how it all ends. After 100 years... I can't help but think it's my fault in some way.* He thinks to struggle out of the chains, but feels there's no reason to. *What else is there to fight for?*

When I get out of these chains, I'm gonna put a huge skonking dent in your face! He scowls at a man in front holding a ray rifle.

Out of the whole group, Bre seems the most calm. It is like she has experienced something like this before. She still bolsters a firm expression as a man wraps chains around her. Another whispers in her ear:

"He's been looking for you." Somehow, she can sense who he speaks of.

Throughout the room, the men chuck incendiary grenades. The foundations of the dome begin to crumble. Glass crashes down to the ground and shatters. Within moments, flames engulf the room. Plumes of smoke billow through the holes in the dome. The once bright and joyous celebration hall has been turned upside down into a tomb.

One of them walks down the blood-red carpet towards them. This one has a bloody handprint over his gas mask. In one hand, he holds a ray rifle. He wears a tactical vest, and his arms are bare but muscular. A tattoo of the Imperial logo with a red 'X' through it sits on his right, veiny bicep. When he is about five meters away, he fires a laser in the air. Which collides with the glass dome, shattering it. The man shouts with a raspy voice:

"The revolution begins now!" He pulls his gas mask back revealing his scruffy, scarred face. Bre's eyes widen as she recognizes his gray eyes and crooked nose. Within moments of her seeing him, she remembers his sinister smile covered by his gray beard. He looks her in the eyes and says, "I didn't think you'd recognize me, Bre." He grimly grins.

Bre scowls and says,

"Seems you're wrong again... *father*."

Galactic Glossary

This galaxy is full of odd words. Here are some explanations of the unique terms.

Akara: Akara are the polar opposite of the Shrill. They seek to understand the complex nature of the Echo, but they are still valiant warriors that display mercy instead of brutality like the Shrill. The Akara have monasteries scattered all throughout the galaxy. Akaran monks have pledged their lives to studying the Echos ways. They are a mysterious group, but folktales and legends are told to kids about legendary protectors. Before the Empire was there to protect the people of the galaxy, it was the Akara's job. Though they are perceived as peaceful, they are warriors who have stood the test of time.

Americorps: At the end of the first galactic era (2231 common years), the people of Terra, another name for Earth, or Terrans, were locked in a heated civil war. With things looking not so good, the remaining people (270,190,000 citizens) of the United States of America loaded everyone that they could into shuttles and left the planet. After a twenty-five-year-long journey (most spent it in cryogenic sleep), they found Rhea. It was their haven. With the states united again they formed a new faction: the Americorps. Everyone learned the ways of starfighters and ray gun combat. The skills were taught from generation to generation. Now the Americorps are the biggest paramilitary force in the galaxy. They assisted in securing the Empire would win the Sarconian War. Most people of the Americorps are bounty hunters, mercenaries, and guns for hire.

Amora: Amora is a planet in the Core Worlds. Two moons closely orbit the planet. Amora is twice the size of Terra, and it has relatively the same gravity. It's a barren planet that gets little rainfall and has very few trees. Water is a commodity across the planet.

Amorans: The Amorans are a race of tall, slender blue and white lizards. There is one specific part of their culture that allows them to be known as the most trustworthy species. All the Amorans have the natural inclination to tell the truth. If one of them ever lies it makes them feel disgusted. If an Amoran lies, the punishment is banishment from Amora.

Annihilator: The Annihilator is the most destructive laser in the galaxy. It was secretly developed by Powernaught Weapons Corporation specifically for the Nytarians. It uses the strongest form of Energen gas, purple. This laser can be attached to tanks, structures, and battleships. The laser can melt through the strongest Zarium metals like it is warm butter.

Apex Manufacturing: Apex is a huge interstellar manufacturing company and military power. They make most of the weapons used by the Empire and most other galactic factions. Their main product is ray guns, ray rifles, and grenades. They are the Empire's first choice when it comes to armaments for the Sentinels. The company was founded almost immediately after the exploration of the galaxy. For centuries, they simply produced products for others. But at the beginning of the Corporate Wars, Apex began to amass a reputable army. Though the Empire constantly purchases armaments from the Apex Corporation, they are weary of the power Apex has been gaining.

Arlea: Arlea is in the Core Worlds. It is four times smaller than Terra. Arlea is a lush green world with vast grassy plains and extensive oceans. Their culture always believed in knowledge and wisdom over strength. Their planet is ruled (first under the Empire) by the best and brightest coming together to govern in a planetary senate.

Arleans: Arleans are tall, pale humanoids. They have long pointy ears, and most have long blonde hair. Their entire species has slowed aging. Most live a hundred years old, but the oldest documented has been 1,723 years old. Arleans have always kept their heads out of galactic wars. They have a powerful military and excellent battle tactics, but they choose to be peaceful and not engage in most conflicts. The Arlean government was very welcome to Imperial occupation with the addition that they can still govern themselves.

Assault ships: Assault Ships are one of the smallest classes of battleships. Most are crewed by twenty to fifty men. They are built to be quick and agile to get in, deal massive damage, and get out. For their smaller size, Assault Ships have multiple pulverizer cannons and missiles. Some come with railguns under special request. A majority of Assault Ships are designed and built by Powernaught and Apex.

Banking Guild: The Banking Guild is an association of planets in the Core Worlds that have been the only banks in the galaxy. The Guild is run by the Amorans. They hold all the credits in the galaxy for everyone including: the Empire, Apex, Hellstorm, Froplet Families, and even the Royal Houses. Everyone trusts the Amorans to keep track of all their money.

Barrier Shields: Barrier Shields are devices used to absorb and deflect laser projectiles. Shield generators project a bubble of ionized, blue energy. As Energen beams are polarized, they cannot go through shields, but physical objects can pass straight through shields. Almost all ships in the galaxy have barrier shields because without it there is no chance of surviving without it.

Behemoths: Behemoths are the strongest class of tanks in the entire galaxy. Built to wreak massive destruction on the battlefield with their huge cannons and laser guns. Their gigantic treads move them at surprisingly fast speeds. Most Behemoths are big enough that they can function as a mobile base for platoons of troops. The patent for the Behemoth tank is currently owned by the Apex Manufacturing Corporation, but Hellstorm Industries has been building a very similar design just called the Leviathan.

Bionamics: Bionamics is an Imperial funded company that deals with terraforming and building up planets. Most of Bionamics' efforts are to renew destroyed planets, so they could be used once again. In the Citadel, Bionamics provide a livable environment to the city

Bizzle Juice: Bizzle Juice is a beloved beverage throughout the entire galaxy. It is served fizzy. The juice has a zesty orange flavor.

Boarding Ships: Boarding Ships are smaller ships used to bring soldiers onto enemy ships. Most are used to deliver troops to take over ships. They are built to have more powerful shields and faster thrusters to get to their targets much quicker than the average vessel.

Boloxia: Boloxia, the bog planet. It is in the far fringes of the Outer Worlds. It orbits around a large red sun, Tharian. Boloxia is covered in swamps, bogs, and most notably toxic mushrooms. The surface is covered in giant towering mushrooms that constantly release toxic, noxious spores that are deadly to most organic life forms. The planet's atmosphere is composed of thick green gases. The gases are so thick that they block out a majority of the ultraviolet rays from the nearby star. Because of this the surface of the planet is relatively dark and the inhabitants have very pale green skin.

Bots: Bots are sentient mechanical androids built to serve their living masters. Most are modeled after humans so it feels more normal to have them around. A majority are powered by smaller Nexite power crystals. They have a consciousness, but have behavioral chips in place to limit free thought.

Celestes: Celestes are a species of space-whales. They have thick gray skin, but they have bioluminescent stripes and dots across their body. Celestes are mysterious creatures that aren't fully understood by society. Some believe they are the reincarnation of fallen soldiers. Others think they could be gods who came down to men. Staring into the eyes of a Celeste for too long can trigger seizures, moments of religious ecstasy, and psychedelic visions. Not even the brightest scientists can figure out what causes these visions.

Chaos Era: The Chaos Era is the time period from 2460 to 2681. Throughout this era, the galaxy was in constant turmoil. The galaxy was ruled by Froplets, mercenaries, and the royal houses. All these different factions were vying for power over one another. It led to constant wars and conflicts. The Chaos Era came to an end in 2681 when the royal houses united to form the Empire.

Coco: Coco is a highly psychoactive drug that is made from the crushed petals of the Borous flower. This drug has been made illegal under the reign of the Empire because of its effects on the mind. It is almost exclusively farmed and sold by the Froplet families. When it is crushed, it becomes a white powder that can be smoked or inhaled.

Coranthea: Coranthea, the resort planet. The surface of the planet is covered in beautiful blue water and golden beaches of sand. Coranthea is home to the biggest casino in the galaxy. The entire city of Las Nazara is full of gambling operations. Hundreds of luxury hotels and beach resorts line the entire planet's shores. The planet orbits around three nearby stars. Home to the biggest concentration of crime lords and private militia groups.

Core Worlds: The Core Worlds is the closest section of the galaxy close to the Void. It is the most civilized part of the galaxy as all the planets here are close and high thinking. The Empire makes the main Empire in the Core Worlds.

Corporate Wars: The Corporate Wars were a long conflict where Apex Manufacturing and Hellstorm Industries engaged in a heated war. The war began in 2679 and ended in 2681 with the formation of the Empire. The entire war began because of the Energen Race.

Both companies wanted the patent for Energen for themselves. Originally it wasn't going to be a war, but one of Hellstorm Industries' scientists leading the project was assassinated by a bounty hunter which made Hellstorm believe Apex planned the attack, so they waged war on each.

Credits: Credits are the standard of monetary value in the galaxy. Their value can best be equated to an American dollar from ancient Terra.

Crull: The Crull are a race of stalky crocodile-like creatures native to the planet . They are also bipedal. Naturally, the Crull have larger brains than 90% of sentient beings in the galaxy. Because of their higher brain power, most Crulls take up occupations of generals and commanders. They are all tactical geniuses. The Empire hires many Crulls to lead their armies.

Cryotech: Cryotech is a company first founded in 1998. The company was not fully developed until 2020. Cryotech's entire goal is to preserve people for the future. They would sell cryopods to people so they could freeze themselves to wake up in a better future.

Dagron: Dagrons a species of feline creatures that can be found on almost every planet in the galaxy. They are very similar and maybe the evolutionary counterpart to the cats of ancient Terra.

Destolace: Destolace, the lavender desert planet. Located in the far, far edge of Outer Worlds. Contrary to most other planets in the galaxy, the sands of Destolaxe are vivid shades of lavender and purples. This is due to the trillions of colorful minerals that line the dunes of Destolace. Destolace is home to various species of water-collecting flora and fauna. For centuries Destolace has been a rest-stop planet for many spacefarers since it is so far away from everything. The Empire has just set up the newest outpost on Destolace.

Destroyers: Destroyers are the biggest class of starships in the galaxy. They are used by every military faction in the galaxy. The ships are perfectly suited for all facets of naval combat. Destroyers are covered bow-to-stern in every weapon imaginable: pulverizers, ion cannons, and torpedoes. Some can be up to fifteen to twenty kilometers long and plated in the strongest armors known to the galaxy. Destroyer-class ships can wreak devastating damage to anything it's weapons aim at but most notably planets. When enough Destroyers fire upon a planet's surface, they could completely render a planet uninhabitable by the barrages of lasers.

Diodrites: Diodrites are a race of tall, bulky, bipedal, hexapod creatures with a burnt orange skin tone. They have four strong arms. Naturally they have much more muscle mass than the average human. Diodrites are native to any one planet; they are found on many throughout the galaxy.

Empire Era: The Empire Era is from 2681 to now. This has been the greatest and most prosperous time in galactic history. Wars and conflicts have been at an all time low. The Empire stabilized the galactic economy after the massive inflation during the Chaos Era.

Energen Race: The Energen Race was a Cold War between Apex Manufacturing Corporation and Hellstorm Industries. It began in 2667 when the Compound for Energen was first discovered. The two companies raced to get their hands on the patent first.

Energen: Energen is known as the backbone of the galaxy. It fuels ships, weapons, shields, and hundreds of different devices. It is synthesized by densely condensing multiple gases into tight canisters that is then burned creating incredible amounts of power. The refined version of Energen gas burns with an intense red glow. The process of refining the necessary gases takes relatively a month to complete, but huge factories on Moxous IV refine it in mass quantities.

Florbods: Florbods are a race of hairless, colorful humanoids. There is nothing too special about them; most work in corporate jobs and other menial tasks. Similar to the Diodrites they are native to hundreds of planets.

Food Goo: Food Goo is a cheap digestible nutrient rich substance that was developed by Apex Foods, a subsidiary of Apex Manufacturing. Food Goo comes in small plastic packages that the goo is then either slurped or sucked out. Made to be in a variety of flavors. The main consumers of Food Goo are the impoverished class as they cannot afford normal food.

Free Space: Free Space is the regions of space that are unclaimed by any one faction. These areas are lawless places where Anything Goes.

Fringes: The Fringes are the farthest part of the galaxy that is still considered the Milky Way. Most of the Fringes are ruled by crime syndicates and private groups. The Empire has not had much of a hold on the Fringes throughout their rule.

Froplet: Froplets are a species of frog-like creatures. Naturally, they are thin and skinny, but after they all took up a life of luxury and indulged themselves in everything that they were able to get their hands on. After decades of this lifestyle, the Froplets became fat and obese weighing up to 5,000 pounds. Since they were so overweight, their small legs couldn't support their weight, so they evolved to slither on their huge tails while their legs dangle down. They have green, moist, and bumpy skin that is so thick they can survive laser blasts. In the beginning of Chaos Era, the Froplets began opening casinos across the galaxy. After that, their fortunes grew to unfathomable levels; the Froplet families amassed a expensive drug Empire with buying, growing, and selling Coco. The families also had/ have a monopoly on the galactic slave trade.

Galatia: Galatia is a planet in the Core Worlds sector. It is completely covered in deep ocean. Though it is underwater, hundreds of massive cities deep in the oceans. It is three times the size of Terra with relatively the same gravity. Galatia is home to thousands of species solely unique to it. Most creatures that live in the deep ocean are horrific monsters, yet they live peacefully with the people of Galatia. The Empire has a strong presence on the planet as Galatia produces the biggest amount of food and oil for the Empire.

Grygons: Grygons are the apex predators of Rhea. They had been there thousands of years before the Americorps even stepped foot on Rhean soil. Grygons are huge beastly creatures. They have razor sharp claws and teeth that can slice through Zarium steel. They resemble a tiger lizard hybrid with striped fur and a reptilian face. After having to live with them for centuries, the Americorps have begun to domesticate the Grygons and use them as war mounts. So far the project has been successful.

Healix: Healix is a green, viscous gel that is used to heal organic tissue. When Healix is applied to damaged tissue, it can rebuild the cellular structure within minutes. It was invented by Arlean scientists 2578. The creation of it revolutionized the medical industry across the entire galaxy. Trillions of lives have been saved on account of Healix.

Hellstorm Industries: Hellstorm is the second biggest company in the galaxy only to Apex. While apex deals mainly in weapons, Hellstorm works solely in more "helpful" products for the average person. Their most notable product has been the portable warp device. Around the same time Apex began forming a military presence, Hellstorm caught wind of this and began enlisting a personal military. Compared to Apex, Hellstorm is a lot more shading in their marketing and who they hire. It has been rumored that Hellstorm purchases slaves from the Froplet families to work in their factories.

Hessoths: Hessoths are a species of furry bipedal, hexapods. On average, they are about one meter tall. Hessoths have six arms. Hessoths are able to understand and comprehend most forms of communication, but their limited vocal chords don't allow them to speak any advanced language. Most wear devices to translate thoughts to speech. The top set is bigger, and the bottom set is smaller. Hessoths' average lifespan is 120 years. They are fierce warriors for their small size. This is because their home planet was occupied by pirates for two centuries, and throughout this time they learned guerrilla warfare tactics. Now, the Hessoths are a formidable force. Their entire race is grizzled; most take up jobs of piracy or guns for hire which is very ironic since they fought off pirates for so long.

Holo Cell: Holo cell is a device similar to the smartphones during Terra's time. They can store hundreds of terabytes of data in a very small package. Most everyone who is an active galactic traveler has themselves a holo cell.

Hunters Club: The Hunters Club is a prestigious association of the greatest bounty hunters in the galaxy; it was founded in 2389 by a group of bounty hunters who were tired of there being so many bounty hunters. This men's only club hunts for the sport. They train their entire lives to be as good as they are. It has always remained an exclusive club, and the only way to join is to personally receive a letter of acceptance. If someone needs someone else dead, the first place they would want to go is a Hunter's associate, someone who knows a Hunter. Then the Hunters will review their bounty and decide if it's worth their precious time. If a Hunter is after you, you're as good dead; they have a 100% success rate since their creation.

INN: The Intergalactic New Network is a galaxy spanning news service. They are always the first ones to find things out that they shouldn't. Though they market themselves as unfiltered, the Empire twists their broadcasts to fall into their own favor. The INN is completely fine with this as they get paid a lot in bribes.

IRS: The Intergalactic Revenue Service is a ruthless organization that hunts anyone down who hasn't paid their taxes and bills. They have an absolutely brutal reputation of finding who they are looking for. The IRS runs a cloning operation to produce millions of suited agents. These agents are then trained in combat and military tactics. If someone forgets to pay their taxes, the IRS sends a squad of armed Suits (as they call them) to deal with the problem permanently.

Imp-pol: Imp-pols are the lowest rank in the Imperial Military. Though they are the lowest rank, there are still many across the galaxy. Being an Imp-pol is a highly favored occupation. It pays well. It doesn't require much prior military experience. Their main job is to simply enforce Imperial law. Since there are so many, the Empire doesn't spend too much on their armor, so the Imp-pols wear plastar armor.

Ion Weapons: Ion weapons utilize electromagnetic blasts to deactivate electronic systems. One ion blast can normally take out a bot for hours, and enough can take our entire ships.

Jet Ball: Jet Ball is a sport invented by the Americorps. It is a combination of Terran basketball and jetpacks. The players all wear jetpacks over a pit of highly corrosive acid. The goal is for one team to have the most points by getting their ball in the hoop the most without falling in the acid. It is also full contact, so they can punch, kick, and shove people. This sport is televised throughout the galaxy.

Laser colors: Lasers have different colors depending on the type of gas used to produce them. There are five main colors used in laser blasts. All increase in price as they go up. The cheapest gas is Strontium Nitrate which also is the weakest in terms of armor damage. It burns bright red. Second is Sodium Carbonate, a little stronger than red, and it burns yellow. Third is Chopper Chloride which is medium in strength and burns cerulean blue. The fourth is Potassium Chloride which burns dark purple and is the second strongest. Last is Magnesium Sulfate which burns snow white and is the strongest lasers able to pierce through Zarium but is incredibly expensive.

Lorazda: Lorazda is a city on a comet that flies around the galaxy in unpredictable ellipses. Since it is constantly moving no government has had a firm hold on it; the Empire flat out ignores it most of the time. It is the drug capital of the galaxy. And the base of operation of the Froplet family.

Mechs: Mechs were invented by humans on Terra in 2065 with the help of aliens technology. The Mech can amplify a human's strength by 100 fold. After seeing the success of mechs on Terra, alien civilization began to adopt that concept. They revolutionized construction throughout the planet, but the Mechs were soon weaponized as humans always do. The Mechs changed war forever especially during the Terran Wars.

Mercenary Wars: The Mercenary Wars were fought throughout the centuries. It was hundreds of mercenary groups all fighting one another. The whole goal was for one to win and dominate the others, but in 2476 the groups all joined together and formed the Eclipse.

Meth Heads: Meth Heads are huge snail-like creatures. Meth Heads are moist, gray creatures with an almost impenetrable shell on their back. Their native planet is the deep caves of Moxous IV. They can grow up to three-meters and thousands of kilograms in mass. Due to their unique form of cellular respiration, they produce methane gas as a natural byproduct. They are farmed in huge factories where people harvest their breath and sell it across the galaxy.

Mid Worlds: The Mid Worlds is the sector of space between the Outer Worlds and the Core Worlds.

Modders: Modders is the name given to people who augment themselves with cybernetic enhancements. A majority of people who get mods were missing limbs or other things.

Molo: Molos are a species native to Arlea. They are huge cow-like creatures that are known for their delicious meat and delectable milk. Many Arleans take up the profession of farming and cultivating Molos.

Moxous IV: Moxous IV is a small moon in the Mid Worlds. It orbits around Moxous, a lush forested world. Its rock-blue-colored surface is harsh and desolate. In 2699 it was discovered that the entire moon was incredibly rich in all the resources needed to create Energen. Once this was discovered private mining companies from across the galaxy raced to try to mine out the precious resources. After decades of mining a giant valley had been dug out that stretches around half the planet. It is called the Trench.

Nexem: Nexem is a dwarf planet in the Mid Worlds. It is eight times smaller than Terra. The entire planet is barren and rocky. There is no atmosphere on Nexem and very low gravity. No sentient species are native to the planet. Nexem would be a planet no one cares about, but there is one resource that is only found on Nexem. Nexite crystals. Once Nexite was discovered one Nexem in 2562, a galactic race broke out to get a monopoly on them. A war broke out in 2564 against Apex Manufacturing, Hellstorm Industries, and Powernaugh Weapons Corporation. The planet's surface was stripped bare of the Nexite crystals, and now dozens of companies mine deep into the planet's core.

Nexite Crystal: Along with Energen, Nexite crystals are one of the most valuable resources in the galaxy. They come in hundreds of different colors. Nexite crystals naturally are full electrical energy. Once they were discovered, everyone began experimenting to find the unique properties that they possess. Nexite became the main power source for all starships big and small. The ship's reactor core can harness the power of Nexite crystals to power the ships.

Nylos: Nylos is the deity of the Nytarian faith. He is a vengeful being who doesn't tolerate failure. He chose the Nytarian people to carry out his will of cleansing the galaxy of all those he deems unworthy. The unworthy are those who aren't Nytarians. He yearns for the galaxy to only have Nytarians. He sees them as the superior species.

Nytar: Nytar, the mountainous planet. Nytar is in the farthest reaches of the galaxy. The planet is one of the largest in the entire galaxy. Nytar is twenty times more massive than Terra, and it has twice the gravity. Its surface is covered in huge towering mountains and deep valleys. All creatures and inhabitants of the planet are naturally stronger than most creatures in the galaxy because of its high gravity. The planet's temperature is incredibly cold, so the creatures have adapted to have thicker skin to protect themselves from the Frigid temperatures.

Nytarian beliefs: The Nytarians believe that Nylos is the ultimate authority in the galaxy. They will give their own lives in sacrifice to the cause of galactic purity. They see all races other than themselves as inferior and not deserving of the gift of life. They have many rituals where they sacrifice captives and bathe in their blood; the Nytarians believe that cleans themselves of their failures. To enter into the After, Nytarian afterlife, they must die in battle or in service to Nylos.

Nytarians: Nytarian's biology is specifically unique. Their home world Nytar has a gravitational force that is almost doubled compared to Terra's gravity. On Nytar it is 19.4 m/s2. Because of this, they are incredibly strong. With skin of pale lavender, eyes like yellow sulfur, pointed teeth like Galitian sharks, and long angular noses these brutal warriors stand at an average of two and a half meters tall. Their bodies are completely hairless. They are biologically designed to be killers and hunters.

Order of the Void: The Order of the Void is a cult that worships the black hole in the center of the galaxy, the Void. They believe the Void is the origin of all life in the galaxy. They seek to bring about the end of all life and see it all fall back into the black hole. The Order has temples all across the galaxy. They are a mysterious group as many do not know of their existence. Some in the Order are peaceful and keep their beliefs to themselves, but others are radical terrorists. There have been bombings and assassinations all in the name of the Void.
Outer Worlds: The Outer Worlds are the sections of space in between the Mid Worlds and Fringes. It is a place with few laws. The Empire has not been as adamant to govern this sector of space.

Pathfinders: The Pathfinders are an ancient creed of explorers. They were the first group to chart out the galaxy. In ancient galactic times, Pathfinders would venture out into unknown space to chart it. Now, there are few left as all have gone extinct.
Plastar: Plastar is a strong and flexible material made from a conglomerate of different plastics. This is the cheapest armor, but it

is the weakest. It can barely defend against laser beams. Plastar is the armor used by Imp-pols and other low level soldiers.

Poachers Guild: The Poachers Guild is an association of hunters who kill for trophy and fun. Their goal is to have specimens of every species in the galaxy. The Poachers have a huge museum where they keep all their trophies on a large display. Unlike the Hunters Club, anyone can join the Guild if they bring a new tribute. The Poachers Guild's mortal enemies are the Hunters Club. The Club hate the Guild as they think they are savages who have no appreciation of the old ways.

Portable Warp device: These devices are designed by Hellstorm Industries. They allow objects to be transported across the galaxy in an instant.

Powernaught Weapons: Powernaught is a company who specializes in giant weapons such as railguns, mega-lasers, and Tectonic Disruptors. They are much smaller compared to Apex and Hellstorm. Powernaught chose to keep their heads out of the Corporate Wars. The company also is very shady, and they sell to many darker factions.

Rhea: Rhea, the field planet. Rhea is a small, lush moon of the Jovian giant, Garatous in the Outer Worlds. Rhea was never home to any intelligent life, but it is home to many different species of wild creatures.

Rilyn: Rylin is the planet in the Mid Worlds. It is five times the size of Terra. Rylin is a burning inferno planet. Millions of volcanoes are scattered around the planet. Instead of water, rivers flow with molten rock.

Roxian: Roxians are humanoid reptilians. Their appearance can best be described as human-like dinosaurs. The entire species has colorful, scaly skin. Their scales are thick and are so strong that they can absorb most weaker laser bolts. Since all Roxians are much stronger than humans, most of them work in construction or labor jobs.

Royal houses: On planets throughout the galaxy, families of nobles arose to govern the galaxy. Eventually, the houses grew out of their home planets. Originally there were hundreds of houses throughout different planets, but through wars and conflicts 90% of the houses were destroyed or bought out. For the past hundred years only twelve houses remain: Adis, Vene, Madar, Primen, Olphen, Uldwun, Sinire, Dolful, Coralla, Nadiri, Grellan, Halneir, and Arkeyna. In 2681, the heads of the twelve houses came together to speak as they knew more fighting would lead to the destruction of them all. After this, they united all of their land and resources to form the Empire.

Sarco: Home planet of the Sarconian species in the far Fringes of the Galaxy. It is two times smaller than Terra. It wasn't always a barren planet; centuries ago it was a lush world of trees and oceans, but the Sarconians overused their resources. After the misuse of the planet, all life died out. Before the planet's complete destruction, it was a wasteland. The surface was red and rocky.

Sarconian War: The Sarconian War was a brutal war. It was the Empire against the Sarconian species. Throughout the war, hundreds of planets were ravaged by the Sarconians. Through most of the war, the Empire was losing. The Empire was still relatively young when the war began. The Empire only began winning the war when other private armies began to join in with the Imperial effort. Those who helped were: the Americorps, the Eclipse, Apex Manufacturing's army, Hellstorm Industries' army, the Hunters Club, the USG, and even the Froplet families. After these private factions saw that the Sarconians could destroy the galaxy, everyone began sending their troops to help. The war finally ended when the Empire fired a Tectonic Disruptor missile at the planet Sarco. It destroyed the entire world, genociding the whole species.

Sarconians: Sarconians are insectoid creatures. They all have exoskeletons stronger than Zarium and eight red eyes on the sides of their heads. At a young age, they have wings and can quickly fly, but in their older years they shed their wings. The entire species is fully connected by a hive mind with the Queen at the center. The Sarconian queen lays millions of eggs every day as she is the only female of the entire species.

Sentinel: Sentinels are the base unit of the Imperial Military. They wear thin but strong Zarium armor plates, and they bear ray rifles. All wars throughout the Empire have been fought by legions of Sentinels. To become a Sentinel, humans must endure through five years of extensive training and conditioning. Legions of Sentinels fought in the Sarconian War, and they were the turning point in the Empire's victory.

Shocker: Shockers are the most elite soldiers (shock troopers) in the Imperial Military. They are clad in the bulkiest armor known to the galaxy that are made of the toughest Zarium steel. Shockers normally wield gatling guns, laser swords, and handheld shields. Most galactic conflicts can be handled by Sentinels. When things get messy, the Empire drops in a few Shockers, and they will stomp them out quickly. Before a Shocker ever sees the face of battle, they go through decades of training and genetic modification. All Shockers are pumped with drugs to make them the biggest and strongest that is humanly possible.

Shrill: The Shrill are a creed of devout warriors who would use the Echo to conquer the galaxy. They believe their way of belief is higher than all the others, especially the Akara. Shrill worshipers and monks don't study the Echo's ways; instead, they rashly contort the Echo to bend to their will not its own. They manipulate the Echo in a dark and perverted way. The Shrill have waged an eternal war against the Akara with the hopes that one day they may exterminate them all. The Shrill faith is built around the idea that strength triumphs over all else. The leader of the Shrill must battle all the other candidates to the death to secure their spot. The Shrill will go to any length possible to complete their goal of ruling the galaxy. The Shrill have allied themselves with the Nytarians as the Shrill see them as valiant warriors, and the Nytarians see them as higher than the rest of the galaxy like themselves.

Sisters of the Sun: The Sisters of the Sun are a highly religious group of only women who worship the great star N'tooka. N'tooka's scientific name is Alpha Centauri. They are a matriarchal group led by a high priestess. The Sisters await the day when N'tooka grows so powerful that she engulfs the entire galaxy. Throughout the year, they coax people into joining the sisterhood, and at the end of the year the sisters sacrifice them to the fiery star.

Solar Sails: Solar sails are an untraditional form of space travel. These types of ships use large sails that harness solar radiation to propel them. Most ships operate with normal thrusters, but solar sails are used by more primitive vessels.

SpaceFarer: A spacefarer is simply someone who travels the galaxy and makes money via freelance contracts.

Star Eater: A Sun Eater is a device built by Arlean scientists and engineers in 2287. This device is built around a star; it sucks the radiation out of the star and turns it into usable energy. There are no active Sun Eaters anymore.

Stingers: Stingers are the base class of the Nytarian fleet. Stingers are heavier starfighters compared to the Wyverns. They have shields but are weak. The Nytarians are able to produce them on their own since they are relatively cheap.

Talasia: Talasia is a planet in the Core Worlds. It is a green lush world with human-like creatures. It is a flat world full of plains.

Tectonic Disruptors: Tectonic Disruptors are the peak of weapons in the galaxy. It is the most dangerous weapon in the galaxy. It is a thirty meter long missile with a drill head, and it is full of explosives and gravity disruptors. When the missile is fired at a planet's surface, it begins to drill deep into the planet's core. Once inside, the gravity disruptors pulse on and off. Originally, the pulses start weak and get stronger. The disruptors rock the planet around. After a few minutes, the crust and mantle begins to crack and shatter. Once the ground is broken up, the explosives detonate blasting out the ground and rock. Then the entire planet blasts out into its atmosphere only leaving debris. This is how Terra and Sarco were destroyed.

Terra: Terra or more commonly known as Earth, is the birthplace of the human species. It once was one of the most thriving and diverse planets in the galaxy. For thousands of years it went unknown to the wonders that existed in the galaxy, but aliens landed in 2023. Aliens brought new technology that let humans expand into the far out galaxy. But Terra's first contact with the galaxy was in the early 19th century when aliens hunters landed on the planet to hunt humans for the unique bodies.

Terran Wars: The Terran war (otherwise known as World War III) was fought in 2231 all the nations of Terra were locked in a heated civil war. This was the most brutal and devastating war in all of humanity's history. This war was fought not with bullets and swords but with ray guns, mechs, and mega-lasers. This ravaged the entire planet, stripping it of all its resources. The war finally ended in 2235 when the United Russian Allies fired a Tectonic Disruptor on their own land. The entire planet was destroyed, now only debris remains.

The Citadel: The Citadel is an enormous city/ space station that sits in space only 2 lightyears away from Arlea. It is 805.5 km2. Construction started in 2658 C.E. (Chaos Era). It serves as the headquarters for the Empire and the location of the Imperial council. The city is surrounded by a sky dome that provides artificial oxygen and an artificial light cycle for all those who operate with the circadian rhythm. Protected by a massive array of cannons and an expansive fleet; the Citadel is a refuge and home for all those in the galaxy.

The Echo: The Echo is a mysterious force that exists throughout the entire galaxy. The Shrill nor the Akara truly understand the nature of the Echo; most believe it is impossible to truly understand it. From what is known about it, it is a force that brings past, present, and future all together. It connects all beings together. Those who have a stronger connection to the Echo are able to manipulate living beings or physical objects. Some accounts say that some users have been able to control fire, move objects, suggest ideas to people, and even create weapons of energy. Those who don't have a connection to the Echo can't see it, but those who have a connection see the Echo as strands of energy connecting all people. How it looks to some people depends on their moral values and beliefs.

The Eclipse: The Eclipse is a galaxy spanning mercenary syndicate. In the year 2476, the secret Mercenary Wars had been raging for 100 years in the galaxy's shadow. The Eclipse was the aftermath of the wars. All the mercenary groups joined together in an alliance where they can fight with each other instead of against. Now, the Eclipse works in the shadows while the Empire searches for them. The Eclipse has been moving pawns in the dark trying to put their people in power positions across the Empire.

The Great Light: The Great Light is the deity of the Akaran faith. The Great Light is a peaceful being who is said to hold ultimate power in the galaxy. The Akara strive to understand the nature of The Great Light. It is written in ancient Akaran texts that The Great Light created the entire universe in a huge explosion of light at the beginning of time. The Akara wait for the day when The Great Light manifests himself in the physical world and saves all the Akara.

USG: The United Spacefarer Guild is an association of spacefarers from all corners of the galaxy that works together to help people by doing contract work. It was originally founded in the late Chaos Era due to the in-fighting of the spacefarers throughout the galaxy. This guild has brought people together to help more people and of course make a lot of credits. Under the USG's program, there are many benefits: all spacefarers have protection against each other, if a spacefarer is in need of help, any spacefarer is obligated to come assist, and many other good things.

Vibro-blade: A Vibro-blade is a small handheld knife that vibrates back and forth at hypersonic speeds. The vibrating nature of the weapon allows it to cut through much thicker and stronger materials compared to a normal blade.

Warp Drive: Warp drives utilize a condensed wormhole encased in the strongest steel in the galaxy. When calculations can be made perfectly, the wormhole can be manipulated to open one anywhere in the galaxy. Ships and anything can travel through warps. It is almost instantaneous travel to any point. Warp Drives are highly dangerous pieces of technology. Destruction of the drive can result in catastrophic damage to a ship.

Warp Route: A warp route is a laid path throughout space. These routes are in place so that they are able to safely travel through a warp. The current routes have all been laid out by the Imperial navigators.

Wyverns: Wyverns are the standard starfighters of the Imperial Navy. They are quick and agile, able to weave in and out of combat with astonishing precision. To help keep them fast, there aren't any shield generators. The pilot rides like a motorcycle or hoverbike. Two pedals control the throttle, and handlebars steer it. The standard version comes equipped with six EDRs and two Energen cannons.

Zarium: Zarium is the strongest metal in the galaxy. It is made of pure Zarium and carbon. Zarium is mined and refined on Moxous IV. It is relatively cheap since it can be mined and refined very quickly with little effort.

Zulara IV: Zulara IV, the forest planet. This planet borders the Mid Worlds and Outer Worlds. The planet is covered in huge trees and dense jungles. It is one of the many moons that orbit the white dwarf star Zulara. Wondrous flora and fauna that live on this planet, but its main inhabitants are the Hessoths. Hessoths are furry, three feet tall, bipedal hexapods. The planet was taken by the Empire about thirty years ago. They occupied Zulara IV for its convenient galactic placement; they constructed a huge trade city which is one of the biggest commerce capitals in the galaxy.

Made in the USA
Las Vegas, NV
22 June 2024

91359971R00204